Her Grisly Grave

A GRIPPING CRIME THRILLER WITH A TWIST

TANYA STONE FBI K9 MYSTERY THRILLERS

TIKIRI HERATH

ACADEMY PRESS

Her Grisly Grave

Tanya Stone FBI K9 Mystery Thriller Series

www.TikiriHerath.com

Copyright © Tikiri Herath 2025

Library & Archives Canada Cataloging in Publication

E-book ISBN: 9781990234347

Paperback ISBN: 9781990234330

Hardback ISBN: 9781990234323

Paperback Large Print ISBN: 9781990234477

Hardback Large Print ISBN: 9781990234590

Audio book ISBN: 9781990234316

Author: Tikiri Herath

Publisher Imprint: Rebel Diva Academy Press

Back Cover Headshot: Aura McKay

❀ Created with Vellum

The Red Heeled Rebels Universe

The Red Heeled Rebels universe of spine-tingling mystery thrillers featuring your favorite female sleuths are available in e-book, paperback, hardback, and large print editions, globally.

~

The Tanya Stone FBI K9 Mystery Thrillers

This pulse-pounding series stars Tetyana from the Red Heeled Rebels as undercover federal agent Tanya Stone. With her is FBI-trained K9 Max, her loyal and lovable German Shepherd dog. Serial killers prowl the wealthy small towns along the coast of Washington state. Can Tanya and Max hunt them down before the killers turn on them?

Her Deadly End

Her Cold Blood

Her Last Lie

Her Secret Crime

Her Perfect Murder

Her Grisly Grave

This series is now complete.

~

The Asha Kade Private Detective Murder Mysteries

This series contains standalone murder mystery books featuring Asha Kade and Katy McCafferty, the sassy smart Red Heeled Rebels. A secret benefactor's estate deposits one million dollars into their favorite children's charity every time Asha and Katy solve a cold case. But do they know the deadly the odds stacked against them?

Merciless Legacy

Merciless Games

Merciless Crimes

Merciless Lies

Merciless Past

Merciless Deaths

This series is now complete.

~

The Red Heeled Rebels International Mystery & Crime - The Origin Story

This is the award-winning origin saga of the Red Heeled Rebels. Meet the Rebels in their youths, a ragtag group of trafficked orphans who unite to form a found family and fight for their lives. For freedom. For justice. The books in this origin series must be read in order for your best enjoyment.

The Girl Who Crossed the Line

The Girl Who Ran Away

The Girl Who Made Them Pay

The Girl Who Fought to Kill

The Girl Who Broke Free

The Girl Who Knew Their Names

The Girl Who Never Forgot

This series is now complete.

Tikiri's books are available globally in e-book, paperback, hardback, and large-print editions. They are also available in libraries everywhere. Ask your friendly librarian or your local bookstore to order a copy for you via Ingram Spark.

Note from the Author

Dear reader friend,

Thank you for picking up my book.

Do you enjoy twisty thrillers with feisty detectives who hunt the villains and make them pay? If you do, you're in the right place. In my books, justice always prevails.

My stories are for smart readers who love pulse-pounding thrills, nail-biting twists, and strong female leads. There is no explicit sex, graphic violence, or heavy cursing in my books, and no animal is ever harmed.

I'm not a marketing agency or a branding firm that employs ghost writers or artificial intelligence machines to create books. I don't hide behind a pen name or a fake avatar. I am a human author with human experiences, and I write my own stories.

Just like you, I'm also a reader. And I'm delighted to meet you.

Enjoy the read!

Best wishes,

Tikiri

Vancouver, Canada

~

PS: I wrote a special bonus story for this novel. You'll find the secret link to this story gift at the end of this book.

PPS: All my books use American spelling because the majority of my readers live in the USA. But I am a Canadian who went to international schools around the world, so I write mostly in British English. I know. I'm a mixed-up gal.

As soon as I finish writing a book, my spell checker changes everything to American spelling. After that, my wonderful American editor underlines any missed words with her sharp red pen.

But words can be sneaky. And insidious.

If you see a funny-looking word anywhere, please report it to me. Rest assured, I will give it a sound talk to and banish it from my books.

~

Tropes you'll find in this mystery thriller series include: female protagonists, women sleuths, police officers, police procedurals, detectives, serial killers, small towns, dark secrets, family lies and deceptions, plot twists, shocking endings, missing people, creepy cabins, fast-paced action, vigilante justice, crime, murder, kidnappings, revenge, intrigue, and psychological suspense.

There is no explicit sex, heavy cursing, or graphic violence in my books. There is, however, a closed circle of suspects, twists and turns, and nail-biting suspense. NO DOG IS EVER HARMED IN MY BOOKS. But the villains always are.

Her Grisly Grave

HER GRISLY GRAVE

AGENT TANYA STONE FBI K9 MYSTERY THRILLER

A killer's deadly riddle. An agent's dark secret. A twisted psychological game gone horribly wrong...

In the affluent seaside town of Black Rock, beautiful blond women vanish, one by one.

The murdered victims are found blindfolded, their heads crowned with sunflower garlands. The chilling calling card of a twisted mind.

FBI Agent Tanya Stone hunts the cold-blooded

criminal, with her faithful police dog, Max, by her side.

But the psychopath is always one step ahead, taunting them with cryptic riddles sent to a true crime podcaster, exactly one hour before each death.

As the body count rises and suspense reaches fever pitch, Tanya fights to unravel the dark secrets of this small town. But it's hard to say who's telling the truth.

The stakes are deadly. And personal. Tanya doesn't know the shocking truth lies in her haunted family's past.

And the clock is ticking....

Will Tanya pay the ultimate price for a tragedy that happened years ago?

Day One

Special Agent Tanya Stone
&
K9 Max

Chapter One

I s she dead?

Agent Tanya Stone squinted through the trees at the woman in the red bikini.

The woman was lying face down on a towel that had been carefully draped over a flat rock on the beach. Her golden-toned skin was evenly tanned. A small sunflower was stuck in her pretty blond hair.

From the back, she looked a lot like Deputy Shawn Fox's wife, Zoe.

This was a favorite spot for sunbathers from the affluent seaside town of Black Rock, but the early morning sun was low, partially shrouded by gray clouds. It would rain soon.

It's an odd time to sunbathe.

Something about the woman on the rock

bothered Tanya. It was the way she was lying. It wasn't natural.

Tanya emerged from the wooded trail she had been running along and jumped across the train tracks onto the beach. She stepped toward the rock to get a better look at the woman.

Two seagulls squawked and bickered above her, while the waves of the mighty Pacific crashed against the shoreline, spraying mist everywhere.

But the spray didn't seem to bother the woman sleeping on the rock. Tanya narrowed her eyes.

That's not Zoe.

A chilly wind whipped through Tanya's hair. Something felt wrong about this place today. She couldn't shake off the feeling of dread coming over her. It was like someone was watching her. She was wearing her running leggings and windbreaker, but she shivered.

Her gaze returned to the woman on the rock. She had no visible injuries. Besides, if this was a cadaver, Tanya's FBI-trained K9 dog would have been the first on the scene.

Most of Black Rock's denizens got along with their law enforcement team. But the police chief, Jack Bold, had received a handful of complaints over the years. Hard core libertarians considered even a simple question from a deputy an affront to their privacy.

Tanya licked the saltwater from her lips and

stepped away from the woman on the rock. She swallowed her unease and silently scolded herself for being paranoid.

Not every body I see is a corpse. And not every person I meet is a killer.

Her brow furrowed.

But why do I feel like I'm being watched?

She spun around.

Where's Max?

He usually trotted ahead of her on the trail and had disappeared a while back when he had spotted a squirrel.

"Max?" she called out.

A bark came from behind her. She whirled around to see her German Shepherd running down the beach, away from her.

Is he after a crab again? He's going to regret that.

Tanya glanced at her phone. She wasn't done with her morning run, and it was already time to get back to the precinct. Jack liked his team to be on time.

She was about to call her dog and return to the parking lot when she heard the muffled cry.

"Help me!"

Chapter Two

Tanya whirled around.

She scanned the beach, but all she could hear were the waves crashing against the rugged shoreline.

Did I imagine that cry for help?

This area was deserted on weekday mornings. Normally, it was just her and Max on the running trail by the tracks.

Sometimes, she would glimpse kite surfers taking on the ocean's rolling waves. While it was breezy that morning, it wasn't windy enough for surfing.

Tanya narrowed her eyes and peered in the direction of her dog.

Max was making a beeline toward a boulder the size of a compact car that jutted out of the beach. His nose was stuck to the wet sand, like he was following an invisible trail.

"Max?" she called out. "Where are you going?"

He stopped and glanced back at her. With a short bark that seemed to say, *Follow me, Mom,* he turned around and scampered toward the boulder.

The tide was rising, and the waves were coming up to Max's feet, but he kept moving, a determined expression on his face.

Tanya knew that look.

He's caught a scent.

She raced down the beach toward him. "What is it, bud?"

The muffled cry came again. Closer this time.

"Help!"

Goosebumps sprang up on Tanya's arms. The voice was vaguely familiar.

Max trotted up to the boulder and sat down next to it. He turned his head in her direction and barked three strong barks.

Tanya's heart raced.

He's found someone.

She dashed over and scrambled onto the boulder.

The waves were rolling in faster now. They crashed against the rock, spraying seawater on her face. Tanya wiped the droplets from her eyes and got down to her knees.

That was when she spotted the woman crouched by the foot of the boulder.

She was struggling to keep her head above the waterline. It took Tanya a horrified second to realize why. Her hands were tied, and her eyes were blindfolded.

"Help me!" cried the woman. "Someone help!"

Tanya leaped into the sea. A gigantic wave rolled in and slammed her against the boulder. "Hang on! I'm coming!"

The bound woman gurgled and spluttered.

Tanya grabbed her by the shoulders and pulled her to her feet. The woman opened her mouth and vomited seawater.

Tanya's eyes bulged as she recognized the victim.

Chapter Three

"Zoe!"

Zoe's swimsuit was torn, and her hair was stuck to her scalp. She was trembling hard, like she was on the brink of hypothermia.

Tanya ripped the blindfold off her eyes. Zoe blinked rapidly, like she couldn't see. Her chest heaved as the water drained from her limp lips.

Tanya pulled off her jacket and wrapped it around Zoe's shoulders. "I got you."

She plucked out the Swiss Army knife she always carried with her and cut the rope that bound Zoe's hands. "You're safe now."

With a cry, Zoe fell into Tanya's arms, sobbing. Tanya pulled her friend in and held her tightly.

How did this happen?

The last time she had seen Zoe was at Lulu's cafe, a month ago.

Everyone had been there to celebrate her cancer remission. Zoe's husband, Deputy Shawn Fox, and their seven-year-old son, Zak, had looked cheery for a change. Tanya remembered how weary they had been from Zoe's grueling treatments at clinics all over Washington state.

Tanya slipped her army knife into her pocket and pulled out her phone. Holding Zoe with one hand, she clicked on the precinct's number with the other.

"Tanya Stone. Code eleven eighty," she barked. "East Beach. By the woods. I repeat. Eleven eighty. Paramedics and police. ASAP."

As soon as the dispatch confirmed the message and Tanya slipped the mobile into her pocket, a large wave rolled in and crashed against the rock. Seawater sprayed over them. They swayed on their feet as the wave pulled back into the ocean.

Tanya pulled Zoe closer.

"We need to get you to a dry spot. Can you walk?"

"He... He h-hit me in the h-head," stuttered Zoe. "I didn't... even see him coming."

"Hang tight, okay? Walk with me."

With an arm around Zoe's shoulders, Tanya waded with her through the rising water, step by step. Max barked and wagged his tail as they maneuvered around the boulder.

Tanya shot him an appreciative glance.

You deserve a big treat today, bud.

Zoe stumbled and leaned against the rock, like she couldn't move any farther. "My feet..."

Tanya buttoned up the jacket and rubbed her arms, knowing her priority was to keep Zoe warm till the medics arrived.

"It... was a... a shadow." Zoe's lips trembled as she whispered. "I-I think it was a man. I felt... a pain in my head. Next thing... I wake up in the water. He tied my hands and blindfolded me. Why? Who?"

Tears streamed down her blotchy cheeks.

Tanya wiped the tears away, trying not to choke up herself. If she hadn't been on her daily run and Max hadn't been the smart pup he was, Zoe could have drowned.

From somewhere nearby, Max started barking.

Backup, thought Tanya.

"He was too s-strong," whispered Zoe. "I tried... to fight... back... but he was... big."

Tanya's instincts had been right the first time.

Something was wrong with this place today. Very wrong.

"What were you doing here at this time, hon?"

"I wanted so badly to... to... go swimming as soon... as I got b-better." Zoe sniffled. "I asked my sister to come with me. Nicole thought it was too... cold, so I told her to go back home... I s-swam a bit. I was... just coming out of the water, when... when... that... man... attacked me."

Tanya's throat tightened.

Nicole?

"Was your sister with you, hon?"

Zoe nodded. "She... came to... to spend the summer with me. She's a teacher in Seattle. School's closed."

Tanya's eyes flew to the flat rock where the woman in the red bikini lay.

Max was twirling around the rock, barking nonstop. Her heart skipped a beat. She knew exactly what he was trying to tell her.

She turned to Zoe. "Hey, hon, is Nicole wearing a red bikini?"

Zoe nodded and clutched Tanya's arms like she was scared she would abandon her.

"It's okay. I won't leave you," said Tanya, but her eyes were on Nicole. The sleeping woman hadn't moved since she first saw her, even with all the commotion around her.

Zoe clung to Tanya. "Where's she? Did... Did she send you to h-help me?"

Tanya wrapped Zoe in a tight hug, unable to answer her. Somewhere in town, sirens began to wail.

Backup. Finally.

Tanya's eyes flittered back to the flat rock and her dog, who was trying hard to get her attention.

Max had done the right thing. He had known to search for the human in trouble first before indicating the human who was dead.

A shiver went through Tanya as she realized Nicole might never wake up again.

Chapter Four

Zoe's sister is dead.
But she doesn't know.

Tanya pulled her phone out and mentally crossed her fingers that Zoe wouldn't recognize the local police code for *Possible Dead Body*.

She was about to dial when Max stopped barking.

Tanya whipped her head up.

Max was staring into the darkened trail behind the tracks, his ears perked, his muscles taut, and his snout forward. He looked like a wolf ready to attack.

Tanya froze.

Is the man who attempted to kill Zoe back?

She scanned the section of the trail where Max seemed most interested. Someone was standing among the fir trees behind the trail, watching them.

She made out an outline of a person, a faint silhouette inside the woods. Woods was a big word for the stretch of trees that lined the tracks by the beach, but it was still hard to say if that was a man or a woman.

It was impossible to tell if this was the killer who had targeted Zoe and Nicole, or if this was an accomplice. But even with the low cloud cover, Tanya noticed the glint of steel.

The silhouette was holding a rifle.

Max erupted into a flurry of angry barks. He bounded around the rock, ready to dart into the woods.

"Max!" screamed Tanya. "Get back!"

She pulled Zoe down to the watery floor. Zoe cried out in surprise and pain, but Tanya held her down.

"Max!" she hollered. "Come back here! Now!"

Max's barks stopped, and soon, his furry head popped up by the rock. Tanya grabbed his collar and yanked him close. She wrapped her arms around him and Zoe, shielding them with her body.

"Heads down!" she screamed.

The gunshot rang out, echoing through the beach.

Chapter Five

Tanya held her breath, anticipating a second shot.

All she could hear were the sirens wailing on the road.

She hugged Zoe and Max tightly as the waves rolled in, swaying them back and forth.

Her own Glock was secured in her belly holster. But to get to it, she would have to let go of Zoe and Max and make sure they wouldn't rush into danger.

Zoe was shaking uncontrollably, but Max was wiggling in her arms. She knew her dog wanted nothing more than to nab the shooter, but that was a risk she would never take. "You're not getting killed today, bud."

The sirens got louder. Soon, brakes squealed in

the parking lot. A car door banged open. Then another.

Relief coursed through Tanya's veins.

"Shooter!" Chief Jack Bold's voice rang from the parking lot. "Everyone back!"

Tanya released Zoe. Zoe curled up against the rock and hugged her knees, sobbing. Tanya placed a hand on her arm. "Stay right here. Don't move till I tell you."

Tanya turned around and peeked out from behind the boulder.

Two squad cars had stopped next to her Jeep in the parking lot. She spotted the chief and a deputy hunkering behind their open cruiser doors, their bulletproof vests on, sidearms drawn, searching for the perpetrator.

An ambulance had stopped on the road, its engine still running and its lights flashing. Two frightened faces peered out of the front windshield.

"I said, get down!" That was Jack. The paramedics ducked in their seats.

Tanya scanned the running trail, but the silhouette with the gun was no longer visible. She thrust her head out and hollered.

"Shot came from the woods."

"Copy that," called out a male voice from the parking lot.

"Shawn?" Zoe struggled to sit up. "Is that Shawn?"

"Hang on," said Tanya. "He'll come over when it's safe—"

"Shawn!"

Zoe's screech made Tanya's ears ring.

"Zoe!" Deputy Fox's panicked voice came from behind his squad car. "Where are you? Zoe!"

"I'm here!"

Before Tanya or Jack could do anything, Deputy Fox bolted out from behind his car and raced toward the boulder where Tanya and Zoe were hiding.

"Get back, Deputy!" bellowed Jack, but Fox didn't seem to hear.

He came crashing down the beach and dropped to his knees by the rock.

"What happened? Didn't I tell you not to go swimming alone?"

He reached over to his wife and pulled her in.

"I- I was with Nicole." Zoe collapsed into his arms. "I think she ran away when... when that...that... man came."

Her words were warbled and tears streamed down her cheeks.

"Don't anyone move till I clear the area," came Jack's furious voice.

Tanya peered out from behind the rock again.

The chief had stepped around his vehicle, his weapon drawn. He was heading toward the trail.

Tanya pulled her Glock out from her holster.

He needs backup.

She turned around to Fox, who was hugging his wife.

"Stay right here."

Without waiting for a reply, she hunkered low and peered out, scanning the woods for the figure with the rifle.

Whoever you are, you're not getting away.
Not today.

Keeping her head low, she scrambled over to the next boulder, her Glock aimed forward.

Chapter Six

Tanya felt something furry brush against her legs.

Max was following her. He was in stealth mode, his stomach low to the ground, his head down, and his ears back.

Good boy.

Using the large rocks on the beach as shields, Tanya moved closer to the trail. Max kept close to her heels, mimicking her movements.

Several yards ahead of them, Jack had stepped onto the trailhead. He trained his weapon forward and surveyed the trees.

When Tanya got to the boulder closest to the woods, she raised her head and whistled.

Jack turned.

"Coming over," said Tanya.

He nodded. "I'll cover you."

Tanya turned to Max. "Let's go!"

Max rocketed toward the police chief. Tanya darted after him, her gun in her hand. They stopped by the tree Jack was using for cover.

"Did you see the guy?" he asked.

"I was sure I saw the barrel of a shotgun," said Tanya. "I heard it go off, but I don't think it hit the rock we were hiding behind."

"That's strange." Jack frowned. "How could anyone miss a boulder the size of a car?"

Tanya scanned the stretch of trees in front of them, searching for shadows.

"This isn't our typical criminal. Something strange is going on here."

I can feel it in my bones.

"Stay with me," said Jack as he stepped onto the trail, his sidearm at the ready.

They crept around the trees, their weapons aimed ahead, their heads swiveling back and forth, ready for a suspicious movement or sound.

Max trotted quietly next to them, no longer in alert mode. Tanya glanced down as he sniffed a dry leaf.

"The shooter's gone," she said, feeling deflated. "He would be barking like mad if they were still here."

"They may have left a casing," said Jack. "Keep

your eyes peeled so we don't step on potential evidence."

Max whirled around and trotted over to a large pine tree. He smelled the base and circled the trunk. Jack and Tanya stepped up to him and scrutinized the ground.

"Nothing to see here," muttered Jack.

Tanya turned to her dog. "What is it, bud?"

Max thumped his tail and barked softly as if to ask, *Don't you smell what I smell?*

Jack and Tanya examined the nearby trees to see if there were clues there. Max watched them work, his head cocked to the side but not moving from his position by the pine tree.

Tanya walked back to her dog and crouched low at the spot where he had taken a keen interest. She peered through the foliage toward the boulder where Deputy Fox was hunkered with Zoe.

"Given the angle from this tree to the boulder, this is the most probable location of the shooter when I saw them last."

"But there are no footprints, no disarrayed leaves, no shell casings," said Jack, surveying the ground. "Nothing to indicate anyone was here, let alone fired a weapon. Whoever it was, they knew what they were doing."

Tanya narrowed her eyes. "Now that I think of it, the gunfire was muted, like the weapon had a suppressor."

Jack sighed. "The shooter picked up the casing and took off when they heard the sirens."

The feeling of dread came over Tanya again, the same unease she had felt when she had discovered Nicole lying on the rock.

What am I missing?

She lifted her gaze to the branches above them.

Jack followed her eyes and whistled.

"Is that what I think that is?" he said, peering upward.

Tanya leaped to her feet and squinted at the tree branches that spread over their heads several stories high.

"What is it?"

He pointed. "Look at that spot on the branch to your right. I'd bet all of my pension that's a fresh bullet hole."

Tanya's eyes widened.

"The perp fired the gun in the air?"

"This gets stranger and stranger." Jack turned to her. "That was a warning shot."

A shiver went down Tanya's spine.

A warning for what?

Chapter Seven

"Next time, try to find the victims in more accessible venues, would you?"

Dr. Chen grumbled as she waded toward Nicole's body on the rock. A rookie intern, masked and gloved, followed the medical examiner, carrying the death investigation kit.

The tide had surrounded the flat rock now. The wind had also picked up, making it an even more miserable place to be. Everybody was cold and wet, their feet sinking farther into the sand the longer they stood at the crime scene.

"State Patrol is sending a team," said Jack, slipping his phone into his pocket. He rubbed his forehead. "I need all the help I can get."

An earsplitting wail echoed from the parking lot. Everyone turned to look.

The ambulance driver had just turned on her siren. She gave them a somber wave before rolling onto the road, her red lights flashing.

Though they were short-staffed, Tanya was glad Deputy Shawn Fox was accompanying his wife to the hospital.

"How interesting," murmured Dr. Chen, her head bent low over the body. "Warm to the touch. No rigor has set in yet. From a preliminary glance, I would presume the time of death to be within one hour—"

Tanya's eyebrows shot up. "She was killed while I was on my run?"

"Let me finish, Detective. I was about to say any time between one to three hours."

The doctor gestured to the intern, who stepped up to her. Between the two, they turned the corpse over.

Tanya gasped out loud.

It was hard not to remember her mother whenever she saw a blond murder victim of forty years old. It was the bullet hole in Nicole's temple that made her stomach turn.

Just before the medics shooed her out of the ambulance, Zoe had told Tanya that Nicole had come to celebrate her win over cancer. It broke her heart to see a family get torn apart so brutally, like her own family had.

Tanya turned away and closed her eyes. Jack's hand brushed her arm.

"You okay?"

Tanya nodded, but kept her eyes averted from the victim.

She clasped the gold pendant she always wore. It was the only memento she had of her previous life, this single piece of jewelry she had taken from her mother's bloodied body the day she was assassinated by a Russian gang. Tanya had only been eighteen.

Nicole's eyes were wide open, terror etched permanently on her lifeless face.

"Clean bullet wound to the temple," said Dr. Chen, her gloved finger grazing Nicole's forehead. "This dark stippling around the wound tells me the shooting occurred at close range."

The physician looked up at Tanya and Jack.

"She saw her killer. Too bad she isn't alive to tell you what he or she looks like."

She placed Nicole's head back on the rock. The sunflower in her hair fell off and slipped into the water.

The intern grabbed it before the waves washed it away. "Was she taking pictures for social media or something?"

Tanya stared at the wilted flower in the intern's hand, her mind buzzing.

"I think the killer posed her body after he shot her."

Jack jerked his head back.

"How so?"

"Zoe and Nicole walked down the hill from their home for a swim. They didn't bring any flowers."

"How do you know?"

"Because Zoe told me. All they had carried with them were their towels, keys, and ID in waterproof cases, pinned to their swimsuits."

Jack frowned. "Are you telling me the killer shot the victim in the head, placed her face down on the towel to make her look like she was sunbathing, then stuck a sunflower in her hair?"

Tanya sighed. "If we had security cameras around here, we would know what really happened."

Jack rubbed his forehead again.

"I've been demanding that from the city council for years. This might be the trigger they need to get off their bureaucratic bums and do their job."

He turned to the doctor.

"Any signs of assault, Doctor?"

Dr. Chen didn't look up.

"At first glance, I'd say no. There are no telltale bruises. Clothing is intact, but they could have dressed her after the assault." The physician spoke in a crisp, no-nonsense tone. "You'll have to wait until I examine her properly at the morgue, but all I can say now is you have a curious case on your hands, Chief."

Tanya scanned the area, trying not to feel

discouraged. She and Max had done two rounds along the beach, but the waves had erased footprints or other evidence that might have helped them.

"Why pick on a cancer survivor and a school teacher?" said Jack. "Two suburban victims with no criminal records or past deviances. Was this the work of a random killer?"

Dr. Chen tsked and shook her head as she stared down at Nicole's face.

"A random killer playing a random game. What a horrid thing to happen."

Jack reached into his pant pocket, pulled out a small evidence bag and held it up for Tanya.

"This was on your windshield when we came in. Recognize it?"

Tanya peered at the crumpled piece of paper inside the bag.

"There was nothing on my Jeep when I went for my run."

"I thought it was a prank at first." Jack offered the bag to her. "Maybe by a kid. But after what has happened now, I suspect something more."

Tanya squinted at the printed words. They were in comic sans font, the kind used for jokes online. She read the lines out loud as the others listened.

"*I have no form, but I can take any shape. My touch is cold and my embrace unforgiving. Though I have no voice, I will roar in your dying ear. What am I?*"

Dr. Chen frowned.

"What in heaven's name is that?"

Jack turned to her.

"It's a riddle."

Tanya stared at the words, her heart ticking faster.

"A killer's riddle."

Chapter Eight

A small army of state officers trooped into Black Rock's old precinct building. Jack divided them into teams.

One group was to guard the crime scene until the state forensics team completed its work. Another group was tasked to comb the beach, the woods, and the trail for clues they might have missed, and two officers were to dig into cold cases to check similar past homicides.

"Book whatever rooms you have available." Katy was speaking into her phone, her beautiful red hair more frizzy than normal.

"If these guys and gals have to bunk it, that's fine. You've got to have something for us at the motel, Marty. Come on. This is urgent police business."

Tanya stood next to Katy's desk amidst the

bustling office, one hand absentmindedly sliding her gold sunflower pendant back and forth. Max was at her feet, slurping a bowl of water, splashing most of it on her boots.

The ambulance had returned to retrieve Nicole's body and had taken it to Dr. Chen's clinic for the autopsy. Zoe and Fox were still at the hospital in the county over and weren't expected to be home till the next day.

"Interview all past and current boyfriends. Male friends of any kind. Let's start with the usual suspects."

Jack was addressing the two research troopers who stood at attention by his office door.

"Given both sisters were targeted, this must have a familial connection. Do background checks on each adult family member you can find."

"Yes, Chief," chorused the officers.

Jack took his ball cap off, wiped the sweat off his brow, and turned to Katy, his office manager.

"I'm off to notify the parents. They need to know. They might have info to help us out."

Katy nodded. "I'll hold down the fort."

Tanya furrowed her brow as she listened in, her brain buzzing.

Zoe's parents were retired city employees. They were quiet, elderly folk who gardened and played with their grandkid.

Zoe's sister, Nicole, had been a math teacher in

Seattle and a single girl for a long time. Zoe's husband, Deputy Shawn Fox, had joined the police academy soon after graduating. He had a stellar work record. Zoe, herself, wrote romance novels as an escape from her disease.

Other than Zoe's recent battle with cancer, they were the most unassuming and ordinary family Tanya knew.

She realized the chief was only covering all the bases, but this couldn't be a family affair.

Her gut stirred. In her bones, she felt something bigger was at play.

What was the significance of placing a flower on Nicole's hair? Was the killer trying to throw them off by making it look like a crime of passion?

No. This wasn't a random attack, either.

Tanya glanced down at the paper in her hand. It was a photocopy of the bizarre riddle left on her Jeep. Katy had bagged the original and sent it by secure courier to the state forensics lab.

Jack had tasked a junior trooper, who had more tech skills than the others, to scour online sites for the riddle. She was still looking, but had come up with nothing so far.

Tanya's past as a rebel fighter in Ukraine had sharpened her vigilance. Some days, to the point of paranoia. When something was amiss, she always felt it.

Like she was feeling now.

Nicole's killer saw me park the Jeep and placed the note on my windshield while I was on my run. They planned this, so I'd find the dead body and then the note. But why?

She gazed down at Max, who whined and thumped his tail.

Tanya crouched low by her dog and ruffled his head before reaching into her pocket for a treat.

"You were the goodest boy today. Thank you for finding Zoe in time, bud. I'm so proud of you."

Max swooshed his tail in reply and snapped the snack in his jaws.

Tanya rested against Katy's desk with a heavy sigh. The new tech-trooper had taken over her own desk, so it wasn't like she had a place to sit anymore.

She read the riddle again, racking her brain for an answer.

I have no form, but I can take any shape. My touch is cold and my embrace unforgiving. Though I have no voice, I will roar in your dying ear. What am I?

Tanya sat up as she realized she knew someone who could help.

Asha.

She plucked her cell out of her pocket, muttering to herself.

"If anyone can figure this out, it would be her."

Asha had followed her to Black Rock and had moved in only a week ago.

She had already rented the old train station as her

headquarters and hung up her private detective shingle to the curiosity of the locals.

Asha's longtime fiancé, David, was still in New York, wrapping up his martial arts business so he could join her soon. It would be good to have her found family close by again.

The phone rang.

And rang.

Tanya gritted her teeth.

Pick up, Asha. Where are you?

Chapter Nine

"Hey, Tanya!"

Asha sounded breathless, like she had been running.

The noise level inside Black Rock's police precinct had ratcheted up over the past hour, Tanya could hardly hear anything. She pressed the phone to her ear.

"I need your he—"

"I hit a milestone!" Asha's excited voice came down the line, interrupting her. "My first podcast episode is in the bag. I was live too."

"Asha—"

"I'll be the queen of true crime on the West Coast. Just wait."

Tanya sighed. "Don't you have enough of real life crime as it is?"

"You'd never guess who my first interviewees were."

It seemed like her friend hadn't even heard her.

"Ocean and Sahara were amazing. We discussed the incident at the Silver Serenity retirement residence. A few live calls came in too. One was super weird, but hey, trolls are part of the podcast world, right?"

"Asha, I need you to—"

"Hey, ladies!" Asha was calling someone near her vicinity. "It's Tanya. Say hi."

The giddy voices of the two septuagenarians came down the line.

"Hello, my dear," said Sahara. "How are you?"

"Hope you're keeping out of trouble, sweetie," said Ocean.

Tanya shook her head.

Not really.

Sahara and Ocean's personalities were as flamboyant as their bright clothes and oversized jewelry. No one knew their true names or their mysterious pasts, but everyone in town seemed to have an opinion—and not nice ones. But small-town gossip didn't faze these women who carried themselves with power and dignity.

Tanya let out a heavy sigh.

She couldn't share the riddle in front of these two socialites. The entire town would know in seconds what had happened at the beach that morning. That would only create havoc and increase calls to the precinct.

We have enough on our hands already.

"Where are you?" said Tanya in a tired voice.

"Just locked up the studio," said Asha. "We're going to celebrate with high tea and cakes at Lulu's. Want to join us?"

"Listen. Can we talk privately—"

"Is that Asha?" came a frazzled voice from above Tanya's head. She looked up to see Katy leaning over her desk. "Put her on speaker, please."

With a resigned sigh, Tanya clicked on the speakerphone.

Katy leaned closer.

"Asha? It's Katy. Can you pick up Chantal from school? It's a really bad day today."

"Sure thing, sweetie."

A high-pitched chirp came through the speakerphone like Asha had just unlocked her car.

"What are you guys working on over there? Did you find a dead body or somethi—"

The sound of an explosion blasted through the speakerphone.

Tanya reeled back and almost dropped her mobile.

Katy's eyes widened in shock.

Ocean and Sahara's terrified wails came through the phone.

They were screaming Asha's name.

Chapter Ten

Tanya raced across Black Rock, her heart in her mouth.

What in heaven's name just happened?

Everyone at the precinct had mobilized into action the second the blast came through the phone's speaker.

Jack had run out of the precinct and dashed toward his cruiser while Tanya and Katy had jumped into the Jeep with Max. They were all speeding toward the old train station.

"Fire trucks and ambulance are on their way," said Katy, her voice strained.

She placed her phone on her lap and dropped her head in her hands.

"Was that a bomb? What are we going to do if she's... she's—"

Tanya slammed on the brakes as two teens wearing oversized headphones darted into the street. Katy grabbed the door handle, and Max dug his claws into the backseat.

Tanya honked her horn and glared at the errant pedestrians. Max barked in the back.

"Sorry, bud." Tanya checked him via the rearview mirror. "Hang tight."

News of the murder on the beach and the blast at the old train station had gotten around, and the folks of this normally sleepy town were coming out to gawk.

Jack's squad car was ahead of Tanya's vehicle. He had sirens and lights. She didn't. She kept her Jeep's nose as close to Jack's bumper as she could so local traffic wouldn't get in her way.

"Try her number again," said Tanya as she pressed down on the gas pedal.

"Pick up, Asha!" cried Katy into her phone. "Pick up."

"What about Ocean and Sahara?" said Tanya. "They were with her."

"I've tried, but they're not picking up either." Katy let out an exasperated sigh. "They must have left their phones at home."

Tanya slowed down as she approached the town's elementary school. The kids were having their playtime. Their screeches and hollers came from the playground.

Katy turned her head and stared at a group of children on the mini basketball court. Her brow furrowed with concern.

"They don't seem to have heard the blast. If anything happened to Asha, how am I going to explain it to Chantal?"

"First, Asha's probably okay," said Tanya, speaking with more confidence than she felt. "Second, kids are more resilient than we think."

She revved up as she got out of the school zone. "Almost there."

Three minutes later, Tanya raced into the old train station's parking lot and screeched to a stop by a red sports car. It was the only other vehicle in the lot, besides Jack's police cruiser.

Tanya jumped out, her heart filled with dread. Inside the Jeep, Max howled to be let out, but she barely heard him.

Asha's cherished silver convertible was blazing in the center of the station's parking lot. Dark gray fumes hovered over the mangled wreck.

But Asha was nowhere to be seen.

Chapter Eleven

"Let's go!"

Jack slammed his door and dashed toward the burning vehicle.

Tanya raced with him.

Ocean and Sahara were dangerously close to the fire, flailing their arms, shrieking Asha's name.

Red-hot sparks flew from within the wreckage, like someone had lit a mini fireworks display inside.

"Get back!" Jack grabbed the two women.

"But we need to find her!" cried Sahara, struggling to get out of his grasp.

He pulled them away to safety, ignoring their protests.

Tanya whirled closer to the crumpled car, her heart pounding. The fire raged around the vehicle, and the searing heat beat on her face, but she barely felt it.

"Asha!" she shouted. "Asha! Where are you?"

Ignoring the flames, she bent down and peered into the mangled machine, scanning for signs of life. The acrid odor of synthetic fertilizer was strong in the air.

A pipe bomb?

She squinted through the twisted metal, but there didn't seem to be a body inside the wreckage.

Tanya frowned. Asha was petite but not that small. A pipe bomb couldn't blow a human into nothingness.

There would be remains and....

She choked up to even think of it. For one moment, she couldn't breathe.

"Stone!" hollered Jack, still holding on to Sahara and Ocean. "Get away from there!"

"She's not here," cried Tanya. "What happened?"

Ocean twisted around.

"She was on the phone with you."

Tanya stomped over to them, sweat pouring down her face.

"Tell me exactly what happened."

"She was half way down the parking lot when she pushed the remote to unlock her car," said Ocean, "and—"

"The whole world blew up." Sahara threw her arms in the air.

Tanya and Jack exchanged a glance.

"Hang on," said Jack. "She wasn't inside the vehicle when it—"

An incoming firetruck blared its horn, drowning out his voice. Ocean and Sahara slapped their hands over their ears as emergency sirens screeched around them.

The first responders spilled out of their vehicles, hollering to each other and grabbing their equipment. The fire chief jumped out of his truck. Jack spun around on his heels.

"John," he called out, waving to the head of the town's firefighting team.

Katy came over and ushered Sahara and Ocean to the far end of the parking lot. This time, they didn't protest.

Tanya stepped back to the wreck. Fire Chief John Marks would soon close off the scene to anyone but his team, so if she wanted to find Asha, it would have to be now.

She got to her knees and squinted through the flames. She put an arm up to shield her face as the fiery heat blasted around her.

"Asha?" she hollered. "Asha?"

She caught a movement from the corner of her eyes. She braced for yelling from the fire chief but instead heard a bark. A furry brown blur flashed across the parking lot and disappeared around the station building.

Tanya hopped to her feet.

Max?

"I couldn't stop him. He was howling!"

That was Katy. She was calling out anxiously to Tanya from behind the yellow tape barrier the fire team had put up.

"He was about to rip your car to shreds. I had to let him out. Sorry."

Tanya whirled around and narrowed her eyes. Max had made a beeline to the other end of the station, deliberately avoiding the burning wreck.

She caught sight of his tail from the corner of the building. He was sniffing something concealed by the side wall.

"Clear the way!" yelled a firefighter from behind her. Someone shoved Tanya in the back.

"Out of the way!" came another shout.

Tanya heard the loud whoosh of the water hoses opening up, but she didn't hang around. She pushed through the firefighters, almost tripping over their equipment, and darted toward the corner of the building.

"Max?"

Max looked up at her and barked three times.

Tanya's heart dropped.

He was sitting by a prone body. No one had noticed it as it had been hidden by the station's side wall.

It was the body of a small woman.

Chapter Twelve

"Asha!"

Tanya dropped to her knees.

Her friend was lying on her back. Her face was blackened and her eyes were closed. Her jeans and shirt were torn from the force of the blast.

Tanya jerked back as Asha stirred. A trembling hand reached up and touched Max's nose. He wagged his tail and sneezed a happy sneeze.

Tanya's heart skipped a beat.

She's alive.

Max licked Asha's face while Tanya examined her friend.

"The blast wave from the explosion threw you here," she said. "Don't move."

Asha turned to her and blinked. "My b-baby girl's gone."

Tanya bent over, taking stock of the cuts on her face and the bruises on her arms.

"Is anything broken?"

"I was just about to get in and drive to Lulu's," said Asha, stroking Max's nose, "when it went b-boom."

"Stop moving. Where are you injured?"

"My poor baby girl," whispered Asha, blinking away tears. "I loved her to bits."

"You can always get another darned car." Tanya shot her a stern look. "Let's focus on you right now. Where are you hurt?"

"I always w-wanted a convertible. Did you know that? She was my best f-friend... after you and Katy."

Tanya clenched her jaws, but a smidgen of relief crept into her heart. If Asha was so upset about her precious cabriolet, she was alive and alert, and that was all that mattered.

Tanya turned around and gestured to Jack who was marching over.

"She's here!" she hollered.

"Get paramedics now!" Jack shouted to the emergency crew.

Tanya glanced back to see Katy waving desperately from across the lot, held back by the fire chief himself. Two medics ducked under the tape and ran over.

Asha turned to Tanya and grabbed her arm. "He warned me."

Tanya frowned. "Who?"

"The troll. The weirdo who called my podcast."

Tanya wondered if Asha's injuries were worse than they looked and she was hallucinating.

"I should have guessed," whispered Asha.

Tanya leaned closer.

"What are you talking about?"

Asha's eyes flickered.

"Tanya," came Jack's stern voice from behind. "The medics need to access her."

Asha licked her dry lips.

"He said something about having no blood, but a heart of fire. No voice but something about thunder.... And then, the day you meet me is the day yours end."

Tanya's pulse quickened.

"A riddle."

Like the one left on my Jeep by the beach.

The medics pushed Tanya aside and unzipped their first aid kits.

Tanya stumbled back and got to her feet. Asha looked up at her and gave her a weak smile.

"Figured it out too late. The answer is a bomb."

Chapter Thirteen

The medics lifted Asha onto their stretcher. Tanya and Jack stepped back to offer them space.

Asha gave them a feeble thumbs-up as the paramedics carried her away. Max trotted alongside, as if for moral support.

The small group treaded along the edge of the parking lot, ushered by a firefighter, toward the ambulance parked behind the fire trucks.

Tanya turned to the police chief.

"Another riddle. There has to be a connection."

A somber expression came over Jack's face.

"A murder on the beach. An attempted drowning in the ocean. A shooter in the woods. And now a car bomb. All in a day in our little town."

Tanya pulled out the photocopy of the riddle from her pocket.

"It's a psychopath," she said. "They're playing with us—"

"Hey!" called out an angry voice. "You can't go in there. It's a crime scene."

They whirled around.

Sahara and Ocean were ducking under the yellow tape with Katy behind them. The fire chief had been preoccupied with the burned shell of the car so he hadn't noticed, but another first responder had.

"Get back, folks!" he bellowed. "You're not permitted there."

Jack turned to him and waved, to say *it's okay*.

"Didn't I tell you people to head home?" The chief glowered as the trio ran up to him. "I'm not going to be responsible for any more civilian deaths."

Katy turned to him, panting from her short exertion.

"Ocean saw something. Please listen."

Ocean grabbed Jack's arm. "I spotted the guy who did this."

Sahara grabbed his other arm. "It was just a shadow though."

Jack extricated himself from them, pulled out his phone, and switched on the audio record button.

"Can you tell me exactly what you saw?"

"I saw the gangster who tried to murder Asha," said Ocean.

Jack stared at her.

"Did you recognize him?"

"I've never seen him in town before."

Sahara turned to her friend with a flinty look.

"It was just a shadow in the corner. Don't make things up. You have to give them the facts."

"These are the facts." Ocean glared back at her friend. "It was a big, bald guy with a beer belly. He was by the building. I'm sure of what I saw."

"When did you see this... shadow?" said Jack.

"Soon after we arrived for our interview. We were parking the car when I spotted him. It was just before we walked in to say hello to Asha. I didn't think much of it then, but...."

Ocean grabbed Jack's arm again.

"He looked like the typical Mafia goon. Organized crime is targeting Asha because of her new true crime podcast. They're worried she'll expose them."

Jack frowned.

"How do you deduce all this?"

"Here's what I suggest you do, Chief." Ocean wagged a finger in his face. "Ferret out the gangs in town and interrogate the members, one by one. I'd bet you'll find the criminal who did this through my description alone."

Jack let out a sigh. "If only it was that easy."

Tanya leaned toward the women.

"You were there when Asha did her live podcast, right?"

Sahara nodded. "We were her first guests."

"Did a troll call in?"

Sahara's brow furrowed. "Sounded more like a robot. I thought it was some idiotic kid in their basement using one of those electronic voice disguise things."

Jack's brow furrowed. "Was it a male or female voice?"

"If robots can have a gender, it was undeniably male," said Ocean. "A very creepy male."

"What did he say?" said Tanya.

"He was the third caller." Sahara put a finger to her chin, like she was trying to remember. "Asha interviewed us before opening the phone lines for questions. She was expecting a dozen calls, but got only three. It was a bit disappointing, but it was her first time."

Ocean pursed her lips. "She hung up on him."

Tanya tried again. "Did he say anything before she hung up?"

"He said big things were going to happen in Black Rock," said Sahara.

"Asha asked him to elaborate," said Ocean. "He said she had to answer a question first."

Sahara scrunched her brow. "He rattled off something weird...I couldn't make head or tail of it."

"Was it a riddle?" said Tanya.

Sahara snapped her fingers. "That's it. He prattled something about blood, and thunder and voice, and ended with *what am I?*"

"Did Asha give him the answer on air?" said Jack.

"She was as puzzled as we were," said Ocean. "We were sure it was a prank."

Jack's phone rang, startling them. He put his mobile to his ear. Everyone waited quietly, listening to the incomprehensible high-pitched voice on the other end.

"Right away, Doctor," he said, hanging up.

He looked at Katy. "Can you coordinate the teams at the office?"

"Not a problem."

Katy spun around to Ocean and Sahara, but Sahara spoke up before she could.

"Yes, sweetie, we can pick up Chantal from school. Don't you worry now. Go, do your job."

"Peace is still out of town," said Katy, flustered. "He's at business meetings all day. Otherwise—"

Sahara squeezed her shoulder.

"We're taking care of Zak till Zoe and Shawn come home. I'm sure he would love to have Chantal as a play date. They'll get to camp out in our living room."

"Please make her finish her homework."

"We got the kids, honey," said Ocean. "You get the sick bastard who did this."

Jack, Tanya, and Katy walked briskly toward their

51

vehicles across the parking lot, giving wide berth to the firefighters assessing the bomb damage.

"What did Dr. Chen want?" said Tanya.

Jack didn't slow his pace.

"The hospital discharged Zoe. They just got back in town."

He paused as he reached his cruiser.

"Zoe might have something for us."

Chapter Fourteen

Max was waiting for Tanya by the Jeep. He whined happily to see her. Tanya opened the back door for him while Katy got in the front passenger seat and put her belt on.

"Thank goodness it's only a concussion," said Katy. "She could have gotten killed."

"Not everyone would have survived unscathed," said Tanya. "She's young, healthy, and fit. Plus, it was pure luck she landed on the soft lawn, and she was at least twenty feet away from the vehicle when it blew up. Any closer and...."

She shuddered to think of the consequences.

She turned around to pet Max. He always made her feel better. She clipped the loose pet-safety mesh back in position and bopped her dog on his nose.

"This is your seatbelt, you big doofus. Stop pulling this out or I'll have to ticket you."

Max turned his head away, but not before she noticed his side-eye roll. She ruffled his ears and gave him a treat.

"That's for finding Asha. You were a real good boy today."

Katy turned around and smiled at Max.

"He deserves all the treats. He's our secret therapy dog, just by being here."

Max barked and wagged his tail like he understood.

Tanya put her Jeep in gear.

A crowd had gathered by the old train station, kept at bay by a handful of junior troopers and the yellow tape. Other than the lone reporter from Black Rock's weekly newspaper, there weren't any cameras or television vans stalking the scene.

Jack had already taken off to Dr. Chen's clinic. Sahara and Ocean had left in their red sports car.

Tanya maneuvered her vehicle gently through the crowd. The journalist spotted her, rushed over, and knocked on her window. Tanya kept her eyes in front and inched her vehicle forward.

The Black Rock's ocean promenade usually buzzed with activity in the afternoons. It was the time of day when people got off work, picked up their kids from school, and went for ice cream, fish-and-chips, and walks along the beach.

But that day was different. A subdued unease hung heavy in the air as news of the shocking incidents trickled through the small town.

Tanya parked her Jeep next to Jack's cruiser at the clinic.

Katy stepped out and opened Max's door. Tanya was about to lock her vehicle when a furious female voice rang from inside.

"Asha Kade, I demand you get back in here!"

Tanya and Katy whirled around. A petite woman in a wheelchair rolled out of the front sliding doors.

With her singed hair, dusty face, and torn clothes, Asha looked like a refugee from a war zone, but she held her chin high. She was pushing the wheels with all her might.

Max darted over to her with a joyful bark, like he hadn't seen her in ages.

Dr. Chen stomped out of the main entrance, her face flushed.

"This is my clinic, and you must obey my rules!"

"Get me out of here," said Asha, rolling over to Tanya and Katy. "She's going to kill me."

Katy stared at their friend. "*Kill* you?"

"She shot me with morphine."

Dr. Chen stomped over. Tanya and Katy took a cautionary step back. For a diminutive woman, the physician had an explosive personality that packed a powerful punch.

The doctor spun around to Asha and placed her hands on her hips.

"Do you have a death wish?"

"What?"

"You're in no state to be on the streets. What part of that simple request don't you understand?"

Asha tapped her ear.

"You know I can't hear anymore. Besides that, I feel fine."

"Huh!" Dr. Chen scoffed. "You feel fine because of my painkillers."

"I have to get back to the studio," said Asha, turning her chair around to Tanya, ignoring the physician. "We might be able to trace that troll's call. It could point us to the bomber."

The doctor leaned over to her with a scowl.

"And give them another chance to finish you off?"

Asha turned her wheelchair away from her once again.

"Sorry, Doctor. Can't hear a word you're saying."

Dr. Chen's face turned red.

"You'll crawl back, crying for help when things feel worse, and things always feel worse before they feel better."

Tanya stared at the two women. Both were at least a head shorter than her and small in stature, and one of them was injured, but she wondered if she would survive breaking up a physical fight between them.

She tapped Asha on her shoulder.

"You just survived a bomb blast. The medics said you're lucky to have gotten off with no broken bones."

Asha squinted at her.

"What? Speak louder."

Tanya raised her voice.

"You have a concussion. You need rest!"

Asha's eyes flashed.

"Are you people going to hang around here chitchatting, or are you going to figure out who destroyed my car?"

The physician glowered at Tanya like this was her fault.

"Your friend is as bone-headed as you are. I can't be responsible for her irresponsible decisions."

With a furious hiss, she whirled around and marched toward the entrance, bumping into the intern who had come out to find what the commotion was about.

"Roll that patient back in," shouted Dr. Chen as she stomped inside. "Strap her down if you have to. I'm not having my patients run around, willy-nilly, before I give the green light to discharge."

The intern stared at Asha but stood rooted to her spot, like she couldn't decide which would be worse, tackling a headstrong patient or disobeying her boss.

Katy put her hands up.

"I don't have time for this. I've got work to do at the station."

She spun around. Tanya watched her hurry over to the police precinct next door.

Everyone's on edge. And for good reason.

Tanya turned to her friend in the wheelchair. Asha was stroking Max's head, a stubborn expression on her face.

"What were you thinking?" said Tanya, spreading her hands out.

Asha turned around and squinted.

"Why are you mumbling?"

Tanya raised her voice.

"Because you were thrown in a blast!"

Asha pointed at the clinic doors, where the intern was hovering, looking like she was trying to rustle up the courage to come over.

"There's a murder victim lying in the morgue," said Asha. "It's Zoe's sister, Nicole. Did you know that?"

Tanya sighed. "I'm not at liberty to—"

"She was shot this morning at the beach. Why didn't anyone tell me?"

Tanya dropped her shoulders. "It's police business."

"I was targeted too, so I have the right to know." Asha narrowed her eyes. "Besides, I can help. You need me, and you know that."

Tanya stared at her friend. Asha glowered back.

"If you had warned me, maybe I would have known the troll was the killer."

With a reluctant sigh, Tanya pulled out the riddle that had been burning in her pocket.

"Can you figure this out for us?"

Asha grabbed the photocopy and furrowed her brow.

"Another riddle?"

"I'm afraid so, yes."

"Hmm...," murmured Asha as she bowed her head over the paper.

Tanya waited patiently, wondering how much the concussion had impacted her.

Dr. Chen is right. She really should be in bed.

A pang of guilt shot across Tanya.

I really shouldn't be encouraging her. She needs rest, not an intellectual challenge.

Asha slapped the paper on her thighs and looked up, a smug expression on her face.

"What's wrong with you people? This isn't that difficult."

Chapter Fifteen

"The answer to this riddle is ocean water," said Asha.

Tanya plucked the photocopy off her friend's lap and re-read the words.

"I challenge you to prove me wrong," said Asha.

"*I have no form, but I can take any shape.*" Tanya jerked her head up. "Water. I see that now." She frowned. "*My touch is cold.... I will roar in your dying ear.* What does that mean—"

She took a sharp breath in as the realization hit her.

"Waves. Ocean waves crashing on the rocks." Tanya looked at her friend. "Death by drowning in ocean water. That was how the killer had planned to murder Zoe."

Asha nodded. "And I was supposed to die from an explosion. That troll's riddle was a warning too."

Tanya frowned.

"A warning gives sufficient time to get out of harm's way. These are death threats."

"Are you coming?" called a male voice from the entrance to the clinic. It was Jack, waving Tanya over. "She's ready to talk."

Tanya nodded and turned to Asha.

"Zoe might have seen something."

"I saw her and Fox come in," said Asha. "She's not looking great." A grim expression came over her face. "Come hell or high water, I'm going to find the killer and make them pay."

Tanya sighed, knowing she couldn't hold her friend off for long. Besides, she could use her investigation skills and keen brain.

"Come on. You can join us. But if Dr. Chen comes at you with another morphine syringe, you're on your own."

"Let her try."

With a relieved sigh, the intern grabbed the wheelchair's handlebars and rolled Asha in. Tanya followed them, with Max at her heels.

The clinic's receptionist got up as they trooped in through the deserted waiting room. She pointed to the back of the clinic where the examination rooms lay.

"Chief just went in. They're in room A."

Max left Tanya's side and made his way over to her, his tail swishing.

Tanya had long suspected the receptionist secretly fed her dog cookies, even after she had expressly asked her not to. The way Max scampered around her, licking his lips, told her the transgression continued, but she had more important matters to attend to.

She stepped up to the closed door and pushed the handle down.

Four anxious faces turned toward her.

Dr. Chen's examination rooms were small, and this one was already crowded.

Zoe and Fox sat hunched in the patients' chairs while the physician was perched on her stool. Jack was leaning against the counter.

Tanya had visited Zoe during her cancer treatments but she had never seen her this frail. Her heart fell, knowing her sister's violent death would be even harder for Zoe to recover from.

Dr. Chen scowled as she spotted Asha in her wheelchair.

"What is my patient doing here?"

Tanya put a hand up.

"She solved the first riddle. It refers to the killer's methods. She can help us."

Dr. Chen and Asha glared at each other for a second.

"The answer is water," said Asha, turning to Zoe. "Water as in drowning you in sea water."

Zoe turned an anguished face to Tanya, then to Jack.

"What about Nicole? Did he leave something about shooting her, too?"

Jack shook his head.

"Officers are scouring the area for a second note, but they've come up empty handed, so far. We'll keep looking."

"I don't think you'll find one."

Asha wheeled closer to Zoe, her face grave.

"The killer was targeting *you*."

Chapter Sixteen

Zoe gasped out loud.

"Why me?"

Asha shrugged. "That's what we have to find out."

"Why Nicole? What did she ever do?" cried Zoe. "She volunteered at the soup kitchen and taught disadvantaged kids. She is... She was an angel."

"If I have to guess," said Asha, "Nicole saw the killer and most probably tried to warn you. He had to shut her up and... did the unthinkable."

Zoe placed her hand on her face.

"Nicole changed her mind when we got to the beach. She said it was too cold. I was so mad at her because she didn't come swimming with me. I told her to go home. I wasn't really nice."

Her voice wavered and her shoulders drooped.

"If I stayed with her, just a few minutes longer... I left her to die."

Tears rolled down Zoe's cheeks and her chest heaved as she sobbed.

Jack caught Tanya's eye. She knew what he was thinking. In her distress, Zoe hadn't realized she was the one who wouldn't be here if she had delayed her swim.

Fox put an arm around his wife and kissed her forehead. "You can't blame yourself, babe," he whispered.

Tanya felt something catch in her throat.

"What would help us now," said Jack, speaking in a soft voice, "are any details that would help us identify the perpetrator."

Zoe sat up and wiped her face.

"I saw him."

Everyone jerked their heads back.

"I'm sure it was a man," said Zoe, her lips trembling. "I remember his shoes."

Tanya straightened up.

"What about his shoes?"

"They were moccasins. Crimson red-velvet moccasins."

Dr. Chen frowned. "Who in their right mind wears velvet moccasins to the beach?"

"I know what I saw."

Zoe spoke quietly, her face down, her hands folded on her lap.

"It was just a flash, but I saw those shoes, expensive ones too. It's clear as day to me now."

"How do you know they were expensive?" said Jack.

"Because I saw them online last Christmas."

She reached for her husband's hand.

"Shawn needed new slippers, so I looked up moccasins for men," said Zoe. "I found a pair just like that in a fancy online French store. They were almost two thousand dollars."

Dr. Chen scoffed. "Which idiot buys thousand-dollar slippers?"

"They were bright red with a silver skull and bones patch on the lip. They were the exact same ones."

Asha stirred in her wheelchair. She had been leaning forward to listen, a hand cupped to her ear.

"That was a message," she said in a quiet voice.

Jack turned to her. "Can you tell me what this message is, so I can catch the scumbag?"

"We're dealing with a psychopath who believes himself to be intelligent, and who most probably is." Asha spoke slowly, like she was thinking it through. "He's challenging us to identify him."

She turned to Zoe.

"He wanted you to see those shoes, so we would ruminate over them. Worry about them."

"Hogwash," snapped Dr. Chen. "What purpose does that serve?"

"He's toying with us," said Asha. "He targeted Zoe and me. We're pieces on a checkerboard. This is all a game to the killer."

"That's the most asinine hypothesis I've ever heard." Dr. Chen scoffed again. "This sounds like a dumb Hollywood movie made for stupid people by stupid people."

"I'm telling you. This is a cat-and-mouse game." Asha pursed her lips. "We're the mice."

Jack shook his head.

"He's playing with *human lives*."

"He got close enough to shoot Nicole, grab and blindfold you, Zoe, and attach an IED under your car, Asha."

Tanya looked at each person in the room, so they would hear the gravity of her words.

"I think we can safely say the killer is here, walking among us."

The room fell silent.

Chapter Seventeen

A loud bang made Tanya jump.

She slammed on the brakes and scanned the road, one hand on her holster. Max whirled in the backseat, barking.

A rusty pickup truck rolled by, bellowing smoke from under its hood, its tailpipe dragging on the asphalt. The two teens in the front snickered like they were amused by her sudden reaction.

Tanya glared at them as they waved cheekily.

The rolling rust bucket backfired again, and Max unleashed another barrage of furious barks. Tanya turned around and reached for him over the safety net.

"It's okay, bud. Nothing to worry about. Just an old car."

It's not another bomb.

Max gave a final warning bark at the boys, before flopping down on the backseat with a long grumble, as if to say, *What losers.*

Tanya's heart was still racing a million miles a minute. She rested a hand on her chest, willing herself to calm down.

It was late at night, and she had spent all day looking for a homicidal maniac who had shot a friend's sister and almost murdered two people Tanya was close to.

She clutched the Jeep's steering wheel, feeling the day's exhaustion creep into her bones. Her head hurt, her back ached, and her eyelids felt heavy.

She had been in war zones and seen much worse before, but the day's events were getting to her, and she was beginning to see shadows everywhere.

The only relief in the midst of the madness was how everyone pulled together.

With both of their partners out of town, Asha had decided to spend the night at Katy's. A junior officer was stationed outside the house, under orders from Jack.

Ocean and Sahara had stepped up to play foster grandmothers for Zak, Zoe and Fox's son. They had also given their guest room over to Chantal, Katy and Peace's daughter.

Nine-year-old Chantal was too smart to be kept in the dark. She knew something was wrong and had been asking questions no one wanted to answer.

Everyone hoped Ocean and Sahara could keep the kids distracted for a while.

Tanya wanted to scoop them all in her arms and watch over them. They were family, the only family she had left.

But her body and brain screamed for rest. She needed at least a few hours of sleep to clear her head if she was going to outwit the riddle-playing monster terrorizing their town.

She shook herself awake.

Go home, take a shower, and grab some sleep.

Tanya placed her phone on the dashboard before putting the Jeep into gear.

"Dial Ray Jackson," she said, as she rolled back onto the road.

Chapter Eighteen

Max thumped his tail on the backseat as he heard the name of one of his favorite people.

"This is a bad time," came an irritated male voice.

Ray sounded even more like Morgan Freeman, the actor everyone said he was a perfect doppelgänger for.

He hadn't even bothered to greet her. Tanya glanced at her mobile briefly before turning her attention back to the road.

"Hello to you too, Ray. I'm calling for help."

"You're on your own, Agent."

Tanya frowned. "Things are bad here. I need resources. Federal-level resources."

"How many victims this time?"

Tanya exhaled audibly.

"One homicide. Gunshot to the temple. Two attempted murders. One from drowning and one from a pipe bomb under a vehicle. Both survived, but I'm expecting the killer to strike again."

He was silent for such a long time that Tanya wondered if she had lost the connection.

"Ray? Are you still there?"

"Not going anywhere for a while." He sounded annoyed. "I'm stuck here now."

"Where are you?"

"DC."

Tanya raised a brow.

Ray had retired from his role as an undercover FBI agent years ago, shortly after his family was gunned down by a criminal with a long rap sheet. Ever since then, he had been quietly providing support to field agents from his farm base near Black Rock.

Ray was her only communication link to the FBI headquarters in Seattle. He was her lifeline.

Is he looking for another job? Am I going to lose him?

Tanya felt her stomach flip.

"Did you decide to get into politics, Ray?"

A low chuckle came from the other end.

"Not me. But our esteemed director has."

Tanya raised a brow.

"Susan Cross?"

Ray lowered his voice.

"She's been in hush hush meetings all week, talking to the biggest wigs in the capital. I'm playing bodyguard and chauffeur."

"Doesn't she have her own driver?"

"She said she can't trust too many folks, anymore. Politics is a dog-eat-dog world of double-dealers and backstabbers. If you thought our office politics were bad, you should see Washington."

"What's she running for?"

"Congress."

Tanya's eyebrows shot up. "Wow."

"I told you Director Cross has high ambitions. She might even run for president one day. Who knows?"

"Good for her." Tanya furrowed her brow. "What does this mean for us?"

"What this means, Agent Stone, is you can't screw up. If you do anything to make her look bad, or if you blow your undercover, you're toast. Badly burned toast, I might add."

Tanya clenched her jaws.

"I always get the job done."

"Here's my advice to you, kiddo." Ray's voice had softened. "Don't get distracted by the locals. You're a good agent. You've been given a mission. Get it done—"

He stopped abruptly, like someone had entered the room.

"It's our undercover in Black Rock." He wasn't

speaking to Tanya anymore, and his tone had turned reverent, like the Pope and the Dalai Lama were with him.

"Does she have intel?"

Tanya froze to hear the FBI director's sharp voice. Susan Cross was a feared woman—and not just by her direct employees.

Ray Jackson mumbled something.

"Hand over the phone," said Cross.

To Tanya's surprise, the director came on the line. Cross rarely spoke with employees at the bottom of the rung, and didn't contact field agents unless absolutely necessary. That was what the Ray Jacksons of the world were paid for.

"News, Agent?"

Tanya straightened up and almost saluted, though the big boss couldn't see her.

"A firearm homicide in Black Rock and two attempted murders, one with a pipe bomb, ma'am." Tanya spoke briskly, knowing Cross hated to waste time on trivial matters. "We might have a serial killer on our hands."

"One homicide and you call it a serial?" Cross sounded irritated. "Why on earth do you think the good people of Washington pay their taxes? They have the State Patrol, elected county sheriffs, and police precincts to take care of these incidents. This isn't a federal job."

"We don't think the killer's done."

Tanya rustled up her most diplomatic voice which was always hard to do.

"The local team is strapped for resources, even with the state and nearby counties doing their—"

"Let them figure it out," hissed Cross. "Your focus is the Grimwood Estate. Get intel on the organized crime ring we believe to be operating there. Return to HQ with credible evidence I can use to set up a sting op and take these goons to court. Got it?"

"Yes, ma'am."

"Do you enjoy your work?"

Tanya sucked her breath in and closed her eyes. In the backseat, Max whined softly like he knew how she was feeling.

"Yes, ma'am."

"Keep running off on tangents like you've been doing and you'll soon find yourself out of a job. Is that understood?"

Tanya opened her mouth to respond.

But the line had already gone dead.

Chapter Nineteen

S *moke.*
    Tanya peered into the darkness, and her shoulders stiffened.

She was driving along the lonely road that led to her home as usual. But the smoky gray trail rising from behind her cottage was unmistakably different.

A surge of adrenaline shot through her.
Fire!
My house is on fire!
She jammed on the brakes.
Did the killer come looking for me?
She felt a sudden rush in her chest.
I won't be victim number four.
She reached into her glove compartment, yanked out the sheathed knife she kept for emergencies, and

slipped it into her boot. She pulled her sidearm out of its holster and cocked it.

I'm ready for you.

She surveyed the compact one-story house at the end of the street. Her darkened home, huddled among the tall fir trees, remained quiet.

An ominous red glow was coming from behind the cottage, reflecting on the woods in the back. The light flickered in the breeze, creating ghostly shadows against the trees.

Her house wasn't on fire.

Tanya blinked and shook her head to clear it, wondering if her exhaustion was making her see things.

But she didn't imagine the strong odor of smoke. In the backseat, Max was sitting up and sniffing the air. He smelled it, too.

She scrutinized the road, the woods, and her front yard. She squinted at the cottage's facade, looking for signs of a break-in. But the house remained as silent as she had left it that morning.

Ray Jackson had selected this small rental property for her, precisely because of its isolation. Her undercover home in Black Rock was located at the base of a hill and backed into the forest that grew up the steep incline. There were no neighbors for a mile, just the way she and her bureau bosses liked it.

Tanya lowered her window an inch.

The strong scent of burning firewood wafted

into her car. It smelled exactly like when Chantal and Zak came over to roast marshmallows in her backyard.

Someone lit my firepit?

Tanya leaned over to her phone on the dashboard.

"Call Jack Bold."

Max let out a low growl. Tanya whipped her head up.

A silhouette was now visible next to her cottage.

Her heart skipped a beat. Ocean's words swirled into her head.

A big, bald man with a beer belly.

The shadow moved out of the corner and lumbered toward her, his outline growing clearer as he approached her vehicle.

Tanya waited in the car with one hand on her gun. She scanned him for weapons, but he seemed empty-handed.

His shoulders were down, and his posture was hunched. This wasn't the behavior she would have expected from a killer.

Max growled again, more ferociously this time.

Tanya narrowed her eyes. The man looked strangely familiar.

Do I know him?

He was getting closer.

Max let out a volley of warning barks. The man

stopped in his tracks and stared, like he hadn't realized there was a dog in the vehicle.

"Tanya?"

Tanya jumped in her seat. It was Jack. He had finally picked up the phone.

"Hey, Jack, I—"

She stopped in mid-sentence.

The stranger was now trapped in her Jeep's headlights. A wide smile broke across his plump face as he peered through her windshield.

He waved.

Tanya's jaw dropped.

Impossible.

It can't be him.

Chapter Twenty

"Olek?" Tanya burst out.

"Who's that?" came Jack's voice through the phone's speaker. "Are you okay?"

Tanya turned to her mobile.

"It's my cousin. Haven't seen him in years."

Even as she uttered those words, she couldn't believe she was saying them.

"Where are you?" said Jack.

"I'm at home. Max is with me. I saw activity behind the cottage and, er, panicked.... But it's okay."

"Who's this guy?"

"We grew up together." Tanya stared at the apparition in her headlights. "He's the only blood relative I have left."

Olek was standing a few feet from the Jeep's

bumper now, wheezing like the jaunt across the front yard had worn him out.

He waved at her again, like a child would.

"Hope you don't mind," he called out in his familiar Eastern European accent. "I made myself a fire in the back."

He hugged himself and shivered, then gave her a goofy grin. "It was getting cold."

Tanya relaxed her shoulders.

This was exactly what she would have expected Olek to do. Walk in unannounced after years of not seeing her, make himself right at home, and expect that to be perfectly normal.

Jack's troubled voice came through the speakerphone.

"I can come over. Check him out. Make an appearance. I'm still in uniform."

Tanya turned to her cell. "It's fine. I'm a bit jumpy right now. That's all."

"If this guy's family and he's not bothering you, I'm good. But you can call me any time, okay?"

"Thanks, Jack. Good night."

She slipped the phone in her pocket and holstered her weapon. She stepped out of the Jeep. In the back seat, Max was still barking at the intruder.

Olek waddled over to her, looking like the gentle giant she remembered him to be.

"Heya, cousin," he said with another goofy grin.

As if in reply, Max howled. Olek spun around to the Jeep and crossed himself.

"Sounds like you got a werewolf in there."

"You better believe it," said Tanya. "How did you know where I was?"

Olek pointed at her cottage. A bent bicycle was leaning against the side wall.

So that's how he came here.

"Nice digs," he said.

Tanya surveyed her cousin. His clothes were crumpled and dirty, like he had been sleeping in them for days. A slight unwashed smell wafted from him.

"What are you doing here?" she said.

Olek's brow furrowed.

"You're not happy to see me?"

"It's just out of the blue....and no one knows where I am at the moment."

Olek's frown deepened like he didn't understand.

"I, er, found Asha's website. She's a PI now. She even has a true crime podcast."

Tanya nodded.

"I thought if she was in this town," said Olek, "there's a good chance I'll find you here too. And here you are. My only cousin in the world."

"But how did you know I lived here?"

He frowned again, as if to say, *What a bizarre question.*

He pointed with his chin toward the road.

"Knocked on every danged door in this town. That lady down there said she doesn't know a Tetyana, but someone called Tanya lived here alone. Figured I'd take my chances and hang around to see if it was really you. "

Tanya shook her head in disbelief.

Her cousin, whom her village called the local buffoon, the man with a slightly lower IQ than everyone else, had circumvented the largest federal law enforcement agency and had found her.

Wait till Ray Jackson hears of this.

She took a step closer to him.

"Why didn't you call me?"

Olek shrugged. "I-I... got busy, you know?"

He spread his arms wide.

"Can I have a hug from my only cousin in the whole wide world?"

He came over and wrapped his massive arms around her in a bear hug. Tanya felt a lump in her throat. Max howled in the backseat in protest.

Tanya pushed Olek gently away and looked him over.

"Why did you come?"

"You... but, you..." He stopped and swallowed hard. "Just, er, needed, er, a place to rest my head for the night."

"You came all the way to crash on my couch?"

He turned his head away and rubbed his neck.

When he spoke, he wasn't making eye contact any more.

"I'm desperate."

Chapter Twenty-One

"They forced me."

Olek's voice was so low, Tanya had to lean in to hear him.

They were seated around the firepit, two warm beer bottles in their hands.

The flames crackled and flickered, casting an eerie glow on the forest behind the cottage. Shadows that seemed to have a life of their own danced around them. The aroma of the barbecue by the back porch wafted over.

Max had taken a strategic spot nearby, knowing a midnight feast would soon come his way. He hadn't warmed up to the stranger, but had relaxed after Olek had sat down with a bottle of beer.

Tanya placed her bottle on the ground next to her chair.

"When did Chanda find out you were siphoning her funds?"

Olek hung his head. "A year ago."

Strange, thought Tanya. *Why didn't Chanda call me?*

"She was embarrassed to tell anyone," said Olek, like he could read her mind. "She fired me on the spot. She told me I was a monster, but... but I was neck deep in debt."

"To whom?"

Her cousin's eyes flickered. A burning log hissed as if in warning.

"The Bratva Brigade."

"*The Russian mafia family?*" Tanya sat up in alarm. "Why on good earth would you—"

"Because they helped me escape."

Olek hunkered on his log and rubbed his face.

"They put me on a boat and brought me to America. That was the only way I got out alive from Ukraine. They were my saviors."

"They are snakeheads," Tanya snarled. "The lowest scum on earth."

"And the most powerful. I owed them my life, and they knew it. But I couldn't afford to pay them back. That's why I—"

"That's why you took money from an orphanage?" Tanya felt her neck grow warm. "You stole from *children.*"

Olek hunched his back even more, like he was too ashamed to look at her.

"They... They sent a g-goon to the orphanage," he stammered. "Chanda didn't even know. She said he was the best security guard ever, but he was there to intimidate me. He made me steal the money. I was scared for my life."

Tanya inhaled deeply and took stock of what she had just heard.

"Is the Bratva Brigade still on your heels?"

Olek shook his head, but kept his eyes averted.

"I'm done with them."

"But are they done with you?"

"I paid off my debts, didn't I?"

"What do you need the money for, then?"

Olek gave her a strange look, like she should know.

"To... to pay Chanda back and to... to tide me over till I find a job. A real job."

"What kind of work are you looking for?"

Olek gave her that curious look again, then shrugged.

"I...I can deliver pizza. Wash dishes. Mop floors. Anything I can get. I swear, I'm done with being a grunt for the Bratva family."

Tanya didn't reply, but she had noticed how he shuffled his feet and kept his eyes on the fire so she couldn't see into his soul. It had been a long time since she had seen her cousin, but her gut was waving red flag after red flag.

He's lying to me.

The Olek she remembered was a follower, not a leader. He bumbled along and tried his best, but seemed to always make bad choices in life.

Her cousin was a miserable thief.

But is he a killer?

Chapter Twenty-Two

Tanya was fully awake now, despite her exhaustion.

"Hey, remember how you, me, and Yevhen used to play in old farmer Domitrivich's field?" Olek grinned. "Yevhen was always blowing things up. The old farmer was always chasing us out with his gun. That crazy old coot."

Tanya winced.

Yevhen.

She reached for her gold pendant and clutched it tightly. Any mention of her younger brother made her sick to the stomach. He had died a brutal and violent death, and it had been her fault.

Olek was watching her.

"You're thinking of Yevhen, aren't you?"

Tanya looked down and blinked away her tears.

"It was a long time ago. I live a different life now." A tear rolled down her cheek. "Seeing you is bringing it all back."

Olek sat up, like he was eager to please. "I live a different life too, now. My past is my past."

Tanya stared at him, wondering why he was so insistent.

"I promise you I'm turning my life around." His voice was earnest. "I just need another chance. I'll pay Chanda and the orphanage back. I'm ready to go to even cop school, if you can get me in."

Tanya raised a brow.

You wouldn't be accepted even if the king of England vouched for you, dear cousin.

Her brain whirred.

Ocean had been adamant she had seen a big, bald man with a beer belly by the old train station, but she also had a vivid imagination.

Is Olek our killer?

He was a simple man with simple ideas, with the courage of a frightened rabbit. She couldn't imagine him shooting Nicole, tying up Zoe, and blowing up a car, let alone planning these complex crimes.

No, that made no sense.

She squeezed her eyes shut, hoping her own mind wasn't running away from her.

Olek's presence in Black Rock could be completely random. She would be hampering her investigation by jumping to the wrong conclusions.

A ping came from her phone.

She clicked on the message icon, wondering if it was Jack. She stared at the text.

I told you so.

An icy chill went down her spine. Her eyes went to the sender line.

ANON.

It was the anonymous person who had been tormenting her for the past year. She had been receiving bizarre texts from ANON, whoever that was, ever since she had arrived in Black Rock.

The messages taunted her with her past and hinted at her brother being alive. They were like poisoned arrows that pierced her heart.

Asha and Katy thought they were pranks by a bored teen in his mother's basement, a kid skilled enough to hunt down personal information from the dark web. But Tanya couldn't help feel there was more to it. There weren't many who knew of her brother's brutal death at the hands of the red thugs.

She lifted her head and glanced at Olek.

Is it him?

Her cousin was cradling his beer bottle in one hand and poking the fire with the other.

He couldn't have sent me this. He couldn't have scheduled this either.

Olek barely knew how to update his computer.

The wood pyramid she had built in the pit collapsed into the fire, creating a mini fireworks display. A hot cinder fell near Max, who had been napping near the pit. He pulled his paws back in a hurry, got up and shook himself before trotting over to his water bowl near the kitchen door.

Olek had fallen silent again and was staring into the fire, as if transfixed by the flames.

Tanya leaned over to him.

"I need you to tell me the truth."

Olek looked up startled.

"I did. Just like you told me to."

She held his gaze. "When did you get to town?"

"This... er, morning. Why?"

"What time?"

"Ten-ish."

Four hours after Nicole's body was discovered on the beach. But I have only his word for it.

"Were you near the old train station this afternoon?"

He stared at her, confusion in his eyes, mixed in with fear.

"Talk to me, Olek."

"I, er, just got to this town." He looked away. "I don't even know...." He swallowed hard, his Adam's apple bobbing up and down as he did. "I didn't even know you had a train station."

Tanya raised a brow.

Really?

Black Rock's old train station was a fixture in this town. With its quaint wooden facade, green gabled

92

roof, and the large plaque that designated it a heritage building, it was hard to miss.

Olek hugged himself, like he was cold all of a sudden.

"Why are you asking me all these questions? I thought... I thought...."

He let out a heavy sigh.

"Why are you treating me like a criminal?" His voice rose in pitch. "I told you. I'm changing. I'm on the good side now. You know that. Why are you picking on me?"

Tanya sat back in her chair, observing the nervous twitches on his face.

Thou doth protest too much, dear cousin of mine.

You're hiding something from me, but you're not a killer.

She got to her feet.

"Couch is yours for the night."

Without waiting for an answer, Tanya marched through the kitchen door with Max.

She walked straight into her bedroom and bolted the door. She pulled her Glock out of the holster and placed it on her bedside table.

Max trotted over to his large doggy bed and twirled around it.

"You can sleep on the bed tonight, bud."

Tanya slipped under the covers and patted the side. Max jumped on the bed, and with a loud groan, flopped down.

Tanya lay quietly, feeling her dog's weight on her legs. It was comforting to have him close by. She listened to the sound of the fire crackling outside her window, with one thought swirling in her mind.

Why exactly did Olek come to Black Rock?

She reached over, picked up her weapon, and double-checked the chamber before slipping it under her pillow.

Her gut had been warning her ever since she'd seen Olek by her cottage. His story had too many holes.

Someone enticed him here. Whoever they are, they can't have good intentions.

Tanya thrust her hand under her pillow where she could feel the barrel of her gun.

She would be prepared when she needed it.

~

Day Two
At Tanya's cottage

Chapter Twenty-Three

A shrill alarm rang through Tanya's ears. She grabbed her gun and sat up. Her bedroom was empty, but was flooded with light. She raised a hand to shield her eyes from the glare.

She had forgotten to close the curtains, and sunlight was streaming through her windows. She always woke up before the sun.

Did I sleep in?

Max raised his head from the bottom of the bed and thumped his tail.

Tanya's head throbbed like a construction crew was banging inside. That ring again. It hurt her brain. She turned to see her phone buzzing on the bedside table. She picked it up and put it to her ear.

"Morning, Stone." Jack sounded like he had been

awake for a while. "Forensics found the slug up in the tree. It had to have come from the rifle you spotted in the woods."

"That was fast."

"I told them the victim was a family member of one of my deputies. Everyone's chipping in. I'll be buying them more than a couple of rounds of beer after this."

"What type of cartridge was it?"

"A two-four-three Winchester," said Jack. "It's popular with deer hunters."

"So we're looking for someone with access to a sports rifle or has them in their collection." Tanya frowned. "But this particular weapon might not have been registered."

"It's a stab in the dark," said Jack. "One of the troopers is a tech whiz. She created some macros... pivot tables, or something like that, to analyze the records faster. Seems like she knows her stuff."

Tanya's head pounded. She scrunched her forehead to stop the pain, but it was growing. She glanced at her bedside clock but the numerals looked bleary.

"Tanya?" came Jack's voice from the other end. "Everything all right?"

Seeing her cousin again had dredged up dark and disturbing memories of her childhood. Memories of her mother's and brother's brutal murders she had buried deep inside of her.

Olek must be asleep on the couch in the living room.

Tanya lowered her voice.

"I'm nursing a migraine."

"We all had a rough day yesterday," said Jack. "How's your house guest?"

Tanya slipped her legs off the side of the bed and got to her feet shakily. Her joints cracked, like her body had aged overnight.

"You mean, my cousin?" She picked up her soiled clothes from the floor. "We talked over a beer by the campfire."

Seeing her up, Max stretched and yawned. He leaped off the bed and wagged his tail, signaling he was ready to start the day. Tanya nodded to acknowledge him and stumbled across the room to her closet.

"He made some bad choices and needs money," said Tanya.

"The usual family stuff," said Jack.

"I'd like to run a background check on him," said Tanya.

"I thought he was family."

"That's exactly who can lie to your face and get away with it."

"Get away with what?" said Jack.

Tanya sighed.

"My cousin fits the physical profile of the

shadow, the man Ocean spotted by the station an hour before the explosion."

Jack fell silent on the other end, like he was digesting this news.

"I'd like to confirm that he's telling the truth about his whereabouts yesterday," said Tanya. "Does the old train station have surveillance cameras?"

"It's a private building," said Jack. "The owners now live in Australia. They hadn't bothered to add any security features. It's a little late, but Asha said she'll put up cameras after what happened to her car."

"What about witnesses?"

"No one was around that morning. Only the two ladies and Asha."

Max barked as he heard the name of his favorite aunt. He trotted toward the door, his tail wagging. He looked back at Tanya and cocked his head as if to say *Open up, let's go.*

"Hang on, bud," she called out to her pup. Tanya turned her mouth back to the phone.

"Once she's done with your firearm registry, can I get the new tech whiz to check the surveillance feeds in town?"

"She's all yours. She seems keen to help—"

Jack's phone beeped.

"One second," he said before his voice cut off. Tanya waited patiently, listening to dead air, wondering who was calling him.

The chief's voice came back. "I need you at the morgue."

Tanya frowned. "Did something else happen last night?"

"Dr. Chen found another riddle this morning."

Tanya straightened up. "Where?"

"In Nicole's body."

Chapter Twenty-Four

Tanya frowned.

"Nicole was in a bikini. It didn't have any pockets. Other than her keys pinned to her top, she wasn't carrying anything."

"Come down to the clinic. I'd suggest skipping breakfast... because, er, I don't think it's pretty."

Jack hung up. Tanya got dressed quickly, her mind whirring.

Was there something hidden in her hair? Or that sunflower? Did I miss something at the crime scene? I checked everything.

Max barked at her, rousing her from her ruminations.

Tanya furrowed her brow. The house was silent. Olek was a big man who never moved quietly.

Is he still asleep?

Holding her Glock in her right hand, Tanya nudged Max out of the way.

She had gone to bed with the sorrow of the past and fear of the future broiling inside of her. But in the light of a beautiful morning, her paranoia seemed out of place.

Then again, she knew better than to trust anyone. That was how she had survived this long.

Pointing her gun forward, she unlocked the bedroom door and opened it an inch. It was quiet in the living room.

She opened the door a few more inches and peered out.

Where's Olek?

Max wagged his tail. His posture was relaxed. He didn't show the alertness he usually demonstrated when a stranger was in the house. Especially one he didn't like.

Tanya pulled the door fully open.

The living room and kitchen were empty. The neatly folded blanket she had left on the couch was exactly where she had placed it, but the cash envelope was missing.

Olek had come inside to pick up his money, but hadn't slept overnight.

Max trotted over to his food bowl in the kitchen and turned his head, anticipation in his eyes. His tail swayed as Tanya approached.

The kitchen door was still open.

Strange.

Tanya peeked out of the back door. The fire had died down, leaving cinders inside the pit. The empty beer bottles lying on their sides by the log were the only indication of Olek's presence.

The sickly odor of the barbecued meal she had left in the grill the night before wafted over to her. She wrinkled her nose. It wasn't what she wanted to smell minutes after waking up.

Tanya gave Max his breakfast and walked around her yard. Olek's bicycle was missing. The slightly flattened grass on her lawn told her he had cycled back toward the unpaved road.

She glanced around, hoping he had left something that would help Max trace him. A ball cap, a paper, a piece of clothing.

But the only things left were the beer bottles. The odors of alcohol and yeast would overpower any other scent, and Max wouldn't know what to look for.

With a resigned sigh, Tanya locked up the cottage, and bundled Max in the car. She rolled the Jeep onto the road and drove toward Dr. Chen's clinic, keeping her eyes peeled for her cousin.

He can't have gone that far if he's peddling that old bicycle.

Chapter Twenty-Five

Tanya drove quietly, her mind whirring despite her headache.

A vanishing suspect usually signaled guilt.

Olek was definitely hiding something.

She cursed herself for not locking him up when she had the chance. Then again, she had no probable cause to detain him. Her plan had been to talk to him. Make him open up. But now he was gone.

Where did he take off to?

The morning sun beat through her windshield, almost blinding her. She was about to reach for her shades when she spotted the mysterious figure by the curb.

Strangers stood out in this little town.

Tanya had never seen this tall, blond woman before.

She was in her mid to late thirties. With her heavy makeup, pink suit, and white heels, she looked like she belonged on New York's Fifth Avenue, not a small West Coast town filled with retirees and outdoor adventure seekers.

She had a Louis Vuitton suitcase next to her, like she had just arrived in town.

How did she get here?

Tanya pressed on the brakes and rolled the window down.

"Hi there, do you need a ride to town?"

The woman gave Tanya a startled look and stepped back.

She's from the big city, all right.

Tanya bent across the passenger seat to show her face, and wave a friendly wave.

"Sorry. Didn't mean to frighten you. I work at the local police precinct."

The stranger frowned, the creases at the corners of her eyes showing through her makeup. She turned her face away and patted her coiffed hair with a trembling hand.

She's nervous.

Tanya heard a gentle whine in the backseat and suddenly realized not everyone saw Max for the lovable goof he was.

"He's good with people. He won't hurt you."

The woman brought her phone up to her nose and pointedly ignored her.

Tanya leaned away, put her Jeep in gear, and rolled back onto the road, feeling a twinge of guilt for bothering the poor woman.

She had lived in Black Rock long enough now to have gotten used to picking up neighbors whenever they needed to get somewhere. She had forgotten her stranger-danger philosophy that had saved her life so many times.

I must be getting soft.

She knew firsthand what it was like when someone stopped to pick you up on the road, even if it was another woman. That out-of-towner had the right to be suspicious. It was a smart thing to do.

Tanya braked at the cross section and was about to turn toward the clinic when something flashed in her mirror.

She lifted her eyes to her rearview mirror.

A black limousine with tinted windows had driven up to the woman by the curb. To Tanya's surprise, the woman opened the back door and slipped inside the limo, pulling her luggage in with her.

Tanya plucked out her phone and snapped a quick photo through her back window. The picture was blurry. She snapped a second one, but this time, Max's tail got in the way.

"Sit down, bud."

He obeyed immediately, but by then, the limo turned into a side road, obscuring its license plate. Tanya placed her phone on her dashboard with a sigh.

She wanted to follow the limo and find out who that mysterious woman was, but she had bigger matters to attend to. Like find Olek and bring him to the station for questioning.

An angry honk came from behind her.

Max barked.

"Hang on," grumbled Tanya as she put on her signal and turned onto the main road.

The car behind her revved and passed by, the driver flipping her off. But Tanya barely noticed the rude gesture, her mind on the limo and the woman.

The only limousine driven in this town belonged to the very private and unknown owner of the Grimwood Estate. This was the property her FBI bosses had sent her to investigate.

Tanya frowned.

Who is that woman and what connection does she have to the estate?

Chapter Twenty-Six

Nicole's lifeless body lay cut open on the steel gurney.

Her face was covered with a sheet.

The dissections were clean, carried out by Dr. Chen with surgical precision. But Tanya couldn't ignore the gory blood splatters on the table or the bloodied organs inside the stainless steel bowls.

The strong odor of ammonia didn't overpower the fetid stench of putrefied flesh. She tried not to gag.

She pulled her jacket around her as the cool air gnawed at her skin. Dr. Chen's surgery felt like a giant walk-in freezer.

Jack followed Tanya inside the morgue and immediately turned his face away.

The temperature or the smells didn't seem to bother the medical examiner or her two interns. The junior members were examining Nicole's organs with such interest, they hadn't even noticed the newcomers.

Jack cleared his throat.

"Good Morning, Doctor."

Dr. Chen looked up and pulled her gloved hands from within Nicole's stomach.

"About time. Where were you? Out for donuts?"

Jack ignored the jab.

"You have another riddle for us?"

"Found it inside her pharynx."

Tanya's eyes widened.

That's why I didn't see it earlier.

Dr. Chen turned to an intern, who reached for a transparent plastic bag behind him. It contained what looked like a crinkled piece of paper laced with bodily secretions.

The intern offered the bag to Jack. "Covered in saliva but you can still read it."

Jack grimaced and put his hands up. "Just hold it up for us, please."

He and Tanya bent over and squinted at the faint words visible on the wet paper.

"Same comic sans font as the last note," said Jack.

Tanya read the note out aloud. "*I hold whispers of ages past, yet speak no words. I house countless voices, yet remain silent.*"

Jack looked up at the doctor.

"Any idea what this means?"

Dr. Chen shrugged.

"I'm a doctor, not a detective."

Tanya turned to the chief.

"The answer to the first riddle was drowning, which was what the killer had planned for Zoe. The solution to the second riddle was an explosion, hence the car bomb."

"So we know this is a clue to the next homicide." Jack frowned. "But *whispers of ages past* and *countless voices*? What the heck does that mean?"

The room fell silent as if everyone was struggling to decipher the riddle.

Tanya turned to the physician.

"How did this get inside Nicole's throat?"

The doctor narrowed her eyes like she had asked a stupid question.

"The killer stuffed it in there, of course. How else?"

"Did it occur after she expired or before?" said Tanya, undeterred by the examiner's tone.

"There are abrasions inside her cheeks, but given no identifiable skin or cloth remnants under her nails, I would presume it was done postmortem."

"She would have struggled if she had been alive," said an intern. "No one would stand still and have someone stuff something down their throat."

"Unless he coerced her to swallow it just before shooting her," said Jack.

For the second time that morning Tanya let out an involuntary shiver.

"The one thing I can say with certainty," said the doctor, "is your killer is both crafty and wicked."

"Is there any way to extract prints from her skin or inside her mouth?" said Tanya, glancing at Nicole's body on the table.

"We tried the skin," piped up one intern. "Yesterday when she was brought in. We used the iodine fuming method, but got nothing."

Dr. Chen shook her head.

"Unless the forensics world has conjured a magical machine I don't know about, it would be difficult to lift prints now. Certainly not from inside her mouth. Besides, if this killer is as smart as I think he is, they would have been wearing gloves."

Tanya turned back to the plastic bag that was lying on the table and read the riddle again.

"*I hold whispers of ages past, yet speak no words. I house countless voices, yet remain silent.*"

"Strange. The other two riddles ended with *what am I....*" Tanya reached over and turned the bag. "Wait, there's more."

Using her index fingers, she gingerly smoothened the paper through the plastic, trying not to retch as she felt the squishy liquid inside.

"Look at this."

Jack leaned over her shoulder and read the rest of the riddle out loud.

"*This is where you begin your young life. And may end it too. What am I?*"

Chapter Twenty-Seven

Tanya read the last line again.

"*This is where you begin your young life....*" She looked up with a frown. "Young life? Are they referring to a child?"

An intern shivered.

"That's creepy."

Tanya read the riddle again.

"The beginning bit says, *A place that holds whispers of past and speaks no words....* So, it's a location. A venue. If we find out where, we may save the next victim and catch the killer."

Jack pulled out his phone.

"I need that smart tech kid on this. Katy should know where she is."

"Asha can help us," said Tanya. "She solved the other riddles within minutes."

Jack scowled.

"We cannot involve civilians. That would only put them on the killer's path and I won't have that. Not after what I've witnessed."

Just as he was about to click on Katy's number, the mobile rang in his hands. He accepted the incoming call and placed it in his ear.

"All phones stay off in my surgery," snapped Dr. Chen, before turning back to Nicole's body.

Jack listened quietly to the agitated voice on the other end, then turned to Tanya.

"You're not going to believe this."

Tanya's pulse quickened. "Did the search team find Olek?"

"Not yet. But we will." He paused. "This is something else. I didn't expect this."

He put the phone on speaker mode.

"Deputy Fox, we're at the morgue. Stone's here with me. Can you tell us again what you found this morning?"

"I had no idea it was gone," came Fox's distressed voice. "It was Zoe who spotted it first. She saw the shed door open and asked me why I hadn't locked it like normal."

"What's going on, Fox?" said Tanya, ignoring Dr. Chen's glares from across the autopsy table.

"My rifle's missing," came Fox's plaintive voice. "I keep it in the shed at the bottom of the garden. I always lock the gun cabinet and the shed. But someone broke in while we were at the hospital. I didn't even notice."

"When was the last time you were in the shed?" said Jack.

"Last Friday. I think."

"That means the break-in could have happened in the past three days," said Tanya. "Any surveillance cameras?"

Fox sighed heavily on the other end.

Dr. Chen and the interns had stopped working and were listening in with keen interest, their no-phones policy forgotten.

"Should have listened to Zoe," Fox was saying. "These kids smoke weed outside our fence. She wanted to catch them on camera so she could have a talk with their parents. I...I just never got around to it."

Dr. Chen scoffed quietly. "Plucky for the killer to steal from under an officer's own nose, isn't he?"

Ignoring her, Jack leaned into his phone.

"Was the weapon the only item stolen?"

"That's what it looks like, Chief," said Fox.

"What type of gun was it?" said Tanya.

"An old sports rifle with an inbuilt suppressor. It was my father's hunting rifle."

"What caliber cartridge?"

"A two-four-three Winchester."

Tanya and Jack exchanged a glance. That was the same as the slug found in the tree by the beach.

"Dad used to hunt deer in the fall with his buddies." Fox's voice was high-pitched, ringing with nervous energy. "I kept it as a memento of him after he passed away. I clean it once in a while, but haven't used it in years. I had forgotten I kept it in the shed. I swear, Chief."

Tanya faced Jack and lowered her voice.

"The killer used Fox's gun to murder his sister-in-law."

Chapter Twenty-Eight

Tanya's phone rang the second she and Jack left the morgue.

It was Asha.

Tanya turned to Jack.

"I have to take this. I'll join you in a sec."

With a nod, Jack marched out.

He wanted to examine Fox's shed for clues the killer might have left behind. He had already called the forensics team, who were still in town, collecting evidence from the murder scene at the beach and the bomb blast at the old train station.

Max, who had been hanging with the clinic's receptionist, came bounding over to greet Tanya. She noticed the cookie crumbs on his whiskers, but she didn't have time for that.

She brought her phone to her ear.

"Hey, feeling better?"

Asha's voice sounded strong, like she hadn't just been thrown off from an explosion and was on strong painkillers.

"I got another call," she said.

"Was it the same creep who called your podcast?"

"The same warbled robotic voice."

"Another riddle?"

"No," said Asha. "That was a weird thing. I wrote it down as soon as I figured out it was our guy."

"What did he say this time?"

"*You have twenty-four hours to answer my riddle, or another Black Rock woman dies. Who will it be next?*"

A chill went down Tanya's spine.

"Then he hung up," said Asha. "Just like that. I didn't even get a chance to ask who or why."

"What did your mobile screen show?"

"Unknown number. Like it showed up last time."

"Jack has a request in for a warrant to search the phone company's records," said Tanya. "That should help."

"I don't think so. If I have to guess, he uses a new burner phone for every call," said Asha. "After that, he probably pulls them apart, takes the SIM card out, smashes it to pieces, and throws them far into the sea.

That's what I'd do if I was making death threats in public."

She paused. When she spoke again, her voice sounded heavy.

"This isn't your average idiot criminal."

Tanya fell silent for a second.

What does the killer want? Why is he targeting the women of Black Rock?

A tingle came over her back, like someone was watching her.

She glanced up, her heart ticking slightly faster. But she was inside the safety of Dr. Chen's clinic, with her K9 dog by her feet and the local police chief outside in the parking lot.

This is exactly what the killer wants. His goal is to strike fear in us.

She pushed her worries to the back of her head and turned to the phone. She heard an inaudible male voice in the background.

"Where are you?" said Tanya, frowning. "You're supposed to be recuperating at home."

"I, er, twisted Katy's arm," said Asha.

"What did you make her do now?"

"She dropped me off at my studio this morning."

"Jack's going to kill you—"

"The station wasn't touched by the bomb. Just my poor baby girl. Her remains are still in the parking lot. It's so sad. The officers here are very nice. They said I could come in. All it took was a small bribe of Lulu's coffee cakes."

Tanya shook her head, making a mental note to talk to Jack about the new team's lackadaisical policies.

"It's still a crime scene," said Tanya. "And the killer is targeting you. He has your number, Asha."

"It's the number for my podcast. It's on my website. It's public."

"You seem to have forgotten he tried to blow you to smithereens. What about that doesn't make you want to stay away?"

"You seem to have forgotten I helped you with the last riddle. Have I heard one thank you from you or Jack?"

"You're playing with your life." Tanya closed her eyes momentarily. "The killer could have been referring to you with this riddle. Did you think of that?"

"That's why I bribed the cops outside. They're my first line of defense. If he gets through them, I'll fight back."

Tanya knew her five-foot, petite friend could turn into a raging beast when cornered. She was trained in self-defense and weapons. Asha's fiancé, David, taught Krav Maga, the martial arts system employed by the Israeli Mossad itself.

Tanya clicked her fingers to let Max know they

were leaving and marched toward the clinic's front doors.

"If Dr. Chen found out you are running around town, she'd—"

Asha scoffed.

"Blow a gasket like she always does? You all worry too much. I feel fine. Besides, I have a new client. Fox is here, and he needs my help."

Tanya stopped in her tracks. Max sat down in front of her and cocked his head.

"Deputy Shawn Fox?"

"The only one I know," said Asha.

"I thought he was home with Zoe. What's he doing at your office?"

"You forget. I run a private detective agency."

Chapter Twenty-Nine

"Fox's rifle was stolen from his shed."

Asha's voice on the other end of the line sounded sharper.

"Seems like news gets around fast," said Tanya.

"It's the same caliber weapon as the one used to kill Zoe's sister." Asha spoke with a crispness she used when she was negotiating a deal. "He's worried he'll get framed for Nicole's murder."

Tanya picked up her pace. Jack was by his squad car in the clinic's parking lot, speaking to two of the new patrol officers.

"I don't think Fox has anything to be concerned about," said Tanya as she made a beeline to the chief.

"What makes you say that?" said Asha.

"He was at the precinct when Nicole and Zoe

went for their morning swim. He has a strong alibi, backed up by Katy and Jack."

"The thing is," said Asha with a sigh, "he had a major fight with Nicole the night before."

"Oh, no."

Asha nodded. "They were out for beers at the Dog House Pub, so half the town heard them."

"What was the row about?" said Tanya, an unease creeping up her spine.

"Money."

Tanya's apprehension grew.

There were too many coincidences in this case. For one moment, she wondered if the killer was playing mind games with them all.

"He didn't know Zoe had lent her sister some money two years ago," came Asha's voice from the other end. "He confronted Nicole at the pub and asked for the money back. That's when he and Zoe learned she had lost it all in a shady pyramid scam. Let's just say the conversation got heated."

"How much are we talking about?"

"Ten grand."

Ten thousand dollars.

Deputy Fox was a sworn officer of the law, and a friend. Still, he was only human. People have done worse for less.

"He's worried you guys will try to convict him wrongfully," said Asha, like she had an insight into Tanya's thoughts. "So he's hired me to find the killer.

I plan to uncover the truth and save my client from false accusations of any kind."

"If he hasn't committed a crime," said Tanya, "he has nothing to worry about."

"That's what they all say before hanging an innocent man, don't they?"

Tanya shook her head. Her friend could be as stubborn as a bull. "Stay right where you are. *Both* of you."

She stepped up to Jack and tapped him on the arm. He turned and spoke before she could say anything.

"They spotted your cousin."

Tanya's stomach sank. She barely got her words out.

"Where's he now?"

"The suspect was hightailing out of town on his bicycle through the backwoods," said one officer. "He took off into the thicket when he saw our cruiser approach. We followed him on foot, but he was fast on his bike."

"We have a party searching the woods," said the second officer. "Don't worry, ma'am, we'll nab him before nightfall."

Jack gave Tanya a concerned look.

"I have to admit," he said, "these aren't the actions of an innocent man."

Chapter Thirty

Tanya leaned against Asha's mahogany desk and crossed her arms.

Jack glowered at the private investigator from across the room.

"You can't go after him on your own," he said. "That's far too dangerous. You'll only be putting my people at greater risk."

The chief's eyes were narrowed and his jaws were clenched, like he was barely keeping himself from exploding.

He had cordoned off the entire building and had posted officers outside. Yet, here he was, forced to negotiate with a civilian who had brazenly disobeyed his rules.

Other than the loud and shaky breaths coming from Deputy Fox in the corner, it was quiet in this expansive room that overlooked the Pacific Ocean.

Asha had converted the town's former station manager's bureau into her private office.

The ticket box was now a soundproofed booth for her true crime podcast. The waiting area was a carpeted lounge with sofas, a cappuccino machine, and bookshelves filled with forensics textbooks, police procedural tomes, and a rare Sherlock Holmes collection.

There was nothing Jack or Tanya could do with Fox seeking private help, but they knew they had to work together if they were to find the killer.

Asha sat back in her plush leather chair, twirling a pen in her hand.

A black eye had formed overnight, and the red scrapes on her arms were more noticeable. Despite coming across like she had been in a bar fight the night before, her eyes were clear and alert.

Fox was nervously fidgeting with his ball cap in the chair across from her.

Max had taken position next to him, his snout resting on his knee as if to comfort him, but that didn't seem to help much. Fox looked close to a nervous breakdown.

Jack turned to his deputy.

"The killer's taunting us. This was an attempt to frame you, Fox. He's pulling us apart. We need to work together. This isn't helping."

Fox lifted his reddened eyes to him. "I almost lost Zoe. If Max hadn't found her behind that rock, she'd be... she'd be..." He swallowed hard.

Jack softened his voice.

"We're going to find this unsub. I promise you. In the meantime, we have officers stationed by your home. Your family is safe. You need to trust us."

Fox looked down.

"None of that's going to help Nicole. She's gone, killed by my own father's gun."

Asha sat up.

"The killer referred to a riddle when he called me today, but he didn't give it to me." She looked from Jack to Tanya. "Did he share it with you?"

The chief and Tanya exchanged a glance.

"You want my client to trust you?" said Asha. "You want us to work with you? May I then remind you that sharing goes both ways?"

With a resigned sigh, Tanya plucked her phone out and clicked to the photo she had taken at the morgue, only an hour ago. She placed her cell on Asha's desk.

"The riddle note was stuffed inside Nicole's throat."

Asha grimaced. Fox let out an anguished cry and covered his face.

"Sorry," whispered Tanya.

Asha leaned over the screen and read the riddle out loud.

"I hold whispers of ages past, yet speak no words. I house countless voices, yet remain silent. This is where you begin your young life. And may end it too. What am I?"

Jack stepped up to her desk and rapped his knuckles on it.

"Do you know what this means?"

Asha kept her head bowed over the phone.

"I might, if you give me a quiet minute."

Jack turned away from her and started pacing the room impatiently. Max watched him like he was at a tennis match. Fox sat hunched in his chair, a picture of misery.

Tanya was about to step over to Fox to console him, when Asha sat up with a gasp.

Everyone whipped around. Asha's eyes were shining.

"Tell me," she said. "What holds the past, has many voices, but can't talk?"

Fox sat silently, staring at the floor.

Tanya shook her head.

"I have no idea," said Jack. "But I know you do, so please tell us."

Asha jumped in her chair. "Books!"

Jack raised his eyebrows.

"Are you telling me the killer's going to commit his next murder with a *book*?"

Asha lifted a finger in the air.

"This riddle is referring to a place. A *silent* place. What does that tell you?"

"Just give me the darned answer," said Jack, strain in his voice.

Tanya leaned across the desk, her heart beating fast.

"A library?"

"You got it, girl."

Asha turned to Jack, who was looking increasingly irritated.

"Your next murder, Chief, is going to happen in a library."

Jack blinked. He stepped away with a heavy sigh and brought his phone to his ear.

"Katy? Send the team to the city library immediately. The killer may—"

He stopped and frowned as Katy's high-pitched voice came from the other end.

"You heard me right," said Jack, a hint of annoyance in his voice. "The library. The city library. Where they have books. We might prevent the next homicide."

While Jack spoke with Katy, Tanya read the riddle again.

"*This is where you begin your young life.*" She turned to Asha. "What does that mean?"

Asha flopped back in her chair.

"I'm guessing it's referring to the children's

section...." She drummed her fingers on the desk. "I know it's weak."

Tanya glanced down at the paper.

"*And may end it too*?"

"That definitely refers to the upcoming killing," said Asha.

Tanya frowned. "Maybe it's someplace else."

Asha scrunched her eyes.

"What do you mean?"

"There's the pediatrics unit at the hospital and the town's midwifery. Two places where you can begin your young life."

"But there are no libraries in those places...." Asha stopped and her face turned white. "Oh, my goodness. Wait a minute."

She locked eyes with Tanya.

"A school!" shouted Asha.

Tanya whirled around to Jack.

"The school library. That's where he'll attack next."

Chapter Thirty-One

"Oh, look. A doggy."

Tanya whirled around.

She had just parked her Jeep at the primary school's parking lot.

Jack was already striding across the lawn toward the principal's office, his phone stuck to his ear.

Tanya was about to dash after him when she was ambushed by a gaggle of children, clamoring to pull Max's tail, pet his head, or tweak his ear.

Deputy Fox rushed over and scooped his son in his arms. Too big to be carried, Zak struggled, crying to be put down, but Fox only tightened his hold.

He walked over to his vehicle, shoved Zak inside, and slammed the door. Asha got out of Fox's car and glanced around her.

"Chantal?" she called out. "Chantal, where are you?"

"Get back in the car!" hollered Tanya, wishing they hadn't followed them to the school.

Fox whirled around the children who had surrounded Tanya and Max.

"Chantal!" he roared as he spotted her. "Come here!"

But Chantal didn't hear him. She was pushing her way through the crowd, like she was in charge, her ponytail bobbing up and down. She grabbed Max's snout and wrapped her arm around his neck possessively, almost choking him.

"He's *my* friend."

The children shoved Tanya aside, squealing. She hadn't expected to get bulldozed by dozens of rowdy kids, but she was grateful her dog knew to stay calm in the melee. It was like he knew he was dealing with undeveloped little humans.

"Get back, kids," she called out.

A big-sized boy barreled over her as he fought to pull on Max's ears. Tanya restrained herself from grabbing him by the collar and shaking him.

She raised her voice.

"This is important. Please relocate to the rear of the parking lot."

No one listened.

A squad car came screeching to a halt next to

them, and out jumped Katy. She whirled around like an angry dervish and clapped her hands.

"Listen up, everybody!"

Tanya leaned away as Katy's bellows echoed through the parking lot.

"Pay attention!"

The kids stopped shrieking. Their eyes widened as they noticed the red-headed woman towering over them.

Katy gestured toward the far side of the parking lot.

"To the back! *Now!*"

"But Mom," pouted Chantal. "I want to show Max to my friends."

"I wanna play with the puppy," said the big boy who had elbowed Tanya.

Katy placed her hands on her hips and glowered at them. With her mane of red hair and her flushed face, she looked like a furious lioness.

"Didn't you hear me? Get to the back! *Now!* All of you!"

The kids darted toward the perimeter of the parking lot without a glance back. Tanya didn't wait to ask Katy what superpowers she had over children.

"Let's go, Max."

Leaving Katy to corral the kids to safety, she raced toward the main building with her freed dog at her heels.

She had approached the front steps of the entrance when Jack dashed out.

"The library's around the corner."

The school principal stumbled out after him.

She was a short, middle-aged woman with gray hair. She looked the quintessential headmistress, but her bun was askew and her spectacles sat crooked on her nose, like a hurricane had chewed her up and spat her out.

"Adam's been in my office all morning, Chief."

Tanya spun around to her. "Who's Adam?"

"Our librarian. He locked up the library two hours ago. He's protective about his books. Doesn't like the kids going inside when he's not there to watch over them."

Tanya narrowed her eyes. "Did Adam leave your office this morning?"

The principal shook her head.

"We were planning our annual play. This year, the kids are going to perform *Hamlet* at the old theater hall. The city council is reviving it. I'm even making a proper crown—"

Jack put his hand up. "Who had access to the library while you and Adam were at the office?"

"Nobody. There should be no one in the library."

"Get back in your office, ma'am," said Jack. "Make sure everyone remains in their classrooms.

Follow the earthquake drill. Tell them it's a drill so they won't panic."

The principal stared at him for a second, then pushed her glasses up and tumbled inside.

Tanya and Jack ran toward the oversized shipping container that sat on the edge of the playground.

If this had been a big city school, an entire block would have needed to be evacuated. Tanya gave a silent prayer to low-budget, small-town schools.

Max raced ahead of them, making a beeline toward the trailer.

Sirens wailed as firetrucks and police cars pulled in to the school's parking lot.

The public announcement crackled to life, and soon the principal's wobbly voice echoed through the empty grounds.

"This is an earthquake drill. Please stay in your classrooms. Heads under your desks. If you are outside, make your way to the end of the parking lot and stay low to the ground. Don't move until I give the clear. Repeat. This is an..."

"Bomb squads on the way," said Jack, as they jumped up the steps toward the trailer door. "As a precaution."

Tanya's mind buzzed, trying to recollect the words of the latest riddle. Her phone was burning a hole in her pocket, but she didn't have time to analyze the puzzle.

"I don't think it's another bomb," said Tanya.

They positioned themselves on opposite sides of the trailer door, their weapons drawn. Max stood on the top step, his snout pointed at the entrance, his ears alert, and his tail stiff.

Jack locked eyes with Tanya.

"For our sake, I hope you're right."

Chapter Thirty-Two

Jack slipped the library key into the keyhole.

Tanya swallowed hard, knowing the killer could be behind that door, waiting for them. One wrong move, and they could be the next victims.

Jack kicked the door open.

All the lights had been turned off.

The rows of black plastic shelves that lined the inside made it harder to see, but at first glance there didn't seem to be any signs of life.

They stepped inside, guns pointing forward.

The reception desk was empty, and the computer had been powered off. The small circle of chairs in front had been neatly arranged, but the books had been left haphazardly all over the place. There were piles on the floor and some on top of the shelves.

A normal library hummed with low background sounds that signaled life. The silence in here was uncanny, coupled with a spooky feeling that something bad had happened.

Max growled.

Tanya glanced at her pup. He was staring at the farthest bookshelf to their left.

"That way," she whispered.

She stepped gingerly toward the shelf, thankful for the carpeted floors that muffled their footsteps.

Then again, the principal's panicky announcement and the sirens of the emergency vehicles outside couldn't be ignored. If the killer was here, he knew they were hunting him.

Max barred his teeth.

There's someone back there.

Tanya advanced toward the last shelf, feeling Jack's presence next to her. Their eyes swiveled from side to side, ready for anyone to ambush them.

A library ladder was lying at an angle against a bookshelf. She squinted at it. Something was off.

Max growled again, like he was warning her.

Tanya took a step closer to get a better look at what was bothering him. With a startled cry, she tripped over the hidden wire and stumbled, head first.

A booby trap.

Max emitted a barrage of barks.

"Watch out!" Jack grabbed her arm and pulled her back. But it was too late.

The pile of books on top of the shelf rained down and bounced off their shoulders. The ladder tilted and crashed to the floor.

Tanya felt its hard edge slam against her head.

Then, the world went black.

Chapter Thirty-Three

"Save her!" hollered a male voice.

Tanya flickered her eyelids, but she only saw stars.

She squeezed her eyes shut and reopened them. The world was a blur of shapes and colors that blended into outlandish psychedelic patterns.

Did I go blind?

She felt something wet and sloppy on her nose. She turned and squinted. A furry brown shape was moving back and forth, inches from her face.

Max?

"Get that dog out of here," said an unfamiliar male voice.

No!

Tanya lifted her head and opened her mouth to speak.

"Don't move," came the strict voice again.

Tanya didn't recognize him. Whoever he was, he placed his hands on her shoulders and pressed her down. She struggled to sit up.

"I said, lie still," said the man. "Someone get that animal outta here."

"No," Tanya warbled, pushing his hands away. "It's my dog."

"I can't have her die on me!" That was Jack. He was yelling, but he seemed far away.

Who's dying?

Tanya scrunched her eyes, wondering how badly hurt she was.

"Let him stay," came a familiar female voice. "He's a working K9."

Tanya blinked rapidly. She knew that voice. Someone grasped her hand.

"K... Katy?"

"Hang tight, Tanya. I'm going to take you to Dr. Chen's clinic in a minute."

Katy's face appeared in front of her. The image was fuzzy, but that red hair was unmistakable. Tanya shook her head to clear it, but that only made her headache worse.

"You'll need a few painkillers," her friend was saying. "You have a bad bump on your head. Just stay still for me, okay? They've triaged the other victim as a priority."

"What... What happened?" croaked Tanya. "Where... Where am I?"

"You're in the school library. You tripped on a wire, and a heavy bookshelf fell on your head. You were lucky."

Katy paused as if she wanted to explain further but decided not to.

"Did I black out?" said Tanya.

"Just for a few minutes. It's best to get Dr. Chen to check you."

The fuzzy background was coming into focus. The outlines of the bookshelves were now clear. Tanya could see the librarian's desk by the door and the piles of books everywhere.

She lifted her head up. Relief coursed through her to see her dog beside her, his head resting on her stomach.

Max tilted his head and whined as if to say *Are you okay, Mom?* Tanya reached over and rubbed his silky ears, her heart warming to see his big brown eyes watching her.

"Don't worry. I'm fine, bud."

With a happy wag of his tail, he crawled up and licked her face. His whiskers tickled her cheeks. Tears welled up as she pulled Max in for a hug.

"Get her into the ambulance right now!" roared Jack.

Tanya furrowed her brow.
Why is Jack yelling?

Am I dying?

Did Katy lie to me?

She glanced around her. She was lying on a medical stretcher on the floor by the librarian's desk.

She felt her arms and thighs, searching for cuts, bruises, or injuries, but her body was intact. She was sure she would have felt something if she was near death.

That was when it dawned on her.

The medic who had snapped at her earlier had abandoned her. Even Katy had stepped away and was staring with concern at something at the farthest end of the library.

Jack said something incomprehensible. He sounded like he was hyperventilating. Tanya had never heard him like this before.

She raised her head and peered over Max's ears.

A handful of medics and junior officers were crowded at the back of the library. By their feet was a dark lump.

Is that a body?

Tanya pushed herself to a seated position. Her head still hammered, but she could see better. She held on to Max as two medics lifted a stretcher and headed to the exit.

"Make way, ma'am."

Katy jumped out of the way.

Tanya craned her neck to see who they were carrying.

Her jaw dropped.

It was the stranger she had stopped by the curb to offer a ride. It was the same woman who had climbed into the black limo that suspiciously looked like the one belonging to the Grimwood Estate.

That smartly dressed, beautiful blonde was now lying immobile on the stretcher. Stuck in her hair was a yellow sunflower, just like the one Nicole had in her hair at the beach.

The riddle killer has struck again.

Chapter Thirty-Four

A junior officer held up a large leather-bound book.

"There's blood and blond hair strands on the spine, sir."

Jack grabbed a bookshelf to steady himself. His face was gray, like he had seen a ghost.

Tanya blinked rapidly. "Who's that woman?"

But no one was paying her attention.

Hasty steps came from the outside, like someone was running up the stairs. Max turned toward the door and barked once.

"Ma'am, you can't go in there," hollered a stern voice.

The school principal appeared at the threshold of the trailer, her hair and spectacles even more askew than before. She stared at Jack, her chest heaving.

"Chief! Where's the bomb?"

But Jack's focus was on his phone now. He jabbed the screen like he was desperately searching for something or someone.

Katy walked over to the principal.

"There was no bomb. But we did find the victim in here with blunt force trauma to the head."

The principal put a hand over her mouth.

"Is she okay?"

"She's unconscious," said Katy. "The medics are taking her to the hospital."

Tanya called out. "Who's our victim?"

But no one seemed to hear her.

Katy placed a hand on the principal's arm.

"We've instructed the teachers to send the children home. The school is a crime scene at the moment, I'm afraid."

"Crime scene?"

Katy nodded. "A crew is scouring the school yard and the surrounding streets. We suspect the perpetrator is no longer on the premises but we want to check every inch."

The principal gasped. "The killer *was* in *my* school?"

Tanya rose to her feet clutching the nearest chair and took stock.

Jack was on his phone, talking briskly to someone. His face was pale. One trooper was taking photographs, and the other was cordoning off the bookshelves with yellow crime tape.

Beside her, Katy leaned over to the principal like she was about to share very bad news.

"I'm afraid the school won't be accessible until we give the all clear."

The principal stared at her, open-mouthed.

"Why not give the kids a break for a few days?" said Katy. "I'm sure they'll welcome the time off."

"But...but..." stammered the principal. "She said she was heading back to the airport. What was she doing in my library? And why would anyone want to hurt her?" She flailed her arms. "This makes no sense."

Tanya leaned forward.

"You know the victim?"

The principal whirled around to her.

"She's our new child psychologist."

Chapter Thirty-Five

A jolt of energy shot through Tanya. Her headache hadn't receded, but she was beginning to think clearly again.

Katy leaned closer to the principal.

"So the victim is employed by the school?"

"No.. yes... I guess so...." The principal's face scrunched in frustration. "I didn't even know she was supposed to come in today."

Tanya frowned.

"What was the purpose of her visit?"

The principal curled her hands into fists, like she would have liked to punch someone.

"The school board sent her for an interview."

"Did you call the board to check?" said Tanya.

The principal scoffed.

"She showed up dressed like she wanted *my* job. Look, these interviews are shams. They always are. If the board sent her, the decision has already been made and the funding already allocated."

She shot Katy and Tanya a dark look.

"The board only cares to appease city council members and self-entitled parents. The teachers and I are supposed to do as we're told."

"Are you sure she's a child psychologist?" said Tanya.

"She showed me all her fancy certificates from Harvard."

Tanya and Katy exchanged a glance.

Certificates are easily forged.

The principal shook her head and sighed, like she couldn't believe what had just happened.

"The irony is I'll need a therapist for the kids and the staff after this."

She flashed her eyes at Tanya and Katy.

"Do you know how many kids from the East End come without even an apple in their bag?"

They shook their heads silently.

"If the board has money to hire a full-time psychologist, they have the money to feed the handful of kids who come to school on empty stomachs."

The principal threw her arms into the air and stomped out of the library.

"What am I supposed to tell the board now? They're going to blame me for all this mess."

A dizziness overcame Tanya. She clutched the back of the chair to steady herself.

Katy grabbed her by the arm.

"You need to go to the clinic, hon."

"I'm feeling fine." Tanya rubbed the side of her forehead, willing her headache to go away. "I saw her by the road this morning."

Katy stared at her.

"Who are you talking about?"

"The child psychologist. She was standing by the curb, looking nervous."

"What was she doing on the streets?"

"Waiting for her ride. As soon as I passed her, a black limo came by to pick her up."

Katy furrowed her brow. "A black limo?"

Tanya nodded. "If I have to guess, she made a visit to the Grimwood Estate too—"

A loud curse made her turn around.

Jack slapped his phone, like he wasn't getting what he was looking for. Without a word to the team in the library, he marched toward the door.

"Everything okay, Jack?" said Tanya.

He didn't seem to hear.

Tanya grabbed his arm just as he was about to step through the door.

"You know her, don't you?" she said. "Who is our victim?"

Jack blinked like he was seeing her for the first time.

"You... you took a bad hit to your head."

"A minor bump." Tanya leaned over to him. "Who is she?"

Jack swallowed. "My ex-wife."

The Puppet Master

"Everything's ready for you, sir."

The young man stood at attention and saluted his boss.

The boss, not much older than him, nodded briefly.

A woman in a maid's uniform bowed her head demurely.

"The coffee is brewing, sir, and there's more firewood under the mantel, should you wish—"

"Out!" The boss shooed them through the door. "All of you. Get out. I want you out of the property in an hour."

"Yes, sir," came a subdued chorus from his staff.

While the boss was having breakfast, his team had been in his wood-paneled study, cleaning the place and fiddling with his computers.

He was finally alone. He wanted to see this by himself.

This is my game.

A peacock crowed outside the expansive bay windows. The boss picked up a cigar from a wooden box on the mantelpiece and stepped over to take a look.

The peacock fanned his opulent purple and blue feathers, thrust his chest out, and sashayed around the artificial lake. A sense of pride and power filled the man's heart as he gazed at the stunning bird.

After all he had gone through, he had done well for himself. Few knew this place existed, yet here he was, with access to luxuries even the king of England didn't have. The greatest being his precious anonymity.

A low growl came from the middle of the grounds.

The man peered through the window.

Tethered to a steel pole at the heart of the garden was a big cat.

The peacock had veered into her territory just an inch, but it was enough. She growled again. The peacock strutted by her without changing his stride, knowing her massive claws could only reach so far.

If they had been in the wild, the bird would have been her lunch. She was one of the biggest cats of them all, brought into the country in a shipping container with other exotic pets and people. Most times, the animals got auctioned for a higher price than the humans.

The lioness raised her head as if she felt someone was watching her.

She glared at the man behind the window of the mansion. Their eyes met briefly. He wondered if she knew her mate's mane hung on a wall inside this study. The dead lion was his trophy now.

The lioness placed her head back on the ground with a heavy sigh. Her bony frame and listless eyes told the man she had already succumbed to her deadly fate. She would never enjoy the freedom of the vast African savanna lands any more, and she knew it.

The man at the window smiled to himself.

He liked being in control, especially over powerful beings.

He was the puppet master.

With a satisfied grunt, he turned around and stepped over to the bank of screens his tech team had set up that morning.

Let's see what they've got for me.

He peered into the screen on his left. The grainy image of Black Rock's police chief, Jack Bold, came into view. The man's face broke into a grin as the chief dashed out of the library and jumped inside his cruiser.

Still in love with his ex-wife. Heading to the hospital, I presume.

Two female silhouettes appeared by the entrance to the school library. The man's lips twisted into a scornful scowl.

Tanya Stone and Katy McCafferty.

He muttered angrily under his breath.

These two and that Asha Kade. Inseparable, aren't they? Well, they won't be for long.

He swiveled back and forth in his leather chair, his brain whirring.

His mother had always said taking revenge was akin to drinking poison and expecting your enemy to die. A part of him knew vengeance was a bitter pill.

Then why does it taste as sweet as sugar in my mouth?

He watched as Tanya and Katy joined Asha in the school parking lot.

He reached for the mouse and zoomed in on the three women. Asha's black eye, from being thrown after the car explosion, was more pronounced than the day before.

The women hugged each other and climbed into Tanya's Jeep. K9 Max jumped in after them.

The man smiled to himself.

I have eyes everywhere, and they don't even know it.

He leaned back and watched Tanya's Jeep roll out of the parking lot and onto the street.

He chuckled to himself.

Things were going to happen fast. So fast that no

one, not even an all powerful federal bureau, could stop the masterpiece he had planned.

They have no idea what's coming in the next forty-eight hours.

He got up and strolled over to the fireplace in the corner of the study. He picked up the tongs and poked the fire, releasing a subtle aroma of sandalwood in the air.

He poured himself a tumbler of scotch, settled in his armchair, and placed his red moccasin-clad feet on the ottoman.

"The game is on, ladies," said the man as he raised his glass in the air. "Let's see if you can beat me."

Chapter Thirty-Six

"Ladies? We have film footage."

Tanya looked up to see Black Rock's fire chief enter the precinct through the secure door.

A young female trooper in a baseball cap followed him in, her eyes averted like she was self-conscious. She looked barely twenty years old.

Must be the State Patrol's newest recruit.

Fire Chief John Marks dropped a large envelope on Katy's desk.

"There you go. You'll find what you're looking for."

Tanya opened the envelope and shook it. A memory stick fell onto Katy's desk. Katy grabbed it and slipped it into a port in her computer.

Tanya frowned. "The principal said there were no cameras at the school."

"This is from the bomb scene at the old train station's parking lot," said the fire chief. "This is footage of the twenty-four hours before Asha Kade's vehicle blew up."

"Strange," said Katy as she ran a virus check on the new device. "I was convinced the city forbade cameras nearby."

The fire chief flopped down in the chair in front of her and took his cap off, exposing a shock of short white hair.

The head of the town's fire department looked like he had aged a few years over the past twenty-four hours. After what the town had gone through, Tanya imagined they had all gained a few gray hairs and wrinkles themselves.

"The city installed two cameras by the old train station to catch the perverts that have been harassing girls along the beach," said the fire chief, speaking in a low voice. "The council didn't want anyone to know."

"Jack's been asking for surveillance cameras for that exact same reason," said Tanya. "Why would the city install them and not tell us?" She paused. "Does he know?"

"I called him soon after I found out. He's at City Hall right now, lobbying for this footage via the official process, but they're stalling."

Katy looked up, concern on her face.

"So this footage isn't official."

"No, ma'am."

The fire chief sighed and leaned over like he didn't want anyone to overhear his next words.

"I knew Mayor Bailey was nasty, but this takes the cake. He wanted to catch the perverts in action and showcase to the public how bad Jack was at his job. Justification to get him and you all fired, so he can install his goons instead."

He scoffed.

"Petty politics of a petty man."

Tanya pointed at the USB stick.

"How did you get your hands on this, then?"

"I called in a favor from one of the city clerks."

Tanya raised a brow.

The fire chief looked away.

"My wife. She knew what was going on. I think she's ready to retire soon." He rubbed his forehead. "Jack's a good man. He's a friend. I don't like stupid bureaucratic games, and I wasn't about to keep secrets from him."

Tanya nodded. "You're a good man too, Chief."

He turned his tired eyes to Tanya. "Repeat that in front of the mayor, would you? He's cutting my budget again next year."

"Join the club," hissed Katy. "Our shoestring budget is frayed and ready to rip at any moment."

Tanya turned to the junior officer who had

been crouching on the ground next to them, petting Max. Her dog seemed to be enjoying the attention.

Tanya cleared her throat.

The officer got up and stood at attention. Her face turned a beetroot red to have everybody's attention on her.

"How are you involved, trooper?" said Tanya.

The fire chief pointed a thumb at the officer.

"Jack said she was a techie nerd...." He shot the trooper an awkward smile. "That wasn't a nice thing to say, was it?"

"My mom calls me a geek." The trooper shrugged and shuffled her feet. "My gamer handle is Tech Cop. I play online every weekend. My teammates found out, so that's what they call me at the office now."

"What's your real name?" said Tanya.

"Nicole Hall."

Tanya nodded. "We appreciate your help, Officer Hall."

The trooper's face flushed.

"Officer Hall here," said the chief, "went through the files quickly and ferreted the one I wanted. It would have taken ages for the boys at the fire hall. We're not equipped for this sort of work."

He got up with a heavy sigh.

"The state bomb squad's coming over to compare notes on the investigation, but I can't give them this footage because I can't tell them how I, er, obtained it. This won't hold in court and...."

He swallowed hard.

"My wife could lose her job and her pension."

Tanya nodded.

"It's safe with us, Chief."

As soon as the fire chief left, Katy got up and offered her chair to the junior trooper.

"Show us what you found."

Katy and Tanya peered over her shoulder as she pushed the video toggle all the way down the screen to ten minutes before the end.

The camera swept across the beach, stopping for three seconds on a section of the old train station's parking lot. The back of Asha's silver convertible came into view, before the camera panned back toward the beach.

Tanya leaned in, her eyes peeled to the screen as the camera moved across the shoreline and turned toward the train station and its parking lot.

The silver car exploded.

Asha slammed across the lot and landed on the lawn. She lay still, while the fire burned in silence.

The three women watched the footage in horror. The camera didn't linger too long on the car or on Asha. It panned slowly back in the direction of the shoreline.

Katy put her hands on her chest. "If Asha had

been inside when...." She shook her head, like she couldn't finish her sentence.

Tanya turned to the officer.

"A witness said they saw a shadow by the station building an hour before the explosion."

The officer toggled the video back and pressed play.

"Stop." Tanya leaned in. "What's that beside the wall? Can you zoom in?"

The officer clicked several times, pausing after each zoom to check the image wasn't pixelated.

"My goodness," said Katy, pointing with a shaking finger. "There's someone watching them from back there."

Tanya stared in disbelief as her cousin's outline grew bigger right in front of her eyes. His face was hidden, but she couldn't ignore the familiar outline. The beer belly. The bald head.

"Olek," she whispered. "He tried to kill Asha."

Chapter Thirty-Seven

Katy turned to Tanya in shock.

"That's Olek?"

Tanya had held on to a shadow of hope that her cousin was innocent. But any faith she had before had evaporated in seconds.

She turned around and stepped up to an officer who was manning the phones at the next desk over.

"Do we have news from the search party yet?"

"They're still scouring the woods for the suspect, ma'am," said the officer. "They have a shoot to kill order if he attacks."

Tanya's face turned warm.

"Who gave that order?"

"The chief, ma'am. Chief Bold."

Jack gave orders to kill my cousin?

Katy turned to her.

"People change, you know."

She put a hand on Tanya's.

"This is not the cousin you used to know. Remember the booby trap in the library? He targeted you, too. He's already killed one woman and attempted to murder two innocent victims."

Tanya closed her eyes, trying to come to terms with what Katy was saying.

"He's a petty criminal, but he's not evil," said Tanya. "Besides, he doesn't have the skills to plan and carry out any of this."

"Just because he's family doesn't mean he's not capable," whispered Katy. "You have to let him go."

The sting of those words pierced Tanya's heart, but she knew her friend was right.

She turned to the officer at the desk.

"Call the search team. Tell them I'm joining the hunt."

Chapter Thirty-Eight

"Is that fresh blood?"

Tanya crouched to examine the dry leaf that had caught Max's attention.

An officer came over and snapped photos with his phone.

"We inspected this whole area, twice," he said, shaking his head. "Can't believe we missed this."

The small search team had been taking a break when Tanya and Max had arrived. It hadn't been difficult to find them as they had been sprawled in their squad cars, looking haggard.

The afternoon sun was dipping toward the western horizon. Soon, it would get dark, and their task would become even more difficult.

Tanya knew they had been beating the bush all

day, and had brought over a box of energy bars and water bottles. But they hadn't cared for the food.

The second they had spotted the German Shepherd in the back of the Jeep, they had jumped to their feet and cheered. Happy to have found new fans, Max had trotted over to say hello to the tired troops.

Jack's earlier words had flashed through Tanya's mind.

Everyone's chipping in. I'll have to treat them to several beers after this.

She wondered how his ex-wife was faring at the hospital. Tanya hadn't got over the shock of seeing her. She had expected to meet her at a Christmas party, a retirement event, an official function perhaps, or not at all. Never as a victim of an active case on their hands.

Jack had always been tight-lipped about his marriage. All he had said was they had an amicable divorce, after which he had moved to his hometown from Chicago.

A strange thought nagged at Tanya.

First, cousin Olek, whom I haven't seen in years, shows up. Then, Jack's ex-wife comes to town.

Tanya had been around the world enough times to know coincidences didn't just happen. When extraordinary events like this lined up, it was a harbinger for something worse.

Are we being played?

By whom?

A shiver went down her back.

She clutched her golden sunflower pendant and prayed for her deceased mother to protect them.

"Hey, did you hear that?" Asked a voice behind her.

Tanya turned. The search team was squinting at a cluster of birch trees. That was when she realized Max had vanished.

"Where's my dog?"

From somewhere within the forest came a loud bark.

Tanya leaped through the trees.

"Max? Where are you, bud?"

She hastened in the direction of his voice, with the others trooping behind her. Max's bark came again, from somewhere closer this time.

"I see his tail," called out an officer. "Behind the thicket."

Max was sniffing a log. The team circled the log to see what he had found.

Tanya's heart raced as she noticed the rusty spot on the wood. It was blood, fresh blood. But the bigger question was, *Whose was it?*

She turned to the troopers.

"Did you shoot him?"

"Of course not," said the team's lead. "We haven't even spotted him yet."

Max inspected the log for a few more seconds. Then, like he heard an inaudible calling, he scampered through the trees and disappeared from view.

The team scooted after him.

Max headed deeper into the woods, barking every few seconds as if to say, *Keep up, people.* Soon, his barks and the officers' boots crunching on the leaf-strewn floor were the only sounds in the forest.

When they found the K9 again, he was by a colossal oak tree. When Max saw Tanya approach, he sat down and barked three times.

"He's found something," said Tanya, hurrying over to him.

She and the officers congregated by the tree, but there were no clues to the whereabouts of Olek or anyone else. Tanya was about to give the team directions to fan out and search the area when an officer let out a surprised yell.

"Hey!"

Everyone jumped, their hands flying to their holsters. Tanya scanned the woods, but they seemed to be alone.

"What the heck, man?" scolded another officer. "You almost gave me a heart attack."

The first officer pointed up the tree.

"Look up."

Tanya whipped her head up. She stared at the old

bicycle hanging from a leafy branch several feet above her head.

Olek's bike.

Chapter Thirty-Nine

A trooper grabbed the trunk and lifted himself onto a branch.

"Watch it," called out Tanya. "We have to preserve evidence, blood marks, anything that might point to his whereabouts."

"He's not up here. That's for sure, ma'am," called out the officer, squatting on the branch. "The danged perp put the bike up here to hide it from us. If your dog wasn't here, we'd have never spotted it."

Tanya nodded. "Bring it down."

A second officer joined the first in the tree. The two worked in tandem to untangle the bicycle while the others surveyed the area.

"How did he get the bike up there if he was hurt?" said an officer as she took photos of the base of the trunk.

"Maybe that blood wasn't his. Maybe he injured someone else," said another.

"He did a runner, and runners are always guilty."

"I'd bet you he's long gone by now."

Tanya listened to the surrounding chatter, trying to make sense of Olek's odd behavior. Something told her he was still here, in the woods.

"The good thing is we have his bike," she said out aloud. "Max will find him."

The female officer scrunched her forehead.

"Why didn't you send the K9 earlier, ma'am? It would have made our lives a heck of a lot easier."

Tanya felt her neck go warm.

Because a part of me didn't want you to find him. Because I wanted to believe he was innocent.

But Tanya knew the trooper was correct. She should have offered her dog for their search, hours ago. As if he knew they were talking about him, Max barked.

Tanya turned to see him standing in front of a large bush. He barked and wagged his tail as he saw her glance his way. She stepped over to him, taking care to not step on potential evidence. That was when she spotted the red drips on the forest floor.

If someone was holding Olek hostage or if he was feeling cornered, things were about to get serious.

"Cover me." Tanya signaled to the other officers before circling the bush, her gun aimed forward.

Behind the thicket was a mud hill. Max stepped up to it and barked three times.

He's found someone.

A whimper came from nearby.

Olek?

Tanya surveyed the mound that looked like a hibernation den, large enough for a small bear. The drips of blood showed her exactly where Olek had retreated to.

She stepped around the mound, following the blood spots, seeking the cave's entrance. Max followed at her heels, sniffing the ground. Tanya took faith in that he wasn't growling or tensed up and ready to attack.

She stopped and peered at the small opening. The whimpering was coming from inside the darkened den.

How did he squeeze himself in there?

She pulled out her flashlight, turned it on, and bent low.

Olek was cloistered in a space too small to hold him. His right arm was cut, and he was bleeding heavily.

"Don't hurt me. Please, don't hurt me."

He stared at her, tears rolling down his face.

"Why are you punishing me?" His voice was hoarse and shaky, like he was dehydrated. "I followed instructions exactly like you asked."

Tanya wondered if he'd lost his mind. She

171

holstered her Glock and turned the flashlight away from his frightened eyes.

"Hey, it's okay. You're safe with me. We'll get you out of here and get that cut looked into."

Olek pulled his knees up and balled up.

"I didn't mean to hurt her," he croaked. "I swear. Please believe me. I didn't know it was a bomb."

Chapter Forty

"You wanted to kill Asha!" cried Olek.

Tanya stared at her cousin, wondering if she'd heard him correctly.

It was chilly and drafty in the Black Rock precinct jail cell, but rivulets of sweat dripped from Olek's forehead to the concrete floor.

"You hunted me down like a wild hog." He flashed his furious eyes at her. "How could you? *You*, of all people?"

He adjusted the sling on his injured arm and winced. A medic had cleaned and bandaged him up, while Tanya had waited impatiently to talk to him.

Olek had slipped and fallen off his bike while fleeing from the search party, and had cut himself on a sharp rock. That much she knew, but it was the rest of his story that made no sense.

"Why did you keep the bomb a secret from me?" Olek rocked back and forth on the cold steel bench. "Why did you make me do it? How could you?"

Tanya wondered if he was suffering from a brain injury as a result of falling off his bike. She made a mental note to take him to Dr. Chen's clinic and have him checked out.

"But we haven't spoken in years, Olek."

"You called me two weeks ago." His face contorted, like he was about to cry. "Don't leave me out to hang alone. I'm not taking the fall when this was all your idea."

Tanya looked up at Officer Hall, who was standing by the open cell door, instructed to keep an eye on their latest man in custody.

"Where are his things?"

The officer straightened up.

"In the locker, ma'am. I put everything away when we booked him."

"Get his mobile, please."

The officer whirled around and marched toward the back of the precinct.

Tanya turned back to her cousin, her mind a whir. He was sitting slouched, his arms on his thighs and his shoulders hunched, looking like Quasimodo imprisoned in Notre Dame.

Her heart fell to see him like this. Olek was a petty criminal, not a killer.

Or is he?

She knew better than to make baseless assumptions, especially of someone she hadn't seen in a long time. She leaned closer to him.

"Tell me exactly what happened."

"I came to town and went to the old train station, just like you told me to."

He swallowed and wiped his mouth. Tanya nodded to urge him to keep talking.

"I slipped the tracker under Asha's car, the one you mailed me." He spoke in a low voice, like he was afraid someone might overhear him. "I thought it was a cool spy gadget. That's what I figured."

Tanya listened quietly, but her brain was swirling, trying to piece this puzzle together.

"Go on."

"I stuck it in the Audi's undercarriage, and then... and then... I ran to get my bike and get out of town."

That's when Ocean spotted you.

Olek looked up at her. His eyes were clear. Tanya wondered if he had smartened up and become the best liar on earth. Or if he was simply telling the truth.

He rubbed his bloodshot eyes.

"That tracker you sent me wasn't a spy gadget, was it?"

Tanya didn't reply.

"It was a bomb!"

He yelled so loudly, Max barked from the office area where Tanya had left him with a bowl of water.

"I know you told me to get out of town." Olek's voice turned shaky. "You told me not to contact you, but I had to see you. I had to look in your eyes and ask why you made me do that... but I chickened out."

"That's why you came to my house."

He sat up, a red flush creeping up his face.

"I almost killed Asha! You're a murderer!"

His eyes brimmed with tears.

"I like her. A lot. I had a major crush on her when I first saw her. She's a sweet girl. How could you do this to me? How could you plot to kill your own best friend?"

Tanya let out a heavy sigh.

"Whoever asked you to plant that bomb was pretending to be me."

Olek glared at her.

"But I saw your face, and I heard your voice."

Tanya paused. "Why didn't you tell me any of this when you came to my cottage?"

"You told me I couldn't say a word if I bumped into you. You told me your house and your car were bugged. So I didn't. You knew Asha's car blew up, but you played innocent. You questioned me like it was *my* fault. You... you... You're a two-faced witch!"

"Ma'am?"

Tanya looked up to see Officer Hall had returned.

176

In her hands was a plastic bag containing a mobile phone.

The click of high heels came from down the corridor. Everyone turned to see who it was. Katy marched over to the cell and glowered at Tanya.

"The search party just told me what happened. You shouldn't be in here."

Tanya sighed. If Jack had been at the precinct, she would have never been allowed to question her own cousin, let alone someone accusing her of premeditated murder.

She put her hands up. "Just a few more questions?"

Katy glared.

"Haven't you heard of conflict of interest? Nothing you learn here will fly in any court."

"We don't have time. We have to find out who's behind this before we have another victim on our hands."

Tanya turned to Officer Hall.

"Put your gloves on. Check his inbox for a potential note from me."

"When did this email come?" asked the officer.

"'Bout two weeks ago," said Olek, in a defeated voice. "You gave me all the instructions. I was just doing what you told me. You have to believe me."

Officer Hall took the mobile and started swiping through the emails while the others watched in silence. Even Katy looked on, too curious to know what she'd find, to chase Tanya away.

"Got it."

The officer clicked something on the screen.

A female voice crackled through the phone. The officer turned up the volume.

Katy gasped.

Tanya jerked back in shock. She recognized the voice that came out of the speakerphone.

It was her own.

Chapter Forty-One

A shiver ran down Tanya's back.

"That's not me."

But everyone was staring at her, open-mouthed.

"See?" said Olek. "You told me exactly what to do. You told me how to find her car and how to plant that thing."

Tanya turned to her cousin, her heart racing.

"I didn't have your number, your email address, or your social media profiles. If I wanted to get through to you, I would've had to contact Chanda first. I never did."

Olek gave her a doleful look.

"I'm just telling you what happened." He shrugged. "The email proves it."

Katy leaned over Officer Hall's shoulder, and her eyes widened.

"My goodness. It looks exactly like you."

Tanya's eyebrows shot up.

"That was a video?"

The officer turned the screen toward her. Tanya's jaw dropped to see her own face staring back at her. It felt like someone had punched her in the gut.

How is this possible?

The officer pulled the phone back to her eyes and frowned.

"Wait. Something's not right."

"Of course it's not right," said Tanya. "I never made that video."

The officer didn't speak for a minute as she fiddled with something.

"I thought so."

She held the screen up so everyone could see. The video was playing again, but in slow motion this time.

Tanya frowned. "What are we supposed to see?"

"Deep-fake AI," said Officer Hall.

Olek shot her a frightened side-eye.

"What gawd-forsaken witchcraft is that?"

"Not witchcraft. High-tech. Same tool used by identity thieves. Can you hear it?"

Everyone leaned in to listen to Tanya's voice giving directions to Olek.

Halfway through, Katy looked up.

"Something's off. It's creepy."

"There are weird robotic breaks," said Officer Hall.

Tanya nodded. "I don't talk like that."

"No human talks that way," said Officer Hall. "Once I break this down frame by frame, I'll be able to see exactly how this was made." She sighed. "The tech isn't perfect, but give it a few years and nobody will know who's who."

Katy shuddered.

"Explain this to me like you would to my nine-year-old daughter."

"Your daughter can probably make something like this, or even better," said Officer Hall. "She just needs access to the Internet and to know where to find the right tools."

Katy placed her hand over her heart.

Tanya leaned back, feeling like someone had reached into her and pulled her insides out.

"The killer used me to get to Olek, to murder Asha."

The officer nodded.

"This is like robot calls but improved by a magnitude of a thousand with artificial intelligence."

Katy shook her head. "I can't believe how this is possible."

"Anything is possible with AI," said Officer Hall. "The most popular scam these days is to call a grandparent using the voice and face of a grandkid.

The fake kid tells a desperate story and asks for money to be wired ASAP. And the grandparent raids their bank accounts."

Katy made a face.

"Some banks have guardrails, but many don't," continued the officer. "You can lose your life's savings with one click. People have lost millions. The caseloads come in weekly."

"How do the scammers know who to call?" said Katy.

"Social media. That's why it's a bad idea to play online quizzes. It's mainly scammers collecting your data to target you later on."

Tanya frowned. "But I'm never on social media, and no one has photos or videos of me."

Other than my official employer, the Federal Bureau of Investigation.

Officer Hall smiled like she found that amusing.

"It's so easy. Someone could have taken a video of you ordering a cup of coffee at Lulu's. If they're good, you'd never know."

Katy gasped. "That's so scary."

"Most of the time, scammers get info off stolen databases. Hackers auction them off on the dark web. There's a huge black market for personal information because you can make a lot using these fake videos."

Tanya shook her head to shake off the migraine that had come back in full force.

Olek hugged himself, wincing as he touched his injured arm.

"I... I didn't know any of this," he stammered. "You... the fake you, told me Asha worked for the Bratva Brigade. You told me she changed. How was I supposed to know that car tracker was really a bomb?"

Tanya turned to Officer Hall. "We need to trace this email and video ASAP."

A pained expression came over the officer's face.

"That's the hard part. Most of these scammers operate from overseas. My boss says this should be an FBI job. We don't have the resources at the state level."

Tanya stared at her, her mind buzzing with everything that had happened that day.

"Something tells me this came from our own backyard. Whoever they are, they're watching us. Listening in."

Katy shivered.

"Do whatever you can to track it," said Tanya.

The officer stepped out of the jail cell when Tanya's phone rang, startling her. She glanced down at her mobile and put it to her ear.

"Stone?" The police chief's voice sounded strained.

"The killer plans to strike again. Come quick."

Chapter Forty-Two

The blood drained from Katy's face.

"Another victim? Where? Who?"

"Jack didn't share much over the phone," said Tanya, leaping to her feet. "I don't blame him. I get the feeling the killer's watching our every move."

"Oh, man," said Olek, his voice miserable. "I'm beginning to think I'm safer in here."

Tanya stepped outside the jail cell. "I have a long drive to the hospital."

Katy turned to her.

"Jack and Priscilla are at Dr. Chen's clinic now."

Tanya raised a brow.

"Priscilla?"

"Jack's ex-wife," said Katy. "I was at the clinic with them just now. I came here to get you."

"Why isn't Priscilla at the hospital?"

"Jack brought her here for security reasons. We don't have enough resources to post guards all over the place."

Tanya sighed.

They had already stationed two officers at Zoe and Fox's home. More were watching over the crime scenes at the beach, the school, and the old train station. If this carried on, they would have to request resources from nearby counties that were short-staffed themselves.

Tanya walked briskly to the precinct's bullpen, with Katy at her heels. The troopers had taken over their desks and were busy on phones or tapping on laptops.

Tanya snapped her fingers at Max who was sleeping under Katy's desk.

"Hey, there, bud. We have a job to do."

He trotted over and licked her hand, like he felt her anxiety.

Tanya was still coming to terms with the sickening feeling of hearing her own voice give murder instructions. She gave an involuntary shudder.

Katy squeezed her arm.

"I'm coming with you."

Taking a deep breath in, Tanya followed her friend and Max out. They power-walked through the parking lot and around the block toward Dr. Chen's.

Jack's cruiser was parked outside the medical clinic next to the ambulance. As soon as they stepped inside, the receptionist pointed to the door that led to the back.

A dark sense of déjà vu came over Tanya. The last time she had come in here, it was to see a note that had been stuffed down Nicole's mouth, while her body lay cut up on the autopsy table.

"In the morgue?" said Tanya, her dread growing.

"Patient room Two-C," said the receptionist.

"This way," said Katy.

She slipped through the door and hurried down a well-lit corridor. Tanya followed her to room number Two-C.

"Come in," came Dr. Chen's voice, unusually high-pitched. The physician wasn't one to let her nerves get the best of her, but the killer seemed to have even got to her.

Tanya and Katy walked into a private patient's room. Jack and Dr. Chen looked up from across the hospital bed.

Priscilla was lying quietly, covered by a blanket and hooked up to monitors. She looked helpless, her raspy breaths the only signs of her clinging to life.

Jack's pale face and anxious eyes told Tanya everything. She stepped up to the bed and clutched the rail, trying not to choke up.

"Is she going to be okay?" whispered Katy.

"She should pull through." The physician's face

and demeanor told her she was worried. "She's in an induced coma for now."

Induced coma? That didn't sound good.

Tanya turned to the chief whose face was gray and the lines on his forehead more pronounced than before.

"Where was the riddle?"

"We didn't find it," he said. "She spoke it."

Tanya and Katy stared at him.

"She whispered it to me before she went under. It didn't make any sense, but I know it's another riddle."

Jack rubbed his face.

"The killer said something to her after he hit her. She was already on the floor in pain so she didn't catch everything."

"What did she catch?" said Tanya.

"Something about crowns and lights. Does that mean anything to you?"

Tanya and Katy exchanged a confused glance.

"She kept saying those two words over and over." Jack's shoulders dropped. *"Crowns and lights. Crowns and lights."*

Katy glanced down at Priscilla who looked like she was sleeping.

"That's why the killer didn't finish his job. He left her alive, so she would pass on the riddle to us."

"This means there's another victim out there,"

said Jack. "We have to find them before the unsub gets them."

An unsettling sensation came over Tanya.

Crowns and lights. Where did I hear about crowns recently?

She pulled her phone out.

"Asha's supposed to be home on bed rest, but—"

Her phone rang.

Speak of the devil.

She took the call and put her mobile to her ear.

"I was just about to—"

"You won't believe this," came her friend's voice on the other end. Her usual confidence had vanished, replaced by a heightened apprehensiveness.

Tanya's heart ticked faster.

"Did the killer call you, again?"

Tanya heard her gulp.

"He shared the next murder riddle on my live podcast," came Asha's somber voice. "The entire town heard it."

Chapter Forty-Three

"Jack's guard dogs kicked me out of my own studio."

Asha's nostrils flared.

"They pulled the plug from my podcast while I was on air. Can you believe it?"

"Your office building is a crime scene," said Tanya. "You were supposed to be at home resting."

After spending hours at the precinct, pulling her hair out, trying to figure out the newest riddle, Tanya had to clear her head. Max needed a potty break. She knew if they didn't take a breather, neither of them would be alert when the killer made his next move.

Max's barks made her look up. He was playing with Chantal and Zak among the waves. The ocean breeze carried their carefree laughter toward them.

Sahara and Ocean were sitting at the edge of the

pier, following their every move. They had brought the children to the beach, realizing that keeping them cooped up for days on end would only make them restless.

Tanya scanned the shoreline.

Three pairs of officers were patrolling the pier. Other than the police presence, the children, and the two older ladies, the beach was empty.

The sun was setting, and soon it would be dark, but they still hadn't figured out where the killer would strike next. Tanya's anxiety was growing.

She turned to her friend.

"*Crowns and lights.* Those aren't random words. They must mean something."

"There was nothing about lights or crowns in the riddle I got from the troll," said Asha.

She took out her phone and clicked on an audio file. A robotic AI voice emerged from the speakers.

"*I have a heart that roars, yet I'm silent at rest. Though I'm small, I conquer a vast expanse, leaving no footprints—*"

Asha looked up with a scowl.

"That's when the storm troopers barged in and shut me down. They didn't even stop to ask. Idiots."

"We can't blame the crew. They were just following orders," said Tanya.

The chief had held a brief press conference on Nicole's death and the explosion at the train station, an hour after the school was evacuated. He had asked for calm and had shared only so much to not rouse panic among the locals.

Most people had taken heed and were staying inside the safe confines of their homes. This had only made Asha's podcast popular. It seemed like almost everyone had been listening in when the killer had phoned in.

Back at the precinct, Katy was fielding calls from townsfolk, some of whom had teamed up to solve the killer's half puzzle. Even with the entire town involved, no one had been able to decipher the latest riddle.

Asha narrowed her eyes.

"We have two parts of a riddle. Or two parts of two riddles. Which is it?"

"Priscilla was hit in the head badly," said Tanya. "Even if he had told her the riddle, we have no idea if she remembered it with accuracy."

She pointed at Asha's phone.

"Let's focus on your recording for now, or we'll be going in circles."

Asha squinted at the words on her screen.

"A heart that roars could mean an engine of some sort. But what is small that leaves no footprints?"

She sucked her breath in.

"And how small is small? Are we talking child-size small? A Mini car-size small? Or atom-sized small? This is a tough one."

Tanya sat quietly, listening to her friend tear the riddle apart, her own brain feeling as slow as sludge.

She had experienced many disturbing events in her life, but knowing a killer could use her likeness to convince another to commit a horrific crime had unsettled her. She seesawed between anger and helplessness.

Whoever invented deepfake AI should burn in hell.

"This killer is a professional," she said, more to herself.

Asha sat up.

"What about the new tech whiz at the precinct? We should partner up. Two heads are better, as they say."

"Just don't let Jack find out. His priority is keeping everyone in town safe, so he's not entertaining requests."

Asha pointed at the kids.

"He let *them* out."

"Only because Max and I are here. Max needed his walk, and the kids needed some air, but they'll have to return soon." Tanya paused. "You too."

As if on cue, Ocean called out from the pier.

"Chantal? Zak? Say bye. We have to head back."

The children turned and ran toward the women as an officer watched from a few feet away.

"Fine. I'll hitch a ride with them." Asha made a face as she stepped away. "Can't have you get into trouble for aiding and abetting a civilian trying to do the right thing."

With a heavy sigh, Tanya called out to her dog.

She had hoped Asha would figure out the riddle within minutes like the last times. The feeling of dread she'd felt, that something ominous was about to happen, had grown.

"Let's go, bud."

Tanya stomped through the sand toward her Jeep as Max bounded over.

She plucked her phone out of her pocket.

It's time to make the call.

Chapter Forty-Four

Ray Jackson's voice came through the phone immediately.

"I don't have time to chitchat."

"Me neither," said Tanya. "I'm calling to ask for a favor."

"You heard the boss. She's not willing—"

"This is getting serious, Ray. We've had one homicide and two potential murders. One victim is in a coma. Don't you have extra resources you can send down?"

"I thought the State Department is helping."

"They're all green. We lucked out with one tech whiz who plays with computers on weekends. Asha has been helping, but we need a proper team."

"There was a school shooting in Florida," said Ray, "and we have a sniper running around in

Maine. The bureau has its priorities, and their hands are full. You have no case with just one homicide."

Tanya tried not to grit her teeth.

"Would you prefer I call after two more innocents die so this case fits within your bureaucratic jurisdiction?"

Ray groaned.

"I wish I could do more. I'm not as powerful as you think I am. At the moment, I've been demoted to future congresswoman's secretary."

Tanya shook her head. She was about to give up when Ray spoke in a hushed tone.

"I learned something yesterday. I was in the car when Cross took a call from the head of the organized crime unit."

Tanya's ears perked up.

"That's my official chain of command." She frowned. "What did he say?"

"He called about the Crimson King." Ray sounded like he was worried about being overheard.

"Crimson King?" Tanya furrowed her brow. "Never heard that name before."

"He came from nowhere," said Ray, "or so it seems."

"Who is he?"

"Crimson King is the online handle for a powerful international crime gangster." Ray was speaking in a whisper now.

"What's his business?" said Tanya. "Contract killings? Human trafficking?"

"He's a merchant of death."

Tanya inhaled sharply.

"He sells illegal weapons to terrorists," said Ray, "then turns around and sells protection to the rich oligarchs of Eastern Europe, the Middle East, and Africa. Some sources say he has defense contracts with local governments to fight rebels, whom he then arms himself."

"An equal opportunity killer." Tanya hissed. "Why haven't we put this sicko away yet?"

"The man's a genius," said Ray. "He's evaded Interpol for years. No one even knows what he looks like. Some say he wears a mask to veil a tortured face, but I say that's just melodramatic prattle."

He paused.

"Our behavioral analysis unit has pegged him to be a psychopath." Ray's voice was heavy. "Every time his moniker pops up, people start disappearing. Even the bureau gets nervous."

Tanya inhaled deeply.

"Is the bureau getting nervous now?"

Ray was silent for a moment.

"This is confidential information, which means you cannot share this with anyone."

"I have the need to know," said Tanya.

"Your direct supervisor will inform you at the right time through official channels, if and only if, they believe the rumors are true and have any relevancy to your mission."

"That might be too late." Tanya blew a raspberry. "Besides, you are my official channel. You're supposed to be my handler."

"Not anymore, Agent Stone. Until they give you the green light, don't do anything rash. This is just an unofficial heads-up."

Tanya gritted her teeth.

"We might have another homicide victim in our hands by the time the bureaucracy gets its act together."

"One more thing," said Ray.

Tanya clutched her phone tightly.

"The Crimson King has been operating somewhere in the USA for a while, but no one knows where." He paused. "The question is, is your killer the Crimson King?"

Tanya furrowed her brow.

"Why do they call him Crimson King?"

Ray sighed. "Because he leaves a river of blood in his wake."

Chapter Forty-Five

"I can't let you go in there," said Jack.

Tanya dropped her shoulders. "He's my cousin. He's entitled to a family visit."

He shot her a steely glance. "I know you interrogated him in the cell this morning, despite the conflict."

"He's too scared to talk to anyone else. I've known him since I was a kid. He'll open up to me."

The chief shook his head.

"He didn't get that deepfake message out of the blue." Tanya stepped toward his desk. "The killer knew his address and his location, and also knew his connection to me. I need to find out why."

Jack narrowed his eyes.

"That's exactly why it's not a good idea for you to investigate this case anymore."

Tanya threw her hands in the air.

"Come on, Jack."

Max had taken his favorite place at the feet of the chief's desk. At her outburst, he raised his head and cocked it, a concerned expression on his face.

He turned around and glanced at Jack as if to check if his mom was being threatened. But the police chief sat slouched in his chair, his eyes bloodshot from not having slept for two days.

"The entire town is working to figure out that last riddle," said Tanya. "The crime might have already been committed. If it hasn't, it's imminent. We're playing with someone's life. All hands should be on deck, including mine."

"You make it sound like I'm firing you." Jack lifted his tired eyes to her. "I'm simply saying it's not smart to have a conversation with a family member embroiled in this investigation. Defense lawyers will have a field day with that. We need to go by the book."

He leaned back in his chair and crossed his arms. That was never a good sign, because that meant he had made up his mind.

"The killer has hijacked Asha's podcast as his personal communications channel," he said, "and that hasn't helped."

Tanya frowned. "What do you mean?"

"That last podcast has gone viral. Snippets of it are all over social media."

Jack clicked his mouse and pointed at his screen. "Look what's been circulating all morning."

Tanya stepped around the desk and stared at an image of a female body sprawled on a flat rock at Black Rock's beach.

Nicole.

The image had thousands of likes, another thousand hearts, and even some laughing emojis. She shuddered to think of the comments it had racked up.

"Who took that picture?"

"A man who lives on the bluff," said Jack. "The south-facing condos have a straight line view to this spot on East Beach."

Tanya grimaced. "Don't they have any common decency?"

"I have a serial killer to catch." Jack sighed. "I'll deal with these snoopy neighbors later."

He wiped his forehead.

"*Seattle Times* called. The paparazzi are circling us like vultures over roadkill. I'm surprised they haven't descended on us already, but they're on their way, and if I can't help it, we'll be on national television tonight."

Tanya raised her brows.

"This is why procedure is key," he said. "Nothing can go wrong as we find this maniac. We have to give the DA a watertight case."

Tanya sighed, knowing he was right.

She wished she could tell him about the Crimson King. She also wished she could come clean about her undercover role.

But that wasn't possible. Not without breaking her oath to the bureau. The FBI director would come down on her like a thunderclap, and she would be fired from her real job in a nanosecond.

Tanya leaned against the door. She racked her brain, trying to think of how to convince Jack to let her talk to Olek.

"How's your wife doing?"

Jack blinked.

"My ex-wife."

"Sorry," mumbled Tanya. "Why did Priscilla come to Black Rock?"

"She fell into a coma before anyone could ask her."

"When I spotted her on the road this morning, she was getting into a black limo. The only tinted limo around here is the one at the Grimwood Estate."

Jack nodded.

"That connection has crossed my mind."

"Does she have any relations with the estate?"

Jack sighed heavily.

"None, that I know of."

"I know this is hard to take," said Tanya, speaking softly. "But I suspect the estate is run by an organized crime ring."

Courtesy of the Federal Bureau of Investigation.

"They could have coerced her to come here," she said.

Jack looked up, the lines on his forehead deeper than ever.

"Priscilla? Why lure her, then attack her?"

Tanya felt his hurt.

"You may not know who she may have become involved with during the past three years."

He shook his head.

"I know her."

You knew her, thought Tanya quietly.

"She was my high school sweetheart," said Jack. "We grew up together. I loved her."

You still do, Jack.

"She would never socialize with criminals. She's a child psychologist, for heaven's sake."

"Could we at least try to get a search warrant for the estate?"

"Based on what?" Jack shook his head. "No judge worth their salt will sign a warrant just because we have a bad feeling about the place."

Tanya knew he was right.

Her own agency, one of the largest federal law enforcement departments, was having a tough time pinning anything on the estate and whoever lived there. She couldn't expect a local police chief with limited resources to figure it out.

Jack rubbed his face. "Not all limos that drive

through our town belong to the estate. It could have been from Seattle."

Tanya glanced down at her phone.

The photo she had snapped at the crossroads was fuzzy. The limo was at an angle that rendered the license plate unreadable. Even the bureau's forensics team in Seattle hadn't been able to parse it out yet.

"I left Chicago soon after our divorce."

She looked up to see that Jack was speaking softly.

"It was a shock to see her in the school library like that. We're not together anymore, but she's still kind of family, you know what I mean?"

Tanya nodded sympathetically.

"Do you mind if I ask why you divorced?"

"She wanted kids, and I couldn't give her any."

Jack wiped his face, like he wished to wipe that memory away.

"We tried for years until we realized I was the problem."

Tanya looked away, feeling bad for prying into something so personal.

"She loved kids." Jack continued, like he was talking to himself now.

"She had a rough childhood. When I met her, she was adamant she didn't want children because she worried she'd inflict the same pain on them." He paused. "Then, five years later, she changed her mind."

"People change," said Tanya, feeling for him and Priscilla.

They fell silent for a few seconds.

Tanya leaned in.

"Whoever lured my cousin here, sent Priscilla to Black Rock. If you let me talk to him—"

Jack's desk phone rang, making them both jump. He reached for it.

"That must be the school board. I don't think they hired her, but I'd like to hear it straight from them."

Jack took the call.

Tanya slipped out of his office and closed the door gently.

One thought refused to leave her troubled mind.

Something tells me Olek knows who Crimson King is.

Chapter Forty-Six

Tanya's phone buzzed the minute she left Jack's office.

"Aunty Tanya?" came a girl's high-pitched voice. "Where's Aunty Nicole?"

Tanya's heart fell. She could hear the fear in Chantal's voice.

"Why... Why do you ask?" said Tanya, stalling, as she thought of the best way to answer her.

"Ocean and Sahara were talking in the kitchen," said Chantal. "I heard them."

"Did they tell you anything?"

"No, but I heard Sahara say something really bad is happening to everyone. Ocean said it started with Aunty Nicole."

"I, er,... Your mom will tell you when she comes to pick you up tonight, honey."

"She doesn't tell me anything." Chantal took a shaky breath in. "Is Aunty Nicole dead? What about Zak's mom? What happened to her? He misses her."

"Aunty Zoe's just spending a few nights at the clinic—"

"Is she dead? Shouldn't we tell Zak if his mom's dead too?"

"No! She's fine." Tanya's stomach roiled. "Listen. Don't tell Zak anything, okay?"

"Why? How come no one's telling me what's going on?"

Chantal's father, Peace, liked to say he lucked out to have the smartest kid in the state. She was a conscientious and curious girl. It wouldn't take long for her to ferret the truth out.

Tanya's gut tightened to think of either kid seeing that horrible photo of Nicole on social media. Chantal would have more questions if anyone told her Nicole was only sleeping. Sahara and Ocean wouldn't get away with their lies so easily.

Tanya clicked her tongue for Max to follow her. She hurried out of the precinct and into the parking lot, toward her Jeep.

Katy was preoccupied with the new team at the station, and Jack had just told her to take a step back from the case. The least she could do was reassure Chantal and Zak before they learned what had happened to Nicole from someone else.

"I'm coming over." She jumped into the driver's

seat and put her seatbelt on. "Can you tell Ocean and Sahara?"

"Okay," said Chantal, hanging up.

Tanya put the Jeep in gear, wondering whose phone the girl had used to call her.

Katy had given strict instructions not to let the kids have access to phones, watch television, or check out social media for the next few days.

Ocean and Sahara lived a carefree bohemian lifestyle. If they had a religion, it was freedom from social norms. They didn't even like anyone referring to them as aunt or grandma because that was too hierarchical, in their opinion.

But this meant they were also the kind of adults who would give kids whatever they asked for, even if it was ice cream for supper and chicken nuggets for breakfast. They were also likely to leave their phones lying around carelessly.

Tanya glanced at her rearview mirror. Max was standing up in the backseat, his snout pointed out of the window.

"Hey, bud? Chantal and Zak will need you today. Let's make their day a little brighter, shall we?"

Max whirled around and thumped his tail on the backseat, like he understood her. Tanya smiled through the mirror, wondering how she would have made it through the past few heart-wrenching days without him. Her dog kept her sane and grounded.

"Let's hope Jack will forget he asked me to stay

away from the case," she muttered to herself as she rolled down the road. "Give him a few hours, and he'll realize he needs my help."

The memory of Jack hunched over Priscilla's bed at the clinic flashed into her mind. She felt for the injured woman, even though she was a stranger. But to see Jack wracked by worry stung her heart.

She drew in a deep breath. Now was not the time to think about him. She had a job to do.

It took her ten minutes to get to Ocean and Sahara's upscale home at the heart of the affluent West End suburb. She saluted the two officers sitting in the squad car in front of the house. They nodded as she turned into the driveway.

"Hey, Max!"

Zak rocketed out of the front door and raced toward the Jeep before Tanya even came to a stop. She slammed on the brakes, her heart beating fast.

"Watch out, Zak," she called.

Max barked in the backseat and whirled around, excited to see his young friend. Before Tanya could say anything more, Zak had opened her back door.

The dog jumped out and raced after the boy into the yard, barking happily.

Tanya stepped out of the Jeep.

I guess he's the distraction Zak needs right now.

Zak had no idea what his mother had gone through on the beach that day. He also didn't know the lifeless body of his aunt lay in Dr. Chen's morgue, stitched up after the autopsy was completed.

Tanya felt her heart grow heavy as she stepped up to Ocean and Sahara's front door.

It flung open before she could get up the steps.

Chapter Forty-Seven

"You came!"

Chantal skipped through the front door, her ponytail bobbing.

She wrapped her arms around Tanya, and Tanya hugged her back as tightly as she could, giving an extra squeeze for Katy.

The door banged open a second time and out stepped Sahara, looking larger than life, as usual. Her oversized baggy shirt was crumpled, and her hair was streaked with flour. She wiped her face, spreading the white powder across her rosy cheeks.

"Just in time for tea," she said, smiling. "We're baking a strawberry sponge cake."

Tanya put her arm around Chantal and followed her inside the house. One glance at the living room told her the ladies had been lax in following Katy's instructions.

Cary Grant, a large gray Maine Coon, was sprawled luxuriously on the divan in front of the unlit fireplace, his fur draped over something black and shiny.

Tanya poked Sahara in the back.

"Is that your phone?"

"Oops."

Sahara leaned over, plucked the mobile out, and pocketed it. The cat raised his head and gave them all a patronizing look as if to say, *How dare you interrupt my sleep.* Then he settled his head back down, like they no longer existed.

Cary Grant was the reason Max didn't dare enter Ocean and Sahara's home. Her dog didn't hesitate to chase violent men with guns, but Tanya had a hard time persuading him to cross the threshold to this home.

"I was looking for it all day." Sahara gave her a wonky smile. "Must have dropped it on the couch this morning. Oh, well. No harm done."

Too late, thought Tanya as she followed her into the kitchen in the back.

The hum of the stove and the sweet smell of baking filled the house. Ocean was stirring something on the stove. She whirled around.

"A guest," she cried. "I thought you were super busy at the station."

"Yeah, we have several projects on the go," said Tanya. "It's keeping us on our toes."

Chantal climbed onto a stool in front of a mixing bowl filled with half-cut strawberries. On the granite kitchen island was a young adult novel, it's pages streaked with strawberry juice. She looked up at Tanya.

"Is that why Mom is at the office all the time?"

Ocean and Sahara glanced at each other.

Tanya nodded.

"She's an important person of the team. Everyone relies on her. You should be proud of her."

"Is Dad helping too?"

Ocean leaned over to her, her hair almost slipping into the fruit bowl. "Your dad has meetings in the city with a very big client."

"When's he coming home?"

"He'll call tonight," said Ocean, wiping her face. "We can ask him then, okay?"

Chantal turned to Tanya.

"How come there's a police car outside our house? Did we do something wrong?"

"No, hon," said Tanya. "They're here to protect all of us."

"Why?"

Tanya brushed the cat fur off the stool next to her and sat down.

"It's a team effort," she said, remaining vague. "When we have a lot of work, they come over and

212

help us. Whenever they get too much work, we go to their town and help them. Isn't that great?"

Chantal pursed her lips.

"I thought it's because Aunty Nicole is dead."

Sahara and Ocean exchanged a startled glance.

Tanya had interrogated terrorists and criminal masterminds before, but she hadn't realized how much more difficult it would be to tell the hard truth to a young girl.

She leaned over, wrapped an arm around Chantal, and planted a kiss on her forehead.

"I'm sorry, honey."

"I saw it on the news," said Chantal, twirling the fruit knife on the cutting board, her mind elsewhere.

Tanya tried not to glare at Sahara for leaving her phone around.

"I also heard a bomb blew up Aunty Asha's baby girl."

Ocean and Sahara gasped out loud.

A volley of barks and a boy's laughter came from the front yard as Zak and Max played under the watchful eyes of the officers.

"That's right," said Tanya. "But Aunty Asha is safe. Why don't you invite her for cake and tea? She'd love that."

Chantal tipped her head to the side.

"Did you find the bad guy?"

"We're working on it. As soon as we find him, we'll put him in jail where he belongs."

"But, what about—"

Sahara lunged over the counter and plucked the bowl of fruit from Chantal's hands.

"The cake's ready!"

Chantal and Tanya leaned back as the two ladies bustled around the island, their sleeves flapping like sails in the wind.

"We need to whip the cream and cut more fruit," said Ocean in a rushed voice. "It's never good to leave a cake lying around."

"Let's get to work, everyone," said Sahara, clapping her hands. "Chop. Chop."

Ocean turned to the girl.

"Can you arrange the berries on the cake for us, sweetie?"

"Hurry please," said Sahara, in a singsong voice. "Or the cake will go stale. We don't want that now, do we?"

With a sigh, like she knew exactly what the ladies were up to, Chantal slipped off her stool. She turned to Tanya and pulled on her arm.

Tanya leaned over to the girl.

"It's all going to be fine. You and Zak don't have to worry, okay? You're safe here."

Chantal thrust her mouth toward Tanya's ear.

"I know who killed Aunty Nicole."

Tanya's eyes widened.

"Who?"

"Crimson King."

Chapter Forty-Eight

"They told me you weren't supposed to be here."

Olek was hunched on his steel bench, his eyes red and his face puffy.

Tanya closed the jail cell door and crouched low, hoping no one would come this way.

Olek wiped his nose with the back of his hand.

"Why are they keeping me here?" he said. "I didn't do anything wrong."

Tanya offered him a bottle of fresh water.

"I'm going to do whatever I can to get you out as soon as possible."

Olek cradled the bottle, but didn't reply.

A bark came from the parking lot outside, and a pang of guilt crossed Tanya. She had locked Max in the Jeep because having a German Shepherd at your heels attracted everyone's attention—attention she didn't need right now.

She had only a few minutes before someone alerted the chief to her presence in the precinct's prison wing.

Jack was on the phone with a sheriff from the town over, negotiating for more help. That conversation would take a while. The rest of the officers were bustling around the bullpen or patrolling the town, the latest riddle casting ominous shadows over everyone's minds.

Katy, who had taken on the role held by a uniformed sergeant, took calls from the public and kept the teams organized. None of the young officers seemed to show her resentment. No one had time for office politics.

Tanya was certain they, like her, were reeling in shock at the events that had occurred within such a short time frame in Black Rock.

"A city surveillance camera caught you," said Tanya, giving her cousin a pained look. "It shows you placing the IED under Asha's vehicle. Even though you didn't know what you were doing, you need to go through the process."

"But you told me the Bratva Brigade was after you. You told me Asha had joined them," Olek cried, thumping his fists on his thighs. "You told me it was a tracker!"

Tanya kept her gaze steady.

"You know that wasn't me."

"You were our big sister back in the village." Olek's chest heaved. "I always respected you. I looked up to you. We all did."

Tanya's stomach's sank to hear those words. *Someone used that to lure you.*

Olek's eyes welled up in tears.

"How could I think Asha would join the Bratva gangsters? I was so stupid."

Tanya softened her voice.

"Anyone would have been fooled by that video. Katy was, and even that tech-smart officer was, at first."

Olek hunched his back and turned his face away, looking more dejected than ever.

"Can I ask you something?" Tanya placed her hand on his knee. "What do you know about the Crimson King?"

He jerked his head back with a cry and slapped her hand away.

It was such an unexpected reaction, she tumbled back in surprise. He leaned away from her, his eyes wide and filled with terror.

"You've heard the name," said Tanya.

Olek gulped.

Chapter Forty-Nine

Olek was no longer making eye contact. The only sound in the jail cell was his raspy breaths, like he was on the verge of hyperventilating.

Tanya tried again.

"Who is this Crimson King?"

Olek fiddled with the water bottle, his trembling fingers plucking at the label.

"Why are you asking me?"

Because my bureau handler warned me about him.

And little Chantal saw the name in a social media post next to Nicole's dead body.

"Because he could be behind all this," she said.

Olek dropped the bottle on his lap and wrapped

his arms around his shoulders, like he was shielding himself from her words.

Tanya leaned closer.

"He might be the person who sent that video to you."

He whipped his head up.

"He sent that video? He knows who I am?" Olek dropped his head in his hands and moaned. "I'm dead. I'm so dead."

"How did you hear about the Crimson King?"

Olek rocked back and forth like a child.

"Please tell me," said Tanya. "Who is this man?"

"He's not a man. He's a vampire."

Tanya stared at her cousin.

"They say he's the son of a Roma king." Olek shot her a fearful look from under his lashes. "He comes when you're not looking, sucks the blood out of you, and leaves you to die."

"You believe that?"

"Some people think he's the son of a dead Nazi. I don't know and I don't care. All I know is, he's the stuff of nightmares. I shouldn't even be talking about him. They say when you do, you summon him to you."

Tanya inhaled deeply.

"I don't think the Crimson King is some magical being, Olek. He's a flesh-and-blood human. A man who runs an international crime ring. He's someone we can take down."

"I don't care." Olek rocked even harder. "Leave me out of this."

"The more I know about this Crimson King, the sooner we can apprehend him." She squeezed his knee. "If you tell me everything you know—"

Footsteps came from down the hallway, and Tanya fell silent.

She prayed under her breath Jack wasn't looking for her. He would have questions, questions she wasn't ready to answer yet.

She hunkered down and peered over Olek's shoulders to see who it was, but the footsteps receded, and they were alone again.

"He's a leader of the Bratva Brigade."

Tanya spun around to face her cousin.

"You should never cross him," Olek was saying, a tremor in his voice. "He's worse than the Russian militia. He's massacred more villagers than the invaders."

Tanya nodded to encourage him to keep talking.

"No one's seen him, but they say he looks like... What's that show with the pretty singing girl and a man with a mask?"

Tanya blinked.

"The one where the big light crashes from the ceiling?" said Olek.

"The phantom?" said Tanya. "*The Phantom of the Opera*?"

"The Crimson King looks just like that. If he

takes his mask off and looks at you, you'll turn to stone and die." Olek shuddered. "Just like that woman with the head of snakes."

Tanya knew her cousin was the superstitious type, like most folks in her village. But this Crimson King was a mortal human, and he was in Black Rock, watching them.

He might even be walking among them, in disguise.

"Can you tell me how old he is?" she said.

"He's... He's... super smart, young, and rich."

"How young?"

Olek shrugged.

"Does he have a quirk or a special trait? Anything that can help us identify him?"

Olek shook his head mournfully. "Nobody has seen him."

"Does he have a family?"

"He came from nowhere. He's the prince of the underworld."

Tanya sighed.

This is going nowhere.

"Please don't let me go," whispered Olek. "If he finds me, he'll...."

Tanya patted his knee.

"You can stay here as long as you want. I'll get you a blanket and a pillow. I'll even get you a double cheeseburger with lots of pickles, onions, and a Diet Coke. Just the way you like it, right?"

Olek sighed a heavy sigh.

"You know it's only a matter of time, don't you?"

"For what?"

"If the Crimson King sent me to Black Rock, it's because I'm already a dead man."

He paused and slouched even more.

"We all are."

Chapter Fifty

Tanya put a hand on Olek's shoulder.

"I'll protect you."

"That's what you said the last time."

His voice had been so sharp, she pulled her hand off him like it had stung.

"Why do you say that?"

Olek twisted the cap off the water bottle and took a gulp.

"You were supposed to be everyone's big sister."

Why did that feel like an accusation?

He looked up at her, his eyes narrowed.

"He was a real good kid, you know?"

Tanya frowned.

"Who are you talking about?"

"Yevhen."

A pang of sadness crossed her heart at the mention of her dead brother's name.

"He was special," said Olek. "A good-looking kid, too. He had the brightest blue eyes. All the girls in the village were in love with him."

Childhood memories came crashing into Tanya's mind.

"Everyone said he would become a Nobel-winning scientist," said Olek with a sad chuckle. "Remember that rocket ship he made from cardboard and wood? I was sure he was going to burn our village with that thing. But he launched it. Almost killed that poor sheep."

He smiled a small smile.

"When old farmer Domitrivich came out with his hunting rifle, we flew across the field so fast, I thought I'd die. Do you remember?"

Tears filled Tanya's eyes as old memories flooded her mind.

"He would have changed the world if he lived," said Olek. "I went to see him, you know?"

Tanya jerked her head up.

"At the Russian camp?"

"I begged them to let him live. They told me you made an arrangement with them."

Tanya blinked. "I made no arrangement with those thugs."

Olek took a sip from his water bottle and shrugged.

"That's what they told me."

"They demanded a ransom for his life," said Tanya, wondering where this conversation was going. "I did what I had to do to save him."

"Did you, though?"

Tanya opened her mouth, but no words came out. A hurricane of painful memories hurled through her head, so that for one moment, she felt crippled with fear and anger.

The worst scars she had got weren't from fighting the Russian army in the battle fields, but in trying to save her brother's life.

"Seems like you went on a fancy trip to Europe," Olek was saying, "while the Ruskies tortured the boys from our village."

Tanya squared her shoulders.

"I went to find the ransom. They gave me three weeks to bring in one hundred thousand US dollars in exchange for Yevhen's life. I made money in ways I never imagined in my life."

Olek took another sip of water.

"You sold yourself?" He scoffed. "All for what? Nothing. You didn't save him in the end, did you?"

Tanya felt a sharp pang, like someone had shot an arrow through her.

"They lied to you," said Olek. "How could you even believe those barbarians?"

Tanya felt her face go warm.

"I was only eighteen," she said in a low voice.

"My mother was lying dead in a pool of blood on our kitchen floor, and my brother was taken by the militia. I did the only thing I thought was right with what I knew at that time."

Olek breathed heavily.

He looked furious. Furious at her.

"Do you even know what happened to the prisoners?"

Tanya closed her eyes. She didn't want to imagine what her brother and his friends had gone through in that torture camp.

"They were in such horrible shape that the boys who got rescued needed plastic surgery. They had no fingers and toes. Some of them had no hands and feet."

Olek crossed himself.

"They were practicing witchcraft on those boys. Only the creator can say how they survived."

A rush of guilt flared through Tanya. She pressed her hands against her face to contain her emotions, but her body started to shake.

"You know who came to save them in the end?" said Olek. "Was it the Americans? Nope. Was it the Brits? Nope. They were too busy for us. It wasn't even the fancy dancy NATO troops."

He turned to her and glared.

"And it wasn't *you!*"

Tanya sobbed silently, but Olek wasn't done.

"You could have brought them home. You betrayed us all."

He stared at her, a cold expression on his face.

Tanya took a shaky breath in.

"I take responsibility for my mother's assassination and my brother's death," she said. "There's nothing you can tell me to make me feel any worse than I do right now."

"You could have saved Yevhen. You could have saved all the boys."

Olek slammed the water bottle down and lowered his face into his hands, like he was done talking.

"You're right," whispered Tanya, more to herself than him.

"I failed you. I failed all of you."

Day Three

The next morning...
At Black Rock's police precinct.

Chapter Fifty-One

"Katy!" The scream was so piercing, the hair on Tanya's neck stood up.

"Calm down, ma'am," came an officer's voice from the reception area of the Black Rock precinct building.

Tanya had just returned from Lulu's café with a tray of heavily caffeinated drinks for everyone, plus a morning burger for Olek in a brown paper bag.

She had been about to distribute the drinks among the team in the bullpen when the cry came from outside.

Her head was pounding and her vision was bleary from having stayed up all night.

No one had slept. Not even the townsfolk it

seemed, who had been given a lockdown order. The phones hadn't stopped ringing at the station.

The chief, the deputies, and the junior troopers not on patrol duty, had worked through the night, trying to unravel the latest puzzle and find the perpetrator.

But the riddle remained unsolved.

Tanya's search for the Crimson King, or anything remotely related to an international weapons dealer operating in their area, had turned up empty. But one horrifying thought lurked in the back of her brain.

Is Olek the Crimson King?

His character, intellect, and skills were the furthest from that of a calculating cold-blooded serial killer. She had been fooled by highly intelligent megalomaniacs before, but this was too far of a stretch.

I'm letting my imagination run wild.

Like a boa constrictor tightening its hold on its prey, the impact of the past few days was squeezing the life out of them all. Tensions were high, and tempers were short. It felt like the office could burn down with one single lit match.

Jack had ordered half the team to get rest, but no one had left their posts.

The Crimson King, if he was behind this, was living up to his name. He was tormenting the town, and no one was spared.

"We have to speak to her!" came the shriek again.

Max bolted through the open doorway that separated the offices from the public waiting area, barking. Tanya dashed after him, her coffee tray still in her hand.

In the lobby, Ocean and Sahara were struggling with a lone officer who was holding them back. Sahara was beating her fists on the officer's chest. Ocean was crying something incomprehensible, and looked like she was having a nervous breakdown.

Tanya stepped over to them.

"Hey, what's going on here?"

Ocean spun around, accidentally hitting the coffee tray with her arm. The cups tumbled and crashed to the floor. Max jumped out of the way as the hot liquid splashed everywhere.

"I'm so sorry!" cried Ocean, her voice high-pitched and panicked.

"It's just coffee. We can clean it up later."

Tanya pried the two women off the officer and pulled them away from the mess on the floor.

"I heard someone shout my name," came a familiar voice from behind them.

Tanya turned to see Katy stepping out to the reception area. Sahara let out a wail and threw herself into her arms. Katy grabbed her, confused.

"Is everything okay?" said Katy.

Ocean turned to her with feverish eyes.

"We took them to the playground behind our

house. Zak was going crazy, stuck inside. It was only supposed to be for ten minutes!"

Tanya's heart dropped.

"We...We... made pancakes for breakfast," stammered Sahara. "We were supposed to go back in to eat. That's when we...we..."

Katy pushed Sahara away from her and narrowed her eyes.

"What happened to the kids?"

"The two officers were with us. We...we...We were by the jungle gym," said Ocean. "One minute we were watching Zak take a tumble, the next minute Chantal... Chantal...."

Katy's face went white.

She grabbed Ocean by her shoulders and shook her.

"Where's my daughter?"

Sahara and Ocean stared at her mutely, like they were too distressed to speak.

A door banged from behind them.

Jack rushed out, his mobile held to his ear.

"We have a ten-sixty-five," he barked into his phone. "Repeat. Code ten-sixty-five."

Tanya felt nauseous.

That meant only one thing. A child has gone missing.

Katy wailed.

Chantal's disappeared.

Chapter Fifty-Two

Jack strode toward Katy.

"We will sweep every inch of this town. I promise."

Katy wailed, her anguished voice echoing through the empty lobby.

"Find my baby!"

Jack let his phone drop to his pocket and grasped her hands in his.

"We'll get an Amber Alert out. We'll get more boots on the ground." His voice was steady, but that didn't seem to have any effect on Katy.

"That's not enough!" she screeched in his face. "I was sitting right outside your office. Why didn't you tell me?"

Jack held on to her, his face sympathetic. He

didn't answer, like he knew no words would calm her down now.

"Did you call Peace?" spluttered Katy. "Does he know?"

Jack wiped his brow.

"I just found out three minutes ago, myself."

When I was in the coffee shop, thought Tanya.

The chief redirected his attention to Ocean and Sahara.

"Where's Zak?"

"In... In the car, with an officer," stammered Sahara. "We pulled him in as soon as we saw Chantal was gone."

Tanya narrowed her eyes. "Did you see anyone around the playground?"

"The officers were supposed to keep watch," cried Ocean. "Why didn't they do their job?"

Jack clenched his jaws. "Where were they when this happened?"

"One of them went to the squad car to get water," said Sahara, "and the other was on the jungle gym with Zak because he kept falling off. I... I... I should have kept an eye on her...."

Jack's face darkened.

"I'll have a talk with them later."

Tanya was upset too, but she knew blaming anyone wouldn't help them find the girl. She could imagine the rookie cops overlooking a shadow behind a tree trunk, or not noticing an odd movement they should have paid attention to.

They're just kids in uniforms.

Her mind flew to her cousin locked up in the town's jail.

Olek couldn't have done it. Or, could he have?

She shook her head in frustration.

He had neither the smarts nor the shrewdness to organize a kidnapping. Not even by a mile. But the greatest lesson she had learned in the bloody fields of war was to never underestimate your enemy. That was the fastest way to get killed.

"I have a search party to organize," said Jack, plucking his phone out. He stepped out of the precinct door and marched toward his cruiser parked by the entrance.

"Peace," said Katy, in a trembling voice. "He needs to know. I need him here with me."

She pulled her phone out with shaking hands. Tears streamed down her cheeks. Max sat by her feet, his head cocked to the side, like he knew something had gone very wrong.

Ocean beat her forehead with her palm.

"Oh, my Lord, what have we done?"

Tanya faced her.

"Do you have a piece of clothing Chantal wore recently?"

Ocean nodded.

"We brought over a bagful of her stuff."

"I need something she wore, but that hasn't been washed."

Ocean's face fell.

"We did laundry last night."

"What about her pajamas?" said Tanya.

"She was wearing them."

"Okay. What about bed sheets or a pillow case?"

"We, er, slept on the giant sofa bed last night, watching, er, movies," said Sahara. "We piled the blankets on. Would any one of them help?"

Tanya sighed. She was sure the blankets had everyone's scents and were also covered in Cary Grant's fur. She shook her head.

"That will confuse Max. We need something else."

Hearing his name, Max barked and got to his feet as if to say, *Let's go.*

Tanya turned to Katy who was attempting to call her husband, but seemed too nervous to carry out that simple task.

"What about you, Katy?"

Katy gazed at her with her watery eyes.

"Have you done the laundry yet?" said Tanya.

"I...I haven't had time," stammered Katy. "Peace is still in meetings in Seattle. I need to talk to him...."

Tanya put her palm out.

"Can I have your house keys?"

"What? Why?"

"I'll find something from Chantal's room. Max will do the rest."

Katy wiped her face. "They're in my purse."

She stumbled through the secure door toward her desk, moving like a zombie.

Tanya turned to Ocean and Sahara, who were staring at her like prisoners sentenced to death, too numb to speak any more.

"Please write down every little thing you can remember from last night to this morning, okay?"

They nodded, mutely.

"Every detail. I especially want to know if Chantal was on one of your phones again. Email it to me."

"What are you going to do?" said Ocean.

"Find Chantal."

Tanya pinched her lips together. There was something else she didn't want to say out loud.

For that, I'll have to first hunt down the Crimson King.

Chapter Fifty-Three

"The Grimwood Estate," said Tanya, tapping the map on her phone. "All roads lead to this place."

"We don't even know if this property is occupied," said Asha.

The private road around the perimeter of the estate was clear, but everything inside the walls was a swath of gray.

"The Google car definitely hasn't mapped it," said Asha. "For all we know, it's just waste land."

Tanya clicked on the image and zoomed in.

"Satellite imagery shows something like a structure on the grounds. It could be a building or a compound."

Asha leaned over her arm and squinted.

"Hard to say what that is. Do you have a search warrant?"

Tanya shook her head.

"Can Jack get one?" said Asha.

"The estate is owned by a numbered company in the Cayman Islands," said Tanya. "City records have a telephone number to a real estate law firm in London. They would be our best bet, but we'll have to figure out the cross jurisdictional process for search warrants."

"Sounds like a bureaucratic nightmare." Asha frowned. "Do you think Chantal is at the Grimwood Estate?"

"We have these murder riddles, a deepfake video, and a bomb that blew up your car. All this says the perpetrator has the resources, the means, and is organized."

"So you think a wealthy crime ring is responsible for killing Nicole and kidnapping Chantal?"

Tanya's brow furrowed.

"Priscilla and Olek were tricked into coming here by someone who figured out their connections to us. A tinted black limo picked Priscilla up, and the only limo around here comes out of the estate's gates. There has to be a connection."

Asha pursed her lips. "A weak link."

"My gut says they're operating from the estate," said Tanya. "That is the only property in town we haven't searched."

Asha sighed. "The property to which no one has access."

"Stay in your line, everyone," Jack called out from up ahead.

Tanya and Asha had been following a line of a dozen patrol officers. The troopers were stepping in tandem, inch by inch, across the playground, their eyes peeled for clues to find the missing girl.

Max trotted by Tanya's heels, jumping into action whenever Jack called on him to check something.

He had already sniffed Chantal's socks, circled the jungle gym, and led the team toward the narrow road behind the playground. That was where he had stopped. He had turned to Tanya and whined as if to say he wished he could do more.

The trail had gone cold.

There were no tire marks on the pavement or evidence of an abductor's car. There were no houses back there, so no witnesses.

"Why would an organized crime ring target Nicole, Priscilla, me, and Chantal?" said Asha. "It's so random, it makes no sense."

The social media post of Nicole's body with the words, "Killed by the Crimson King," had been posted anonymously. That hadn't elicited much confidence in the crew. Even Jack thought Tanya was following a false trail.

Olek's ramblings about an ancient vampire

hunting for blood would only make him and Tanya a laughingstock. All she had was Ray's warning, but she couldn't share that information with the local crew without giving her undercover role away.

"Criminal organizations are big businesses," Asha was saying. "They have profit-and-loss statements. They keep balance sheets. They even hire certified accountants and MBA graduates to run their departments."

Tanya's mind whirred with what Ray Jackson and Olek had told her.

Is this the work of the feared Bratva Brigade?

Or, is the Crimson King working alone?

"They traffic humans by the containers, sell illegal weapons by the boatloads, and engage in financial fraud by the millions," continued Asha as they stepped behind the officers. "Why would they spend time and money to taunt a small-town police precinct with stupid riddles and target innocent victims?"

"There's a method to this madness," said Tanya. "This crime wave is a message."

Asha furrowed her brow. "What kind of message?"

"That's what I need to figure out."

"Who do you think is doing this?"

"A psychopath," said Tanya in a quiet voice. "A serial killer who enjoys playing with people's lives."

Like the Crimson King.

Suddenly, Max unleashed a volley of barks.

Tanya spun on her heels to see the officers had reached the edge of the playground. They stood in line, waiting for their instructions, shoulders stooped and faces heavy with exhaustion.

Where's Max?

Max was no longer by her side. Or theirs. He was on the road that ran the length of the playground, and was heading toward an old building from across a baseball field, his nose to the ground.

He's picked up a scent.

Tanya hurried over to her dog, with one hand on her holster. Jack raced after her, his Glock out.

"That's the old city theater," he called out as they ran.

Tanya stopped in her tracks.

"Did you say *theater*?"

Jack halted and turned to her.

"Crowns and lights," said Tanya, her gut tightening. "The killer's last riddle."

Jack's eyes widened. "Chantal's at the old theater."

Chapter Fifty-Four

The heavy wooden doors creaked open. Jack and Tanya peered into the old theater.

A musty odor came from within, and an eerie silence lingered in the air.

Tanya's gut tightened. There was something unsettling about this place.

She stood shoulder to shoulder with Jack, as they scanned the theater lobby, their weapons aimed forward. Max stood by them, his ears alert and his muscles tensed.

He feels it too, thought Tanya.

"Priscilla remembered the words correctly," whispered Jack.

Behind her, Tanya could hear the officers shuffling up the front steps to join them. Jack had instructed half the team to guard the perimeter. The remaining half a dozen now flanked them, their weapons drawn.

"Clear," called Jack as he stepped into the lobby.

Tanya followed him in. The worn red carpet muffled their footsteps.

She scanned the empty ticket booth and the popcorn stand that looked like it hadn't been operated in years. The only image whirling through her mind was Chantal's face.

Please be alive.

"What's he doing there?" said Jack.

Tanya turned to see Max sniffing the closed padded double doors across the foyer. Her dog turned to look at her as if to say, *This way, Mom.*

She stepped over to him slowly, taking stock.

Hung above the doors was a torn banner with gaudy gold lettering.

Theater Hall.

Tanya recalled what the school principal had told them the fateful day they had discovered Priscilla in the library.

"*We were planning our annual play. This year, the kids are going to perform Hamlet at the old theater hall. City council is reviving it. I'm even making a proper crown.*"

Jack pulled at his shoulder radio and spoke into it.

"I need three more in the lobby."

244

Hasty footsteps came from the outside. Tanya glanced back to see more troopers rush in and fan out. The remaining officers sidled up behind Jack and Tanya.

Jack turned to his crew. "Open up."

Two officers pulled the old doors apart while everyone hunkered low, their weapons aimed forward, ready for anything.

The heavy doors groaned as they opened, like they hadn't been touched in a long time.

"Empty," breathed Jack as he stepped into the hall. "Look sharp, everyone. Our unsub could be hiding anywhere."

Tanya stood at the threshold while the troopers stepped cautiously around her.

She squinted at the large, open space, taking in the rows of faded red seats and the wooden platform at the far end. It was then she realized the windowless theater should have been immersed in darkness.

It wasn't.

"Someone turned on the security lights," she whispered.

An old chandelier, covered in dust, hung from the high ceiling above them. The stage loomed far ahead, its heavy velvet curtains drawn, like they were cloaking mysterious secrets concealed in the back. But in front of the drapes, on the small section of the platform that jutted out in front, sat a red throne chair facing the empty theater.

Strange, thought Tanya, staring at the chair. It looked brand new. Even from where she was, she noticed it didn't have dust on its surface.

Her heart ticked a beat faster.

A red throne. A symbol of the Crimson King? He's taunting us, again.

She gripped her Glock tighter.

What's he done with Chantal?

She touched her gold sunflower pendant, and silently prayed for her departed mother to look after the girl, wherever she was.

To stop her anxiety from overtaking her mind, Tanya thought of Chantal's parents. When she had left the precinct, Katy had just received news that Peace was scrambling to return to Black Rock on the next available flight. Tanya prayed he would come home soon, so Katy wouldn't be alone during this terrifying time.

She turned her attention back to the theater hall.

Max was in the main aisle, sniffing the floor with interest, but he hadn't alerted her to a human presence yet. Jack and the officers followed him, quietly scanning row after row, checking for anything suspicious that might lie hidden among the dusty seats.

Tanya stepped into the aisle, thinking the hall was quiet.

Too quiet.

She caught up to Jack.

"Why bring her here?" he said as she walked over to him. "This makes no sense."

"Remember what Asha told us?" said Tanya. "He's playing with us."

"I hate games," hissed Jack. "What kind of sick game is this, anyway?"

"Hide and seek," said Tanya. "He hides. We seek."

"Only a monster plays with the life of a child," muttered the chief angrily.

"Did he find something?" came the low voice of a trooper from behind them.

Tanya looked up. Max had stepped onto the platform. He pushed his snout under the heavy drapes, pulled it out, and sneezed. He trotted alongside the curtain, his nose stuck to the floor.

Tanya gripped her Glock.

"There's something behind the curtain."

She and Jack hurried down the aisle and climbed the steps to the stage, their heads on a swivel.

Tanya was about to walk over to Max when something glinted at her from the stage. A folded foil object was stuck under the red throne. She pulled it out.

A crown.

A cardboard crown, painted in gold.

That was when a trooper yelled from the middle of the stage.

"Over here, sir!"

Jack leaped toward him and ripped the curtains apart. A dark lump lay crumpled behind the drapes.

Chantal!

Tanya's heart jumped to her mouth. For one moment, she felt faint.

A ruckus exploded around her as officers talked on their radios and hollered at each other.

Tanya walked over, her heart in her mouth. Jack crouched over the body and gently pushed her shoulders back.

The school principal.

The chief leaned across the woman and checked her wrist for a pulse.

Tanya stared. She had let her terror get away with her.

The principal lay on her side, a sunflower in her hair. Right in the middle of her temple was an open gunshot wound.

Jack laid the woman's wrist down gently.

"She's gone."

Chapter Fifty-Five

"Where's the next riddle?"

Jack stared at the school principal as if he was willing her to talk.

"There's nothing on her," said Tanya.

She had gone through the dead woman's person and pockets twice, hoping in vain to find a clue to Chantal's whereabouts. Other than the killer's signature sunflower stuck in her hair, there was nothing of importance.

Tanya placed the dead woman's shoe back on her foot, feeling a pang of guilt for manhandling the body.

"If the unsub wanted her to send us a message," she said, "like he did with Priscilla, she would still be alive."

"That means the riddle has to be somewhere in

the theater," said Jack, his eyes narrowing. "If not, Dr. Chen might find it inside of her."

Tanya shuddered.

"Then again, our unsub could have changed his modus operandi. He seems to like the element of surprise."

Jack's face darkened.

"This case is beginning to feel like a massive octopus that grows a new leg every time we cut one off. "

"Serial killers are usually set in their ways and select their victims for specific reasons tied to their past," said Tanya. "We need to find the common thread."

Jack nodded.

"There's Zoe, Nicole, Asha, Priscilla, and now our principal." He frowned. "Only one was a successful kill but we don't know if she was collateral. One thing for sure, he's targeting females who either live in Black Rock or visi—"

"Did you find her?"

The shriek came from the open doorway.

Tanya turned around to see Katy running down the auditorium's main aisle. Seeing her, Max darted over, tail wagging.

"Is she here?" called out Katy, her voice panic-stricken. "Where's my girl?"

She pushed aside two officers and stumbled to

the foot of the stage. She stopped in her tracks when she spotted the lifeless body by the curtains.

"It's the school principal," said Tanya.

But Katy swayed on her feet. A trooper caught her before she fainted. Tanya stepped over to the edge of the stage and reached out to her. Katy fell into her arms, sobbing.

"We're going to find her." Tanya clasped her arms around her friend. "Whatever it takes, I will find Chantal and bring her home."

She held Katy, listening to Jack order a thorough search of the theater. Soon, the sound of boots stomping came from everywhere around her.

Two troopers, including Officer Hall, the tech cop, began examining the stage floor for fingerprints or other clues. Four pairs of officers were scanning the rows of seats, their flashlights out. Jack was on the phone to Dr. Chen, informing her to be prepared for another autopsy.

Tanya turned to Katy who was struggling to keep her sobs back.

"Is Peace coming, hon?"

"He's flying in right now." Katy swallowed. "His client offered him a ride in his private jet."

Tanya squeezed her friend's shoulders.

"Why don't you head to the airport to pick him up?"

Katy nodded and wiped her face.

That should keep your mind busy for the time being, thought Tanya.

Officer Hall was crawling across the stage, her phone in one hand, ready to take pictures if she noticed something unusual.

She came within five feet of Tanya and shot her a sympathetic look before pointing at the space she was occupying.

Tanya jumped off the stage and pulled Katy away to give her space to work.

Officer Hall inched forward on all fours before she stopped and frowned. Tanya saw her poke at something on the stage.

Tanya's heart leaped. One second, Officer Hall was on the stage. The next second, she had disappeared with a frightened yell.

Max barked.

Jack and the other officers whirled around.

Everyone gawked at the yawning hole that had appeared in the center of the platform.

Chapter Fifty-Six

"A trap door."

Tanya jumped back onto the stage and peered into the dark void.

A sneeze came from below.

"Help!"

Jack came over, crashed down, and stared into the hole.

"Stay right where you are, junior."

"There was a latch-like thing," said Officer Hall from the darkness below. "I think I pressed it by mistake."

Tanya pulled out her flashlight, switched it on, and leaned in. A damp and musty odor wafted up to her like no one had been down there for years, maybe even decades.

"You okay?" she called out, shining her torch around. "No broken bones?"

The officer sneezed again.

"I fell on something soft."

Jack and Tanya's flashlights caught Officer Hall lying on an old mattress. She covered her face with her hand as the light streamed into her eyes.

The officer rolled off the mattress, sending a cloud of dust in the air, which made her double over and sneeze uncontrollably.

Tanya moved her light away from the trooper.

She shuddered as she spotted a skeleton in a corner. Next to the bones was what looked like a life-sized woman. Naked and dusty. Tanya stared at the dull plastic eyes that stared right back at her.

Officer Hall turned to see what she was looking at and jumped.

"It's just a mannequin," called out Tanya.

"Geez, I thought it was real."

"Stay put. We're coming to get you." Jack turned to the other officers, who were watching them, mouths open and eyes wide. "Get a ladder ASAP."

"Yes, sir," came a chorus of voices.

"There has to be an entrance from the backstage." Tanya looked at the chief. "Old theaters used mechanical contraptions for their plays, but they had to get actors underneath without the audience seeing."

He leaped to his feet.

"Let's find it."

Leaving Katy in the care of a trooper, Tanya and Jack tripped behind the theater curtain and stepped into the claustrophobic narrow halls of the backstage. They walked in single file with Max following Jack, and with Tanya taking the rear.

Tanya swept her torch back and forth as they stepped along a swinging walkway, ducking large coils of cables that hung from the ceiling.

"What's that?" said Tanya as her flashlight caught something on the floor.

Jack shone his light on the dust.

"A shoe print." He paused. "A very large shoe print."

Chapter Fifty-Seven

Jack took out his phone and snapped a photo of the footprint.

Whoever had made that print had taken a step to the edge of the walkway, where the dust remained undisturbed.

What were they doing there?

Tanya aimed her flashlight around and above them.

Is the killer still inside the theater, hiding in the shadows?

Jack zoomed into the photo.

"This is a size fifteen shoe." He lifted his eyes. "If this is our killer, he's a big guy."

"It could be one of our team," said Tanya. "They've been stomping around for the past fifteen minutes."

He shook his head. "This isn't from our crew."

"How do you know?"

"They wear government-issued footwear." Jack stepped away from the print and planted his boot on a fresh dusty spot. "Same as me."

Tanya raised a brow.

"We get our uniforms from the State Department's warehouse, same place the team gets theirs. It's a lot cheaper than procuring our own. Whoever this is, it's not any of us."

Tanya crouched and shone her flashlight on the footprint.

"You're right. This couldn't have come from a work boot. This didn't come from a dollar store, either. The pattern is super intricate. This is a high-end shoe. "

Jack pulled on his shoulder radio.

"I need the forensics team, ASAP." He paused. "Watch each other's backs, people. The unsub might still be in the building."

Tanya furrowed her brow.

Something someone had said about *shoes* niggled in the back of her mind.

She crouched even lower and peered at the print. That was when she saw the faint marks of a skull and bones on the ball of the footprint.

She gasped.

"Zoe saw her attacker's feet at the beach, remember?"

Jack nodded.

"She said something about a red moccasin with a skull-and-bones logo." She pointed at the outline. "Look at that."

Jack squatted next to her and took a sharp breath in.

"I didn't give much validity to her words. Who wears moccasins to a wet beach? I was sure it was her trauma making her see things that weren't there." He shook his head. "I was wrong."

A buzz came from Tanya's pocket. She pulled her mobile out and glanced at the screen.

"Asha."

A sense of dread came over her as she clicked to take the call. The last few times her friend had phoned in, it was to report the creepy caller with a message about another killing.

Her heart ached to think of Chantal.

Please be okay, wherever you are.

Asha was already speaking fast on the other end.

"Hang on," said Tanya as she put her device on speaker mode. "Jack needs to hear whatever you're calling about."

"East Beach," came Asha's rushed voice through the speaker. "We have to head down there now!"

"Slow down, soldier," said Jack. "Did you get another call from the troll?"

"A minute ago."

Jack and Tanya exchanged a quick glance.

That's why the killer didn't leave a note on the principal's body.

"What was the riddle?" said Tanya, her voice shaky.

"Wasn't a riddle this time," said Asha, panting. The sound of running footsteps came through the speaker. "It was pretty dang straightforward."

A car door banged shut and her voice got muted like she had turned her mouth away from the phone.

"East Beach. Now. Hurry."

"But ma'am—" came another voice.

"This is an emergency," hollered Asha. "Go!"

"Wait," Tanya snapped. "What did the caller say?"

Asha's voice came clearly through the speakerphone.

"He said, bring your girl cop pal and that red-headed woman to East Beach in fifteen."

She paused.

Tanya and Jack leaned closer to the phone.

"He also said," came Asha's breathless voice, "that we've been invited to a theatrical spectacle."

Chapter Fifty-Eight

"No one's going down to the beach!"

Jack glared at Asha.

Asha and Katy were standing next to his squad car in the parking lot of East Beach. Tanya had just jumped out of her Jeep with Max, and had come rushing over to find Jack scolding her friends.

"He invited *me*." Asha glared back at the chief. "If he didn't call me, you wouldn't even know to come here."

"He would have found a way to contact us," said Jack. "This unsub is clearly as inventive as he's resourceful."

"He said he wanted to see *me* down at the beach. And Katy. He didn't mention your name, Jack. If we don't get down there, we might not find Chantal."

Jack spread his arms like he couldn't believe what he was hearing.

"What do you think he meant when he asked you to be ready for a theatrical spectacle? I'm betting he's planning on something not very pleasant."

He turned his bloodshot eyes to Tanya.

"Are they trying to get themselves massacred?"

An ear-splitting alarm drowned out Jack's exasperated voice.

The troops were on their way. The chief had commanded anyone not guarding a crime scene or protecting a victim to come to East Beach at the double. He had also called the bomb squad and had alerted the state authorities.

It seemed like the emergency vehicles were arriving at the same time in a parade of sirens and flashing lights. Soon, car doors slammed, phones rang, and team leaders bellowed instructions.

"Make way," shouted someone from the back of the parking lot.

A large white van drove in. It had no identifying decals, but Tanya knew it was armored to the hilt. The three officers crouched in the front seats were wearing combat-style helmets and padded Kevlar vests. The state bomb squad had arrived.

Several yards behind them was the entire fleet of Black Rock's firetrucks. They had parked around the perimeter, their lights flashing.

The firefighters' eyes bulged as the bomb squad disembarked and unloaded their equipment. The fire station crew were mostly local volunteers, used to stamping out unauthorized fires at the beach and giving firm talks to kids who lit campfires during the fire hazard season.

A gut-wrenching sob made Tanya turn.

"Ch... Ch... Chantal...," stammered Katy, her face scrunched in agony. "What's going to happen here? Where is she? Where's my baby girl?"

Tanya's stomach churned at the thought of Chantal being used in the killer's diabolical spectacle, whatever that was supposed to mean. For her friend's sake, she did her best to keep her face straight, but her heart was flaming in furor.

Jack put a hand on Katy's shoulder.

"All the teams are here, and more reinforcements are coming," he said in a soft voice. "We're going to find Chantal and get this guy. I promise you. Right now, I need you to get in my cruiser and stay there. Will you do that for me?"

A loud whir came from the middle of the parking lot, followed by a volley of angry barks from Max.

Five mechanical insects took to the air. The drones hovered above their heads for a second before they fanned out along the shoreline.

An even louder whir came from behind Tanya. Three robotic machines rolled by her. They looked like space rovers mixed with mini excavators.

Bomb diffusers.

Two officers stood by the bomb squad's van, maneuvering the drones and robots with what looked like video gaming controllers. A third stood apart from them, a pair of binoculars on her eyes, scanning the beach from one side to the other.

Max yelped and jumped as a bomb diffuser brushed against his paw. He growled, his hackles up, then snapped at a steel arm.

Tanya hurried over and slipped her fingers around his collar. She stroked his back to calm him.

"It's okay, bud. They're our friends. They're going to help us."

Undeterred by their canine adversary, the machines rolled on by, heading toward the beach.

Max jumped onto a nearby boulder to get a better view of their activities. He sat down, his ears perked and his eyes beady. He would be prepared in case these sinister metal beings turned on his humans.

The air was thick with tension.

The troopers had taken position behind their vehicles or nearby boulders, where they had a clear line of sight to the shore. The firefighters had donned their heavy protective gear, helmets and gas masks included. Their water hoses were at the ready.

No one had smiled or had raised a brow to see Max try to attack the robots. All eyes were focused on the beachfront.

Tanya could feel the nervous energy grow with every passing minute.

They were all waiting.

Waiting for what?

Chapter Fifty-Nine

All sirens had been shut off.

An unsettling silence had fallen over the parking lot.

They were well past the fifteen-minute deadline the killer had given them.

The town was in lockdown, so there wasn't a soul in sight. At least, it seemed.

The only civilians at the beach were Asha and Katy. They were huddled in the backseat of Jack's cruiser. Katy was crying silently on Asha's shoulder, while Asha, who was normally steadfast in a crisis, was staring out at the ocean, her face ashen.

Even through the car window, Tanya could see the heaviness on Asha's face. The killer had delivered the message personally to her. If Tanya knew her friend well, she was taking full responsibility for triggering this expensive operation.

The firefighters stood by their trucks quietly. The junior troopers crouched low, their shoulders taut, their hands clamped around their weapons.

Tanya glimpsed a flicker of fear in everyone's eyes.

It was the fear of the unknown.

Nerves were frayed after several sleepless nights of trying to catch a man who had outwitted them all. She wondered if they were making a big mistake.

Is this a trick?

Is the killer planning an attack elsewhere, while we wait here?

The Pacific Ocean was placid that day, in contrast to the tumultuous feelings inside of Tanya.

White-crested waves rolled in and kissed the sands of Black Rock beach. The ocean water rippled around the rocky formations before withdrawing into the vast sea.

A slight breeze wafted around them. The warmth of the sun was just right for a day at a West Coast beach. Not too hot. Not too chilly.

If they weren't waiting for a serial killer to make his next move, it would have been a pleasant scene.

What does a theatrical spectacle mean?

Tanya jumped onto the boulder and joined Max, touching her mother's pendant for protection as she did. They were exposed up here, but she had a much better vantage point.

She peered into the horizon, her mind buzzing with the possibilities, each of which seemed incredibly improbable. But with two women murdered, three almost killed, and one missing girl, they couldn't take their chances.

Will something rise out of the ocean?
A speedboat filled with detonations?
A torpedo from a submarine?

She scoffed quietly at the ludicrousness of her ideas. Then again, this killer had proved to be as ingenious as he was innovative.

The drones hadn't discovered anything, but kept zooming back and forth in the sky. The bomb-disposal robots rolled across the wet sand, their cameras feeding video footage back to the team inside the van.

Jack was the only one talking, and he was speaking with a quiet intensity into his mobile. Tanya knew he had finally convinced the FBI office in Seattle to send help. Ray had called her to let her know, with strict instructions to remain in her undercover role.

The federal team, should they arrive in Black Rock, wouldn't be permitted to show their recognition of Tanya. And vice versa. She would have to keep Max under control, as he had his favorite agents and would be the first to give his role away.

She rested her hand on his back. Max thumped

his tail, but maintained his focus on a drone hovering nearby.

There was one person Tanya was trying hard not to think about. If she focused on Chantal and what she might be going through in the hands of the killer, she would end up a blubbering mess of wrecked nerves.

Think, girl, think. For her sake. Think.

With one hand on her Glock, she stared out to the sea, teetering between helplessness and untold fury.

How many more innocents have to die for this killer's meaningless cause?

What's this mad man's point, anyway?

Suddenly, Max got to his feet.

He was no longer interested in the robotic machines. His attention was on something in the distance, beyond the horizon.

Tanya squinted to see what had caught his attention. She turned to her dog and whispered.

"What is it, bud?"

Max swayed his tail gently. While his ears were pricked, his eyes wavered back and forth, like he didn't know where to look.

Tanya's heart ticked faster.

Dogs have poor vision during daylight, but could apprehend sounds no human ears could catch.

Max is hearing something.

But he doesn't know what it is.

Chapter Sixty

Tanya put a hand over her eyes and squinted at the ocean.

Nothing.

She bit her lips in frustration, tasting only salty air.

She didn't want to spread panic among the others who were already at the edge of their nerves. She jumped down from the boulder and headed toward the bomb squad team's leader.

She lowered her voice. "How far can you send the drones out to sea?"

The officer looked up from her laptop.

"We've got one fifty yards beyond the shoreline."

"Has it spotted anything?"

"I just reported to the chief. All is quiet on the western front." She paused. "So far."

The officer narrowed her eyes.

"Something we need to know?"

Tanya hadn't seen or heard anything, but her instincts were on high alert.

"I think my dog detected a noise."

"Like what?"

"I don't know. It's a hunch for now. Keep at least one drone focused on the horizon, would you?"

Without waiting for her to answer, Tanya turned around and jumped back up to join Max on his rock. He hadn't focused his eyes on anything yet, but his ears flicked back and forth.

As Tanya sat next to him, watching him keenly, a lesson she'd learned at Quantico, the bureau's training center, popped to mind.

One day, a short man in a crumpled tweed jacket had strolled into her class. He looked nothing like the other trainers at the academy who always dressed in smartly pressed uniforms and shoes polished to a shine. But he had told them a cautionary story she'd never forget.

When the first British settlers arrived in Australia eons ago, swans were considered white. That was, until a beautiful black swan sailed in front of the settlers' eyes. No one, other than the local aboriginal population, had encountered such a rare bird before.

A black swan event is one no one expects to see, but when you did, it blew your mind. Or so, the professor in the crumpled tweed jacket had told them.

Someone had asked how to prepare for an event of such low probability and high impact. The professor's answer had been simple.

You can't.

Tanya's gut tightened.

We're about to witness a black swan.

A faint buzz came to her ears.

It wasn't the mechanical whir of the drones or the robots scouring the shoreline. This was different. It sounded more like an annoying mosquito.

She turned to her dog.

"Do you hear that, bud?"

Max blinked like he still couldn't see anything.

Suddenly, his back stiffened. He got on all fours and barked.

Tanya jumped to her feet and gazed out at the ocean, trying to home in on the unusual noise. That was when she spotted it.

A black speck in the distance, just where the sky met the sea.

Goosebumps sprang on her arms. She whipped around and waved at the bomb squad leader.

"Binoculars! *Now!*"

The officer pushed her laptop away, grabbed the pair of binoculars that lay by her feet, and ran toward the rock. Tanya placed them on her eyes.

A ripple of murmur crossed the parking lot,

drowning out the mosquito sound. "What's she looking at?" came a voice from somewhere behind her. "I don't see anything, do you?" Asked another.

Tanya wished they would stay quiet. She adjusted the eye cups and aimed the binoculars at the black dot on the horizon, but the view was fuzzy.

What is this thing?

She rotated the barrels to get both sides to converge on the single image.

The image came to focus.

Tanya froze.

Chapter Sixty-One

It was an old propeller plane.

Tanya zoomed in. It was too far to see who was inside.

"Small aircraft!" she called out. "Single engine, fixed-wing, two-seater."

The plane was heading straight toward the Black Rock Beach. The drone got louder. Everybody could hear it now. A commotion broke around her, mixed in with Max's barks.

"Where's it going to land?"

"The airport's the other way."

"Is it a seaplane?"

"No floats," replied Tanya, keeping her eyes glued to her glasses. "It has wheels, so it can't land on water."

The aircraft was moving in an abnormal manner.

Something's wrong.

The plane dipped its nose, then tilted upward, before dipping toward the ocean erratically, like a child was at the controls.

Tanya's stomach sank at the thought.

Did the killer put Chantal inside, alone? Impossible. An old plane like this needed someone who knew what they were doing at the controls for it to take off in the first place.

Her mind spun.

Who's the pilot?

Do they have a death wish?

Chantal's little face swirled into her mind, and she felt like throwing up.

Max barked louder.

Something flashed in the sky. It happened so fast, Tanya wasn't sure what she saw was real.

Did someone jump out?

She scanned the sky, searching for a parachute. She surveyed the ocean, seeking for signs of a human body, bobbing up and down among the waves.

Did I imagine that?

"Who's inside?" called out Jack.

"Can't see any souls," said a voice from behind her.

Tanya turned around to see the bomb squad leader was using a second pair of binoculars.

She gestured to her. "Did you see the jumper just now?"

"*What?*" chorused several voices, like they didn't believe what they heard.

"I saw something or someone fall out of the plane," said Tanya.

"I didn't see anything."

Tanya refocused the lenses to see who was inside the cockpit. The plane dipped its wings back and forth, like it had a mind of its own. Its engine roared. It was getting closer.

And closer.

Tanya's stomach flipped.

That thing isn't coming here to land.

She spun around to the parking lot.

"It's going to crash on us! Take cover!"

"Everyone back!" hollered Jack.

People scrambled.

"*Get behind the trucks!*

"*Run! Run!*"

A hand clutched Tanya's arm and yanked her off the rock. Jack turned to face her.

"Are you trying to get yourself killed?"

Tanya lifted her head. Max was staring at her from the top of the rock.

The roar of the plane was so loud, it felt like it was on top of them.

"Max!" she screamed. "Get down here!"

Chapter Sixty-Two

Tanya peeked around the boulder.

The plane was a mile from the shoreline.

It dipped its wings over the ocean, a few hundred feet above the waves.

It was flying low. Too low.

For one split second, she thought she spotted something move inside the cockpit. Her heart raced.

Is someone still in there?

She blinked, wondering if the exhaustion from the past few days had overcome her.

The roar of the plane's engine was deafening now.

A whirlwind of sand swirled up in a mini dust devil, obstructing her view and stinging her face. She brought her hand over her head as the wet sand pummeled against the boulder.

"Get back!" hollered Jack.

Tanya pushed herself to safety, landing next to Max.

She reached out and wrapped an arm around him and held him tightly. She could feel his heart beating fast. Hers was too. She wanted to say something to calm him, but she could hardly breathe herself.

Next to them, Jack was shouting at everyone to keep their heads down.

The plane was very close now.

Its propeller stuttered, and its engine screeched.

With a thundering din, it slammed onto the beach. The ground shook. A storm of wet sand exploded into the air and rained down on the parking lot.

Tanya covered Max's head with her arms and body as the grains pelted her like shrapnel.

The screech of metal bending and glass shattering came next, like a giant was tearing the aircraft apart. It took a second for Tanya to realize the plane was gliding across the sand, forced by its own momentum.

Tanya balled herself up and squeezed Max even harder. He whimpered. She held on to him, fearful he'd panic and dart out, right into danger.

All she could think of was the movement she saw through the cockpit window. Someone had been inside the plane when it crashed.

Chantal?

A loud clang made her look up. A section of the plane's wing bounced off their boulder and hurtled over their heads. It slammed into a parked cruiser, its sharp edges smashing the windows and spraying debris everywhere.

Someone screamed.

Tanya's stomach flipped.

Where's Asha and Katy? Did they get out of the car in time?

She leaned over to look, but Jack pressed her back with his arm.

He shouted in her ear.

"If you injure yourself, you can't help anyone."

Tanya dropped her shoulders, knowing he was right. But the urge to do something was too strong.

Keep Max safe, she whispered to stop herself from running out. She held her dog close, her heart thudding. *Keep Max safe.*

Soon, a disquieting silence descended on the beach. Not even a seagull squawked from above. The sudden quietness was unsettling after what felt like a massive bomb had exploded in their faces.

Tanya couldn't hear the others, but it felt like everyone had deserted the area.

The pungent odor of chemicals and oil filled the air, mingling with the acrid smell of burning metal and melting plastic.

She surveyed the banged-up trucks, the vehicles, and the road behind the parking lot.

Did everyone get to safety?

Where is everyone?

Wherever they were hiding, no one was speaking. Probably in shock, she thought, not wanting to consider the alternative.

Next to her, Jack raised his head.

"Okay, time to triage—"

"Help!"

Jack jerked back.

The muffled cry had been so sudden, it was hard to say where it had come from.

Chapter Sixty-Three

Tanya swiveled her head.

"Did you hear that?"

Jack squinted at the parking lot that looked like a war zone.

"Someone's hurt." He jumped to his feet. "The flying debris must have hit one of the crew."

Tanya got up and pointed behind her with her thumb.

"It sounded like it came from the beach."

Jack frowned. "I thought it originated on the road."

Tanya twirled around the boulder and gaped. Jack stepped up to her and stared at the scene of devastation on the beach.

The rocks had stopped the moving aircraft, but had sliced it into pieces. Its severed nose had dropped a few feet from the flat rock where Tanya had found Nicole's body, only forty-eight hours earlier.

The plane's wings were fractured, and the steel propeller was crumpled like a toy. Both doors were open and hung on their hinges. Other than the occasional hiss of cooling metal, there was no movement or sound from the wreckage.

If the aircraft had flown a few degrees to the west, none of them would have survived.

"That was close." Jack wiped his face.

Tanya noticed the pools of yellow oil forming under the aircraft's amputated wings.

Aviation fuel.

She narrowed her eyes, knowing she wouldn't be allowed anywhere near the crash scene now.

"I think that cry came from there," she said.

"This is the fire chief's jurisdiction," said Jack. "They have the proper equipment."

"But, Jack, if someone's in there—"

"The bomb squad was watching the plane approach, too. The team lead said she didn't see any souls on board."

Tanya frowned.

"I thought I saw movement inside the cockpit after the jumper left."

If my eyes hadn't been playing tricks on me.

Jack shook his head. "If there's a survivor in that mess, it would be a miracle. Let the fire team do their job. We'll only delay their work."

Tanya wished she could tell him and the fire chief that her dog was a federally trained search and rescue K9, not just a smart pup who got lucky. But she knew that wouldn't be possible.

Jack turned away from her and stepped into the parking lot.

"All clear!" he hollered. "Everyone okay?"

The firefighters stepped out from behind their trucks, still in their gear and gas masks. The fire chief took control and started barking orders at his people.

One by one, the junior troopers came out of their various hiding spots, eyes bulging and faces pale, like they were shell-shocked. Officer Hall, the tech cop, stared at the mutilated plane, her eyes wide, as if fascinated by the sight.

Jack stepped up to his crew.

"Everyone accounted for? Anyone hurt?"

Tanya watched him count heads. None of them seemed injured, though she was sure they would all feel the psychological impact later on.

She turned back to the plane, but it was hard to see anything inside the mangled cockpit from here.

That cry for help was a man's voice.

She dug her fingers into her fists.

It couldn't have been Chantal.

The sound of a helicopter's rotors came from a distance. Jack spun around, his face lit up for the first time in days.

"The Feds," he called out, pointing at the sky. "We're getting reinforcement."

About time, thought Tanya.

The fire chief plodded toward the wreck, followed by his team, pulling water hoses behind them. In the parking area, Jack and the troopers started to sift through the rubble.

Tanya stared at the chief's cruiser. Its front windshield was shattered.

Asha. Katy.

They had been inside the car the last time she saw them.

She jumped over a fragment of metal and scrambled over to the cruiser, her heart filled with fear. She reached over to the door, feeling sick to her stomach when someone called her name from afar.

Tanya looked up to see Katy and Asha emerge from the back of an ambulance that had been parked on the road. Relief flooded her body. She was about to join them when an urgent bark came from behind her.

She spun around.

Max?

Her dog had been by the boulder only moments ago, but he wasn't anywhere in the vicinity.

"Where are you, bud?"

Tanya scanned the wreckage scattered across the beach.

The largest pieces of the mutilated fuselage were

concentrated by the big boulders. The smaller debris had been thrown several yards out in all directions.

Another bark came from somewhere along the shoreline, but Tanya couldn't see him.

"Max!" she hollered.

Max replied with three short barks.

Tanya's heart ticked faster. He had found something or someone.

Her heart dropped.

Did he find Chantal?

Chapter Sixty-Four

Tanya slipped behind the boulder and took stock.

In the parking lot, Jack and the troopers were securing the disaster scene with yellow tape, preparing for the forensics team to arrive.

The fire chief was leading his crew toward the main wreckage. They were hauling heavy equipment across the uneven terrain, their focus on not stumbling over the debris.

The fire chief stopped to scrutinize the warped wings of the aircraft. This was where the fuel was usually stored. There was no indication of a fire yet, but it was difficult to predict when the leaking fuel would ignite.

Tanya stepped from behind the boulder and

scurried in the opposite direction of the firefighting crew.

Halfway to the shoreline, she came across a lone wheel from the plane, partially submerged in the wet sand. It was threadbare. She glanced at the ruptured metal fragments around it. The paint was peeling of them.

This was an old flying machine.

She filed that thought in the back of her mind and scanned the area for signs of her pup. After his three-bark call, he had fallen silent.

Where are you, Max?

Tanya hurried in the direction she'd heard him last, suppressing the urge to call out to him. She didn't need to attract any attention.

Her boots scrunched on glass shards. Her stomach sank to think of her dog running around on his soft paws with sharp objects strewn everywhere. She hastened her pace.

Be careful, bud.

She spotted a fresh paw mark on the wet sand. Then, another. Her heart leaped. She knew where he was now.

She headed toward the spot where Zoe had been left to drown, close to the flat rock where Nicole had died.

Did someone get tossed off the plane here?

The sound of whirling rotor blades came from behind her. The noise grew louder. Soon, a large black helicopter appeared over the trees, the yellow FBI decal marked clearly on its belly.

The helicopter dipped to the side and flew toward the far end of the beach, skimming low to the ground. Tanya watched it, knowing the pilot was seeking a dryer and flatter section to land on, away from the disaster scene.

Her federal colleagues would be here soon. She didn't have much time.

She scurried toward the boulder where she had found Zoe.

Where are you, bud?

That was when she spotted her dog's tail.

He was concealed by the rock formation. Ignoring the waves that were rushing up to her ankles and filling her boots with seawater, Tanya squelched toward him.

"Max?" she called out softly.

A furry brown head poked from behind the plane's severed cockpit.

Tanya's heart jumped.

Max let out a volley of barks as if to say, *Quick, Mom, quick.*

Tanya pressed her finger against her lips, but he only barked louder and with more urgency. She cringed as the entire fire team whipped around to see what was going on.

The chief's furious voice rang out.

"Are you planning to get reprimanded by the

287

FAA? They won't think twice about jailing you for disobeying my authority!"

But Tanya's eyes were on her dog.

Max had turned back to the cockpit, and was intensely sniffing a dark-brown object sunken in the sand. She crouched low to see what it was. It was one of a pair of men's leather dress shoes.

Another shoe was sticking from under a gnarled steel rod.

Her pulse quickened.

A body was wedged in between the plane's nose and the rock it had rammed against.

Ignoring the fire chief's angry yells, she jumped to her feet and placed her hands on the side of the cockpit.

"Over here!" she shouted as she pushed with all her strength.

The waves rushed in, making the hunk of metal sway. She threw her weight into it and heaved. The cockpit moved a foot to the side.

Tanya dropped her hands, too shocked to speak.

The blood drained from her face.

She recognized the body.

Chapter Sixty-Five

The fire chief came running over. He shoved Tanya aside.

"Secure the area!"

The crash scene exploded with action. The fire crew dashed in and took over, pushing Tanya and Max to the periphery.

Tanya knew she had to do something, but she had frozen at the sight of her friend's body. It was like every muscle inside of her had seized up in terror.

Peace is dead.

Images of Peace and Katy's beautiful wedding flashed into her mind. Then came a memory of Peace playing peekaboo with a giggling baby Chantal.

Max licked her hands, like he knew. Tanya felt queasy. She wanted to cry out, but she couldn't even open her mouth.

The fire chief knelt by Peace and grasped his limp wrist. Jack dashed across the beach, one hand on his radio.

He halted by Tanya. With one look at her face, he gently placed his hand on her shoulder.

"You look like you need to sit down."

That was when Tanya realized her whole body was shaking.

The fire chief turned Peace on his back so it would be easier to move him onto the stretcher.

Tanya stared at her dead friend's face, and a flash of red fury flared inside of her.

She had met Peace during their troubled youths, many years ago. He had risked his life to help her at a difficult time. Peace hadn't been just a friend. He had been family.

A spear of fury seared through her, she barely heard Jack's voice.

"I'm sorry, Tanya."

Her eyes blazed in anger.

"*This* is the killer's theatrical spectacle?" she spat out. "When I find the psychopath, he'll pay for this!"

"Katy needs to know," said Jack softly, his hand still on her shoulder, trying to steady her.

Tanya craned her neck and looked in the direction of the parking lot.

Katy and Asha were huddled behind the yellow crime tape at the back of the lot. They were gaping at the scene, confusion etched on their faces. They knew something was wrong, but were too far away to understand what exactly was happening.

Tanya's heart sank.

Katy. Oh, my goodness. Katy.

She squeezed her eyes to think of Chantal.

Still missing.

She glanced down at Max, who was by her feet, his ears relaxed and his posture calm. He had stopped barking as soon as she had spotted Peace, which meant there were no others. Dead or alive.

Tanya swallowed hard.

Chantal isn't here. She was never on the plane.

She turned to Jack.

"Katy needs to hear it from me."

Jack nodded and let go of her shoulder.

Tanya grasped her mother's pendant to strengthen her resolve. Feeling like the world had crash landed on her shoulders, she stepped over the debris and turned toward the parking lot.

"Oxygen! Now!"

Tanya blinked and whirled around.

The fire chief was yelling at his team. A firefighter rushed in with an oxygen tank. A second fighter dashed over with a first-aid kit.

Tanya stared at the crew bustling around Peace, unsure whether she was imagining this.

The fire chief turned to Jack.

"We need to get him to the nearest intensive care unit, ASAP."

Jack pulled his phone out. "The chopper. I'll get the Feds to airlift him out."

Tanya ran over to them, her heart thudding. "Is he... Is he...?"

The fire chief looked up. "Faint heartbeat."

Tanya felt something wet on her cheek. She brushed it away and swallowed a sob.

Peace is alive.

Hope soared in her heart. She clutched her mother's pendant.

Maybe Chantal is too.

A strong rush of anger rushed up her spine.

The Crimson King is keeping her alive.

I know it.

I know it in my bones.

Chapter Sixty-Six

"I want to see him!"

Katy screamed.

Tanya and Asha held onto her.

At the far end of the beach, the helicopter's engine whined. The propeller's chug-chug-chug echoed through the shorefront, as the pilot readied to take off with their patient.

Tanya had wanted to confer with her FBI colleagues, but she had given them a wide berth.

She pulled Katy in closer.

"He's going to be fine."

A pang of guilt went through her, for that white lie.

I thought he was dead.

But she didn't know what else to say to a friend whose nerves were already shredded.

Katy's face was pale. Her eyes had that glazed look like she was too bewildered to fathom what was happening to her family.

Asha had kept her composure after hearing Peace had been inside the crashed aircraft, but Tanya could see she was trying hard not to break down.

Asha patted Katy's arm.

"He survived. He's going to get the best care he needs. He'll be okay."

The chopper lifted from the ground, drowning out their voices. It rose above the trees, then, with a slight tilt as if to say goodbye, it took off over the woods and disappeared from view.

The firefighters cordoned off the wreckage while their boss talked on his phone. *Calling the FAA*, thought Tanya.

"I need drones and boats," came Jack's booming voice. "Speedboats, not kayaks, for heaven's sake!"

The chief was pacing up and down the beach, his phone to his ear, shouting to whoever was on the other end.

"I need every vessel in the vicinity searching at least within a fifty-mile radius. Keep an eye out for a discarded parachute. Check Kensington Island. Our perp could have fled there."

Tanya skimmed the destroyed plane on the beach, something nagging at her.

Peace was supposed to have found a ride to Black

Rock on a private jet. How did he end up in this antique flying coffin?

Was he lured?

By someone who used his daughter as bait?

Where is Chantal?

Tanya wanted nothing more than to scour the entire town inch by inch, but she would be wasting time, and Max would get tired quickly. She needed a strategy, a faster plan to find the girl.

But where do I start?

A paramedic came over and turned from Asha to Katy, a questioning look on her face.

"Heard one of you ladies need a ride to the hospital."

Katy turned to her, moving as stiffly as a mannequin.

"My... My husband. They took him...I need... please...I need to be with him."

Tanya let her friend go. The medic took Katy by the arm and led her to the ambulance parked beside the road. Katy hung on to the paramedic like her legs would give away at any moment if she didn't.

"Ma'am?"

Officer Hall, the tech cop, was making a beeline to Asha.

"Fire crew found this under the passenger seat. Chief said to give this to you."

Asha jerked her head back.

"Jack asked for my help?"

"Yes, ma'am." The officer shot her an awkward glance. "He said two heads were better than one."

Tanya stared at the laptop case she was carrying in her gloved hands.

It was wet and had scuff marks, but was otherwise intact. By the handles was a small heart-shaped pink sticker with the words *I love you*.

Asha gasped.

"I saw Chantal put that sticker on it. That's Peace's laptop bag."

Officer Hall placed the case on a nearby cruiser, unzipped it, and flipped the top open.

Tanya raised a brow. "No laptop?"

The officer shrugged. "Maybe he didn't take it with him."

"On a business trip?" said Tanya. "If the crew doesn't find it in the wreckage, that means someone took it."

Officer Hall pulled out two documents from Peace's bag.

"This is a contract for purchasing a bunch of commercial high-rises in the city."

"That's why he went to Seattle," said Asha, taking the papers from her.

"That's funny." Tanya frowned. "Real estate isn't his line of work."

"Katy said a new client had promised him a lot of

money to broker a deal," said Asha, scrutinizing the papers. "It was supposed to be an urgent job."

Tanya wrinkled her nose.

"Something stinks here."

Chapter Sixty-Seven

"This is what the chief wanted me to show you."

Officer Hall reached into the back of the case, pulled out a beige envelope, and handed it to Asha.

"If we figure out what this means, Chief said we might get a raise. Maybe even a promotion."

Asha reached for the envelope.

"*You* might get a pay hike, officer. I don't work for anyone. My work here is pro bono."

She opened the envelope and pulled out a card. She screwed up her eyes.

"Is this a joke?"

"What is it?" said Tanya.

"It's literally a joke."

Tanya leaned over her shoulders as Asha read the

card out loud.

"*Knock, knock.*
Who's there?
Crimson.
Crimson who?
That's for me to know and you to find out."

Tanya felt an electric jolt in her chest. Ray and Olek's warnings swirled through her mind.

"I knew it. The Crimson King is behind this."

Officer Hall's eyes popped.

"Did you say *Crimson King*, ma'am?"

Tanya turned to her.

"You know him?"

"Know him? He's this... Dude, I'm such a superfan of the universe."

"Universe?" Asha wrinkled her forehead. "What do you mean *universe*?"

The officer pulled out her phone.

"He's got an awesome site with downloadable images. They're even creating a new video game featuring him."

Tanya grimaced. "You're going to tell me the Crimson King has a Wiki page next."

"He does."

Officer Hall turned her phone around, her eyes shining.

"He's the master villain of all villains. I used to draw fan art of him."

Asha squinted at the screen and scoffed.

"He's a character in a Stephen King world."

Tanya stared at the young officer.

"We're not talking about a comic book. This isn't a video game either."

Officer Hall shuffled her feet.

"That's the Crimson King I know, ma'am."

"This man is real. He's organized, resourceful, skilled, and a pathological killer." Tanya pointed at the wreckage. "He did this. I'd bet you he commandeered the plane and parachuted out at sea."

The officer gave her a startled look.

"I thought it was the missing girl who jumped out."

Asha's eyebrows shot up.

"Chantal's only nine."

Officer Hall pointed a thumb at the beach.

"The guys back there are saying the father could have stuck a parachute on his kid because he knew they were going to crash."

"Peace would never do that. He'd jump with her," said Asha. She turned to Tanya. "How many could have fit into that plane?"

"Two adults," said Tanya. "No more. There's hardly space for luggage."

"Peace doesn't have a flying license," said Asha. "Plus, he gets airsick. So who was flying the plane?"

Tanya glanced at the wreck.

"That aircraft couldn't have been operated remotely. That means there was a pilot in the cockpit who parachuted out at the right time and right place, leaving Peace behind to crash."

Officer Hall's eyes shone. "That sounds so much like a James Bond type super-evil perp."

Asha sighed heavily. "None of this helps us find out where Chantal is."

Tanya felt desperation claw at her heart.

"At least we know who the perpetrator is now," she said.

"It's a start." Asha blew a raspberry. "A long start."

Officer Hall pulled an evidence bag from her utility belt.

"I'll need to secure the envelope, ma'am."

Asha was about to give the note back to her, when she stopped.

"What's this?"

The officer peered at the card. "There's more on the other side?"

Asha turned to Tanya, her eyes wide in horror.

"He knows you."

Tanya leaned over to see what she was talking about.

She read the words silently.

"*When will you visit, Tanya? The woods are peaceful. I'm not the grim man everyone makes me out to be.*"

Chapter Sixty-Eight

Tanya's heart raced.

She read the note again. But the harder she tried to make sense of them, the more they swam into each other.

Asha was staring at her, her face pale. "There's only one Tanya in town, and that's you."

Officer Hall gave her the side-eye.

"How does the Crimson King know your name, ma'am?"

Tanya didn't answer, her mind a whirl.

The Crimson King had targeted those she was closest to. Peace, Chantal, Zoe, Asha. He had lured her cousin Olek to Black Rock and got him into dire trouble. Nicole had been collateral damage and Jack's ex-wife and the school principal had been anomalies.

Or had they been?

Something Olek had told her by the firepit crawled into her mind. A chill went through her as the realization hit her.

This is personal.

Officer Hall was staring at her.

"He's watching us," said Asha with a shudder. "He's been watching us all this time."

Tanya read the note again silently.

"*When will you visit, Tanya? The woods are peaceful. I'm not the grim man everyone makes me out to be.*"

She straightened up and clicked her fingers at Max. He sprang to his feet and wagged his tail, happy to be on the move again.

"Hey, where are you going?" called out Asha.

"I know where Chantal is."

"Where?"

"It's in the note."

Asha furrowed her brow and glanced at the message again.

"I don't see it."

"It's right there. Staring in your face."

Tanya marched toward her Jeep. "Let's go, Max. We have a job to do."

"Hang on." Asha darted over to her. "Where are you off to, and what are you about to do?"

Tanya opened the back door of her car for Max to jump in.

"The Crimson King has a beef with me. This is

between him and me."

Asha furrowed her brow. "What sort of beef?"

"I don't know yet, but I'll ask him when I see him."

Tanya put a hand on her friend's shoulder.

"Meanwhile, stay away from me. He's been targeting everyone I care about. I can't have you or anyone in his crosshairs anymore."

Asha pushed Tanya's hand off her shoulder.

"I'm not letting you go anywhere near this mad man alone."

She stepped toward the Jeep and reached for the door.

Tanya stopped her.

"Do you want to help me rescue Chantal?"

"For heaven's sake—"

"Then, go to the precinct and talk to Olek. Get him to open up. He knows more about the Crimson King than he's sharing."

Chapter Sixty-Nine

Tanya jumped into her Jeep.

"Ready, bud?"

Max barked from the backseat as if to say, *Let's go.*

Tanya buckled up and put the car into gear. She was about to roll onto the road when her phone pinged.

Is this the hospital?

With a silent prayer to whoever was watching over Peace, she pulled her phone to her lap and clicked on the message app.

Her heart skipped a beat.

It was another text from ANON.

It was the mysterious individual who had been causing her distress ever since she moved to Black Rock. These anonymous messages had been irritating at first, then annoying, then unsettling, given how much the sender seemed to know of her past.

Every time she had called the bureau's IT forensics lab in Seattle, her requests fell further down on their long list. Prank calls weren't a priority, unless they were specific death threats to their agents.

Asha and Katy thought it was a bored hacker kid with access to the dark web at best, or a blackmailing spammer at worst. But Tanya suspected it was someone with more malicious intentions.

Her eyes widened as she read ANON's latest message.

How did you like my theatrical spectacle?

A frisson of fear went through Tanya. She blinked rapidly as the frightening realization surged through her head.

ANON and the Crimson King are the same person.

This meant the Crimson King had been in Black Rock all this time, watching her, taunting her. And now, he had turned deadly.

Tanya went over the jobs she had carried out for the Mossad and the CIA. Her brow furrowed as she dredged up old memory banks, which concealed flashbacks too painful to see.

There were plenty of suspects who would be happy to cause her harm. But she had always worked undercover, and every criminal operation she had exposed had been shut down.

One thing was certain. Someone from her past was now seeking revenge.

"Crimson King," she whispered to herself. "Who are you?"

As much as she racked her brain, she couldn't recall a similar moniker used by any of the crime bosses she had taken down. She clenched her jaws and slammed the palm of her hand on her steering wheel.

He attacked Nicole, Zoe, Asha, and Chantal to get to me!

A blaring honk made her whip her head up.

A red Aston Martin came screeching to a halt in front of her Jeep, blocking her access to the road.

Sahara and Ocean jumped out of the car, arms waving madly. Max thumped his tail in the backseat to see his friends. Tanya rolled her window down, wondering what fresh hell the Crimson King had unleashed now.

"Did you find Chantal?" cried Sahara as she rushed up to the Jeep. "They didn't let us get close to the scene."

"They said someone died in the plane crash," said Ocean, running up. "If anything happened to Chantal.... Please tell us. Is she okay?"

They latched on to her open window and stared at her, anxious lines furrowed deep in their faces.

"Nobody died," said Tanya. "I can assure you of that."

Ocean's blue eyes, normally bright and clear, were filled with tears. Sahara looked like she had aged even more over the past twenty-four hours.

Tanya loved these two women and felt for them. She knew the heavy burden of guilt they carried after Chantal's disappearance.

"Is there anything we can do to help?" said Sahara.

"Yes," said Tanya. "Please move your car."

"We heard someone jumped from the plane," said Ocean, clinging to her window. "Who was it?"

Tanya sighed.

Rumors raced through this town faster than a lightning bolt. Fear was infectious and spread like a virus.

"There was one survivor," she said, choosing her words carefully. "He was airlifted to the nearest hospital."

"Who was it?"

"You're blocking me. I have to go."

Sahara's eyes narrowed. "Have you caught the bad guy yet? Do you know who's doing all this?"

Tanya blinked.

The Crimson King.

The dread she had felt when she read ANON's latest text was growing like a tumor in her gut. But she couldn't show them her true feelings.

She peered into the sports car that was parked directly in front of her. A small face popped up in the front seat.

Tanya's eyebrows shot up.

"Is that *Zak*?"

"We couldn't leave him home alone."

She glared at the ladies. "Take him home and stay there with him."

"We wanted to—"

Tanya leaned over her window.

"If you want me to find Chantal, please move your car and go home."

"But—"

"If you don't, I'll get Jack to lock you up in a jail cell."

Sahara's eyes widened.

Ocean pulled her friend by the arm. "Fine."

Tanya watched the two ladies head back to their car. She now knew this was a personal vendetta. The last thing she needed was to have more of her family and friends getting deeper into danger.

I have to face the Crimson King alone.

As soon as they pulled their vehicle back, Tanya put her Jeep in gear and revved past them, not giving them a second glance.

She turned her face briefly toward her phone on the dashboard.

"Call Ray Jackson."

Chapter Seventy

Tanya tapped her fingers on the steering wheel, hoping Ray wasn't cooped up with Susan Cross and her election strategy team. The phone rang and rang.

She cursed under her breath.

Why couldn't Cross pick some junior muscle from the bureau?

There were plenty of staff who would have jumped at the chance to play chauffeur and bodyguard to the top boss gunning for congress.

But Tanya knew why.

Ray was loyal, especially to his former director. She could imagine the sharks circling Susan Cross in DC right now, ready to tear her into pieces.

Tanya was about to give up, when the ringing stopped.

"What do you want now?" snapped Ray.

"The Crimson King's main target is me."

"That's quite the presumption, Agent Stone," said Ray.

"Do you know how many organized crime heads would like to see me dead?" said Tanya.

"No one knows your real identity." Ray paused. "You didn't blow your cover, did you?"

"As far as everyone's concerned, I'm just another washed up, PTSD-ravaged vet," said Tanya. "Jack appreciates my work and has given me more responsibilities, but he still thinks he's doing me a favor."

"What about your gal pals?"

"You mean my family?"

"How many times did I warn you?" Ray's voice hardened. "You cannot share your secrets with them."

Tanya swallowed. It was hard to keep truths from him.

She had to admit that telling Asha and Katy about her undercover role had been a mistake. But she trusted them with her life. If there was anyone she could rely on, it would be them.

"They were there to help me, when you wouldn't, Ray."

"Not that I wouldn't. I *couldn't*." He sounded defensive. "The bureau has rules, and everyone has a mandate. You are supposed to work alone."

"It's not my friends," said Tanya. "They know how to keep their mouths closed."

"You've exposed them to serious danger, and now, Nicole's dead. Asha, Zoe, and Peace have almost died."

A jolt went through Tanya, like someone had shot her.

"How many more are you willing to sacrifice?" said Ray.

Tanya closed her eyes momentarily.

He was right. Everything that had happened in Black Rock over the past few days had been her fault.

"He's got Chantal," said Tanya, feeling her throat constrict. "When I find her, I'll find him. And I'm going to make him pay."

"You'll be walking into a lion's lair."

"That's why I called." She braced herself. "I'll be at the Grimwood Estate in twenty minutes. I need you to secure a search warrant for me."

Ray fell silent for a second. Tanya crossed her fingers.

"How do you know he's at the Grimwood Estate?" he said.

"The crew found the last riddle—"

"You've got to be kidding me."

"Listen to this," said Tanya, reading from the photo she had taken of the last note. *The woods are peaceful. I'm not the grim man everyone makes me out to be.*

"Grim...wood, eh?" Ray scoffed. "That's a long shot."

"He's been playing with me all along."

"He could be deceiving you."

"I'll take that chance." Tanya took a long breath in and let it out. "This is my mission. I've been waiting for an excuse to search that place. I have a darned good reason now."

"First, no judge will issue a warrant based on a riddle, regardless of extenuating circumstances. Second, a warrant will take a few hours to wrangle, if we're lucky."

He sighed.

"We'll need to fill in paperwork. The judge will need time to deliberate. We can't go crashing into private property like a bad Hollywood movie. There are consequences in real life. Expensive ones. Deadly ones."

"I accept responsibility for my actions," said Tanya. "Pull whatever strings you can."

"You're out of your mind. Susan Cross is in the middle of an interview with NBC news. In ten minutes, I'll be driving her to a fundraiser hosted by a senator. What am I going to tell her?"

"The truth."

Tanya could almost hear Ray gnashing his teeth on the other end.

"And if she shuts you down like last time?" he said.

"Call the judge yourself. You keep pretending to be small fry, but you have more connections than anyone I know."

"You think I can call any old judge and ask them out of the blue to get a search warrant for one of the most closed-off, private properties in the state, based on a flimsy riddle?"

"Warrant or not, I'm going in." Tanya gritted her teeth. "Call every FBI agent in the vicinity. I need backup, and I need it now."

"You're asking for the impossible."

"This is why Susan Cross sent me to Black Rock in the first place. My entire mission is coming to fruition. The least you can do is support me."

Ray sighed.

"Get back to the precinct and do your pretend job, agent. Don't make any moves until I call you back."

"You've got twenty minutes," said Tanya.

"I need more time than that," said Ray.

"I'm done talking," said Tanya. "It's time to face the man we've all been chasing."

Chapter Seventy-One

Max whirled around in the backseat and howled with impatience.

"Hang tight, bud."

Tanya had parked the Jeep a block from the Grimwood Estate. She had a couple of things to take care of before figuring out how to enter the property.

She glanced at her rearview mirror.

The red sports car had been crawling behind her for the past fifteen minutes. It was now parked next to a large willow tree by the side of the road, long leafy branches trailing across the front of the car.

Tanya could easily imagine Ocean and Sahara crouching inside, watching her, believing they were incognito. These two women might be the most indomitable and stubborn septuagenarians on earth, but their sleuthing skills were direly lacking.

I can see you.

Tanya redirected her focus back to the front. She peered through her windshield at the empty road ahead of her.

At the end of that street lay a vast expanse of land, surrounded by a ten-foot-tall electrified wall, topped with barbed wire and fortified by steel bars.

Very grim, thought Tanya. *What an apt name.*

No one from the road could see anything behind that barricaded wall. All that was visible were the tops of massive evergreen trees whose branches swayed to a breeze coming from the ocean. It was like they were challenging her.

Challenge accepted. I will find a way inside.

Tanya had already put on her Kevlar vest and strapped Max's K9 bulletproof gear on him. He knew this meant they were about to jump into action. He twirled faster in the back, whining to be let out.

Tanya leaned over and ruffled his head.

"Good boy. You're going to do awesome. We'll find Chantal and reunite her with her mom and dad."

That last bit she spoke aloud to reassure herself. She was finding it hard to concentrate on her next steps when the grisly image of Peace lying limp by the plane's dismembered nose kept rolling through her mind.

Her phone rang.

Asha.

She took the call with shaking hands.

"Any news on Peace?"

"Katy's at the hospital," said Asha. "She called from outside the intensive care unit. They won't let her in, so she's panicking."

"As long as they're working on him, that's good news."

"That's what I told her, but I'm not sure she heard me." Asha sighed heavily. "First Chantal, now Peace. She's going through a lot."

"What about Olek?" said Tanya.

"He's not the Crimson King."

"I've figured that out, but did he talk?"

"He complained about still being locked up."

"He has to go through the process, and we have other priorities right now," said Tanya. "Plus, we can keep an eye on him."

"He told me how you all used to play together in the fields as kids. He talked a lot about you being the big sis, and how smart and good looking your kid brother was. Olek seems to have admired Yevhen."

Tanya winced to hear her dead brother's name.

"He knew nothing about the Crimson King, other than the urban legends he's heard," continued Asha. "He didn't know much about the Bratva Brigade, either. To be honest, he doesn't come across as the most reliable witness. I got the feeling he was

317

rambling just so he could have some company in the cell."

Asha paused.

"Sorry. I know he's your cousin."

"Don't be," said Tanya. "You've judged him correctly."

"He looks miserable. I'm going to run across the road and get him a cheeseburger and soda. Might cheer him up a bit."

Tanya's eyes flickered to her rearview mirror.

"How quickly can you get to Grimwood Estate?"

Asha gasped. "Tanya, you promised."

"I'm already here."

"I thought you were going to sit tight till the Feds got a warrant."

Tanya narrowed her eyes. "I don't have time to wait."

"Jack wasn't too happy you took off without consulting him."

"He's got a plane crash and a town in lockdown. His plate is full. Besides, I have to take care of this alone."

The sound of a car door slamming came through the phone.

"You're not going in there by yourself," said Asha.

"Max is with me." Tanya paused. "But I have a job for you."

"Tell me."

"Sahara and Ocean have been following me. Their guilt at what happened to Chantal is only putting them and Zak at risk."

Asha took another sharp breath in.

"They brought *Zak* with them? What were they thinking?"

"They probably think he's safer with them."

"How did they evade the surveillance team up front?"

"Their garage opens to the back alleyway. I'd bet they slipped out while the cops were watching the front of the house."

Asha let out a frustrated hiss.

"They're supposed to inform the officers whenever they leave their home."

"The guys are probably still parked in front," sighed Tanya, "thinking all is fine."

Max whined as if to say, *Enough talking already. Can we go, Mom?*

"They're parked under a willow tree, three blocks from the estate," said Tanya. "Can you come over and escort them home safely?"

The sound of a vehicle revving emanated from the other end of the line.

"Roger that," said Asha. "On my way."

"If you can't persuade them, threaten them. Do whatever it takes to get them out of here. And tell the guys watching the house to be more vigilant."

"And you?" said Asha.

"I'm going in."

"*What?*"

"When you come to get the two ladies, don't approach me. Don't honk, don't call, don't acknowledge me. For my own safety, don't do anything that would put attention on me. Is that clear?"

Asha sighed.

"Can you wait until Jack frees up resources from the crash site and sends them over?"

Tanya's eyes swept the lonely path that led to the Grimwood Estate. She pressed her lips into a thin grim line.

"I'm not leaving Chantal in the hands of that killer a second longer."

Chapter Seventy-Two

Tanya hung up the phone and put the Jeep in gear.

She rolled forward, pushing gently on the gas pedal. Her eyes flittered between watching the road ahead and checking the rearview mirror.

The red Aston Martin behind her didn't move.

She was glad the road that led to the estate was straight and narrow. Sahara and Ocean wouldn't dare to follow her where they could be easily spotted. She mentally crossed her fingers they wouldn't be that brazen.

Max barked as they approached the estate.

No one knew who owned this land or who lived inside. But rumors swirled among the denizens of Black Rock.

Some said a Silicon Valley billionaire had

purchased it. Others said a Hollywood celebrity came here to escape the paparazzi. Another rumor said a foreign investor had bought the land to launder their ill-gotten blood-money and get access to the coveted US green card.

Tanya suspected the latter was closer to the truth.

Her shoulders stiffened and her gut tightened the closer she got to the property. Her instincts told her whatever she was about to experience inside those walls would test her skills.

Anonymous tips to the FBI claimed the estate was rife with human and exotic animal trafficking, illegal drug smuggling, and money laundering. One caller had even claimed a cannibalistic cult had taken residence inside the estate.

The FBI's organized crime-fighting teams had been surveying the property for years, but hadn't been able to pin anything down. Director Susan Cross had installed Ray Jackson in a rural farm nearby so the bureau would have a permanent eye on the place, but he had drawn blanks.

Cross was adamant the estate, inaccessible by law enforcement and hidden to the public eye, was a hotbed of unauthorized activity. Tanya was the latest undercover agent commissioned to finish a job that had begun almost a decade ago.

Tanya rolled the Jeep forward slowly, her gaze shifting from side to side, ready for anything. But the road was as quiet as it was empty.

She checked her rearview mirror again. The front bumper of the Aston Martin glinted from under the tree branches.

Where's Asha?

The steel gates of Grimwood Estate loomed in front of Tanya. She stopped the Jeep, lowered her window a few inches, and strained to listen.

Silence.

She turned off the engine and waited, checking her rearview mirror every few minutes. Max was staring intently at the gates, his ears pricked and his eyes beady.

She had been on this road before and had heard dogs barking inside.

Is that what he's hearing?

Her expert eyes took stock of the security layers along the perimeter. The unscalable wall surface, barbed wire, warning signs of potential electrocution, and surveillance cameras on each post made this place as impenetrable as Fort Knox.

The only way to contact anyone inside was via the intercom located on the side of the gates.

What are they hiding in there?

The red Aston Martin had finally disappeared from view. Tanya hoped her friends hadn't just reversed and were lurking somewhere back there. She couldn't afford to split her energy, worrying about them while she rescued Chantal.

Max growled, his eyes fixated on the gates ahead.

"What are you hearing, bud?" said Tanya. "Dogs?"

Max whined.

"You've got to stay by my side, got it? Even if you see other dogs."

Max whined again as if to ask, *What are we waiting for?*

A mechanical whir made Tanya look up. She peered through her windshield.

All the cameras on the wall moved in tandem and stopped as they found their aim.

Her Jeep.

The hair on the back of Tanya's neck stood up.

Someone's watching me.

Chapter Seventy-Three

Tanya switched on the engine, shifted gears, and did a slow U-turn.

In the back seat, Max pawed at the door to be let out.

"One minute, bud," she said as she turned her Jeep around so the front bumper faced the road. Her vehicle was now positioned for a fast getaway.

Tanya removed the safety netting. Max leaped into the front passenger seat and bumped her arm with his snout. She leaned over and checked his Kevlar harness to make sure it covered his vitals.

Then, she plucked Chantal's socks from her pocket and held them to his nose.

"Search."

She felt Max's warm breath as he sniffed the socks, wagging his tail. He barked once in that high-pitched tone he used when he was raring to begin his job.

Tanya pulled out her Glock from its holster.

Her heart beat faster as she checked the chamber. She was about to step into dangerous territory. The Crimson King was no ordinary criminal. Going in guns blazing would be a mistake that could backfire with deadly consequences for Chantal and Max.

Tanya pushed her door open and stepped out, her sidearm gripped in her hands.

Max leaped out after her.

Without hesitation, he trotted directly toward the gates, his nose glued to the ground. His pricked ears and tensed muscles told her he had picked up the scent.

Tanya's heart raced.

Chantal is here.

She surveyed the wall, knowing eyes were watching her through those cameras. Max put his paw on the steel gate and glanced at her.

She stepped up to him. There were no latches or handles on this side of the fence. She pressed and pushed on the surface, but the steel gates remained shut.

Plan B.

She walked over to the intercom and reached for the white button. A sting of static zapped her finger as it grazed the knob. She pulled her hand back.

Why am I so nervous?

She had been in worse situations before, but something about this place unnerved her.

She pressed the button down, cringing at its jarring buzz. Soon, the intercom crackled. Her pulse quickened.

A mechanical voice came through the speaker.

"I've been expecting you."

A tremor went down Tanya's back.

The Crimson King.

It was the same robotic voice that had called into Asha's podcast. This was also the anonymous sender who'd been messaging her for months, tormenting her about her dead brother and mother.

ANON.

Tanya leaned closer to the speaker. "I'm here for the girl."

"She's waiting for you," said the robotic voice.

"She had better not have a scratch on her." Tanya licked her dry lips. "I don't have time for games. Is that clear?"

A hollow cackle came through the intercom, like he was amused.

"Come right in."

The speaker went dead.

Max barked.

Tanya spun around to see a gap in the wall.

A small door had been embedded into the façade, so perfectly camouflaged she hadn't noticed it. It was now opening silently, like someone was controlling it remotely.

Max barked again.

Before she could say anything, he trotted through the opening and disappeared. Tanya gripped her gun tighter. She ducked through the narrow doorway and stepped across the threshold.

She was inside the Grimwood Estate.

Chapter Seventy-Four

Tanya stood by the small doorway, her back to the world outside.

The security cameras on the steel posts whirred as they rotated to her new position.

A cold shiver went through her.

She gazed into the woody thicket beside her, wondering where the killer was watching her from.

But Max hadn't alerted her to anyone or anything. He had trotted a few yards on the path, stopped, and was now waiting for her to join him.

Tanya remained in her position, her muscles tense, staring into this forbidden place she had wanted so badly to get in for months.

She was standing at the beginning of a paved road that cut through a forest. Immense fir trees huddled along both sides of the pathway, which seemed to stretch into the horizon.

The road inclined up a slope and gradually narrowed until it disappeared in the distance. That, she knew, was an optical illusion, but it also meant they were a long way from the main compound or buildings.

A hollow silence hung in the air, like the place had been abandoned.

Where is everyone?

She glanced around, wondering about the security team. During another case, she had met a few of the estate's tight-lipped, flinty-eyed guards. It had taken a lot of prodding to get one recruit to open up.

He hadn't said much, other than the owner employed an armed team and bred Dobermans trained to fight intruders.

Where are the guard dogs?

She glanced at Max who was waiting impatiently for her. He sneezed and pawed the ground as if to say, *Are you coming?*

He wouldn't be this calm if other canines were in the vicinity.

Tanya shook the whirlwind of paranoia threatening to overtake her. After all the macabre events that had happened over the past seventy-odd hours, her nerves were tattered.

She squared her shoulders.

"Let's go find Chantal," she said to Max.

She took a step forward when the phone in her pocket buzzed. She took the call.

"Why didn't you inform me where you were heading off to?" Jack's voice boomed through the airwaves.

"Sorry, Jack. I can't wait for everyone to be ready."

"Is trooper Hall with you?"

Tanya's brow furrowed as she tried to recall the names of the officers who had come to assist them.

"What does he look like?"

"She," said Jack. "She's the whiz kid who's been helping us out."

"Officer Nicole Hall." Tanya's brow cleared. "The tech cop?"

"That's her," said Jack. "She's gone AWOL."

Chapter Seventy-Five

Tanya narrowed her eyes.

Was the tech cop working with the Crimson King all along?

"The team leader took a roll call," Jack was saying. "He can't find her."

"She was with me and Asha when we went through Peace's laptop bag and the latest riddle," said Tanya.

"She and the bag have both vanished into thin air."

Tanya's frown deepened. "Was she with the State Patrol for long?"

"They're new recruits, including the team lead. It's not like I had the pick of the litter. I took volunteers from wherever I could." Jack sighed. "I was really hoping she came with you as backup."

Tanya shook her head. "It's just me and Max."

"Look, I've got a hell of a job to finish here, but I'm coming over. Wait for us."

"Chantal's here. Max is giving every indication of her presence—"

Someone shouted "Chief," in the background. Jack replied, but all Tanya heard was mumbling from the other end.

"The FAA team is here," said Jack, speaking into the phone again. "Stay put till I get there. Don't go inside."

He hung up.

Tanya slipped her phone into her pocket.

I'm already in, Jack.

She gazed into the shadows of the trees nearby, her mind buzzing with questions.

Is the tech cop here?

If she's in cahoots with the Crimson King, why did she help us unravel the riddles?

Tanya stared at the long road ahead of her.

According to the satellite imagery, she guessed the Grimwood Estate to be the size of three Manhattan Islands. She knew a mansion or a compound of buildings lay beyond her view. How much farther, only the Crimson King and his minions knew.

Max barked at her.

Tanya was about to join him when she realized

there was a faster way to travel through this vast property.

My all-wheel drive, all-terrain car.

She turned around and stepped back toward the wall. The opening they had passed through was barely large enough for one adult, let alone her Jeep.

Knowing Max was watching her back, she holstered her weapon and focused on the latches that kept the gates shut. She pushed and pulled, trying to pry them apart, but every piece of fastening on the steel barricade held.

After several minutes of fighting with the locks, she realized what she had feared all along. Everything on this gate was controlled remotely.

Is there a way to override these locks manually?

She straightened up.

Hang on.

My gun.

She pulled out her Glock and aimed it at the largest latch. That was when a cackle came from the intercom just outside the gates.

Tanya froze.

"Your vehicle will remain outside," came the robotic voice through the speaker.

Before she could do anything, the small door they had come in through swung back and slammed shut.

"No!"

Tanya leaped toward it, but there were no

handles or knobs. The surface was too smooth to scale up. Plus, she could never leave Max behind.

Sweat streamed down her back.

We're locked in.

She turned and aimed her weapon on the gate's main latch and fired.

The bullet ricocheted back.

"Down, Max!" she screamed as she slammed to the ground.

Max darted over to her. Tanya grabbed him by the collar and pulled him close, her heart pounding.

"It's bulletproof," she whispered, trying not to shake. "He's playing with us."

Beyond the wall, the intercom crackled to life again.

A hollow robotic laughter echoed outside.

Chapter Seventy-Six

Tanya pulled Max into the woods.

Max whined.

"It's okay, bud." She knelt next to him. "We're safer here."

A black crow on a branch above cawed to warn its clan that strangers were afoot. Tanya wished it would shut up.

Max sniffed a root and gave her a puzzled look as if to say, *I can't smell the socks anymore, Mom.*

She stroked his back. "We'll get on track soon, bud. We'll find Chantal. Don't you worry."

She peered through the foliage at the empty road, only a few feet from her. She couldn't be certain, but she guessed cameras lined that path and their movements would be monitored.

The Crimson King's heartless cackle still rang in

her ear. If he had planned an ambush up ahead, they had to remain in stealth mode.

"The road will be our guide." She patted Max's head. "We're going to walk alongside it. That's how we'll find the compound and Chantal."

She rose to her feet.

"Stay close, bud."

Soon, Max was trotting ahead of her, maneuvering around tree trunks and wayward logs. Tanya stepped cautiously behind him, her head on a swivel and her finger ready for the trigger.

Her worries about the missing girl weighed heavily on her shoulders. She couldn't ignore the terror seeping into her bones at the thought of what she might discover at the end of this road.

Her mind raged at the madman who had wreaked havoc in her town. She gripped her gun tighter, realizing she hadn't desired to put a bullet through someone as much as she wanted right now.

You're a dead man, Crimson King.

She leaned against a trunk for a second to catch her breath. She pulled out the water bottle she carried in her cargo pants pocket, gave Max a drink, and took a sip herself.

"Let's keep going, bud."

They had been walking for around twenty minutes, when, without a warning, Max halted. Tanya stopped herself just in time to not step on his paw.

She peered at their surroundings, her gun aimed forward, but the forest was quiet.

Max turned his snout toward the road and twitched his nose. He barred his teeth and growled a low warning rumble from his belly.

Tanya bent low and peeked from under a pine branch. Massive fir trees huddled close together on the opposite side of the road, forming a dark and impenetrable barricade.

Is there someone on the other side?

She glanced up and down the long road that seemed to go on forever in either direction now, but there was no soul to be seen. She thought she heard a distant bang, but she wasn't sure if she had imagined it.

She bent down and put a hand on Max's neck. "What is it, bud?"

Max flicked his ears, then, whirled around to lick her face. To her surprise, he jumped a puddle and trotted through two large pine trees.

With another glance at the other side of the road to make sure she hadn't missed anything, Tanya hurried to catch up with him. Whatever Max had warned her about had disappeared.

But her troubled mind swirled with fear.

Though she was sweating from the hike, a cold shiver ran down her back.

Who am I kidding?

The Crimson King knows exactly where I am.

Chapter Seventy-Seven

A loud bang reverberated through the woods. Tanya froze.

A murder of crows fluttered from the canopy and took to the air in a black cloud.

Max twirled around, huffing loudly. Tanya grabbed his collar. "Shush," she whispered before he exploded into a volley of furious barks.

Was that a gunshot?

No, it was something else.

Max was facing the road again, his ears pricked.

With one hand on his collar and the other gripping her gun, Tanya peered into the forest across from them. Whatever was going on in this estate was happening on the other side of the road, veiled by the fortress of trees.

She waited quietly, listening, watching, her muscles tense.

Maybe that bang I heard before was real.

But, what was it? Where did it come from?

The crows circled a few times before perching back on the treetops. They squawked and bickered like they were complaining about having been disturbed so rudely, but their initial agitation seemed to have dissipated.

Tanya furrowed her brow.

The birds wouldn't have settled this quickly if the disruption had occurred nearby. That meant the sound had come from deeper within the woods.

She took a long breath in.

The Crimson King was no fool. He was meticulous in his actions and superior in intelligence. And he was orchestrating everything that happened in these grounds.

Suddenly, Max pulled on his collar and barked. Tanya held on to him tightly, her heart racing, her head swiveling.

What is it?

That was when the crackle of a flaring rocket came from the other side of the road. A flaming pyrotechnic blasted from the treetops.

Tanya gasped.

Fireworks?

She lifted her chin and followed its trajectory high in the sky.

A red smoky flame erupted above her head and rained down on the canopy, creating a spectacular backdrop of a bloody sky.

The crows took to the air again, cawing angrily, their harsh cries echoing through the forest.

Tanya's heart pounded. Max barked and pulled at his collar, coughing as it tightened around his neck, revving to rush across the road. She held on.

In war, a red flare indicated distress, an emergency, or danger.

Crimson King.

Tanya clenched her jaws as she realized what else it signaled. He was showing her where he was.

Come to my lair.

Every cell in her body trembled in fury.

I'm not playing into your hands so easily, psychopath.

"This way, bud. Stay close."

Tanya turned and retraced her steps, heading back in the direction of the gates. Max followed by her side.

She marched back thirty yards until she came to the section she had noticed before.

Two mature oak trees flanked the road, their massive branches growing over the pathway. Their leafy branches reached out like fingers, forming a beautiful green arch.

Tanya knew this was a flimsy cover. The Crimson King seemed to have eyes everywhere. Scooting under the archway wouldn't conceal her or Max's movements, but it was better than nothing.

She stepped up to the nearest oak tree, with Max at her heels.

She surveyed both sides of the road. There were no surveillance equipment on the trees, or drones hovering in the skies, but she knew cameras could be hidden anywhere. The latest gadgets were powerful yet microscopic.

If Crimson King was preparing to take a shot at her, all she had for protection was her Kevlar vest. This didn't mean she was going to be safe from being injured or maimed.

She reached down and curled her fingers around Max's collar.

"I'm going over there," she whispered, pointing at the second oak tree across the road. "I want you to stay here until I give the command. Okay, bud?"

Max whined.

She released his collar.

Tanya stood up and stepped toward the edge of the path, her heart thudding. The crows had fallen silent, the woods were quiet, and the road was empty.

Now.

She dashed across the road. She reached the oak tree on the other side and grabbed it for support.

That was when a blur of brown fur bolted by her like a flash of lightning.

Chapter Seventy-Eight

Tanya whirled around, but Max had vanished into the forest.

She stepped around the oak tree, scanning the shadows, her heart thumping.

Where did he go?

The leaves and twigs on the ground were disturbed, but it was hard to see in which direction he had headed.

Tanya knew why he had done what he had done. Her words hadn't been precise, and he was operating under the command of her earlier, more explicit instructions.

Search for Chantal.

Max had caught the scent of her socks.

Tanya squinted into the forest. The trees grew closer on this side. She didn't have a choice. She raised her voice, hoping she wouldn't put her dog in more danger.

"Max?"

Her heart leaped to hear him bark. He was in the thicket farther down to her left. He barked again, as if calling her to hurry. She dashed through the woods, following his voice.

Did he find her?

She was out of breath by the time she spotted his brown tail behind a tree. She stopped, panting.

He was alone. Or so it seemed.

Hearing her, Max spun around and darted toward her. He came to within two feet of her, barked once, and twirled around. He dashed back to his spot by the tree and wagged his tail, as if to say, *Come, see what I found, Mom.*

Tanya scrambled over to him.

Max was gazing at a large clearing. She peered through the trees, but the leafy branches obstructed her view. She crouched low to her dog's level and took a sharp breath in.

This wasn't just any forest clearing. Max had discovered the compound she had been searching for.

An immense manicured lawn sprawled in front of them, with a swimming pool and an artificial lake built in the middle. But it was the massive mansion that rose in the middle of the grounds that caught her eye.

It was a characterless, angular building, the type

that curiously got featured on the covers of modern architecture magazines.

A section of the front driveway was visible from here. A black limousine was parked up front, but there was no one to be seen.

A shudder went through her as Chantal's innocent face floated into her mind.

Where's he holding her hostage?

Tanya's stomach turned to think of how the girl would be faring wherever she was in this forsaken place.

She had learned a valuable lesson over the past two days. The Crimson King liked to play with his victims, like a cat toying with its food.

Her next decision would be crucial.

Chapter Seventy-Nine

Tanya stared at the windows of the home, if this monstrosity could be called a home.

Each window was shuttered with white blinds. The only entrance visible on this side of the building were the wooden double doors on the first floor. They were closed shut.

Tanya clutched her golden sunflower pendant and said a silent prayer to her mother.

Please keep Chantal safe.

The phone in her pocket buzzed, and her heart leaped.

Is it Jack?

Did he get inside the estate?

She scrambled to get her mobile out and clicked on the message app, hoping for good news.

ANON.

She stared at the screen, frozen. *The Crimson King.* She read the message silently.

You're here. Come on in.

She looked up and stared at the mansion, her heart racing.

He's watching me. But from where?

Next to her, Max whined.

"Whatever happens to me, bud," said Tanya in a low voice, her eyes on the building, "you have an important job to do."

She plucked the pair of socks from her pocket.

"Search for Chantal. Protect her. Stay with her till Jack comes."

Max sniffed the socks, making loud huffing noises.

Tanya knew all he probably understood were the words, "Chantal," "search," and "protect," but it felt good to speak to him.

"Let's go rescue our girl."

She got to her feet and stepped out of the safety of the woods. She was ready to face her nemesis.

An earsplitting screech came from the grounds.

Tanya jumped back, startled.

The largest bird she had ever seen scuttled out from behind the mansion and stared in their direction. The peacock stalked across the lawn and stopped several yards in front of them, its beady eyes on the German Shepherd.

"Hush," whispered Tanya. "Stay."

Max remained still, but a low growl came from his belly.

With a shrill squawk that would have curdled anyone's blood, the bird leaped across the lake and landed with a graceless thud at the far end. It cackled angrily at Max from a safe distance.

Tanya glanced down at her dog. He hadn't rushed after the creature, his focus being his job.

Good. He knows what to do.

Tanya scanned the vicinity, searching for booby traps. Seeing nothing, she crept toward the double doors with Max at her heels.

Max sniffed along the bottom of the entrance, sat down, and put a paw on the closed door.

Chantal is inside.

"Good job, bud."

She gripped her Glock and reached for the door.

Chapter Eighty

Tanya pushed the bronze handle.

The door creaked open. The entrance was unlocked.

She wondered what kind of trap the Crimson King had laid for her inside.

Max was trotting around her, wagging his tail, impatient to get in and find Chantal. Blocking the doorway with her body, so he couldn't rush in, Tanya scrutinized the space.

They were at the entrance of a long hall made entirely of marble. It was lit by a row of chandeliers that hung from the ceiling. There were no openings or doors on either side of the hallway.

Tanya shivered as she stared down the cold white corridor. During a raid of a Russian oligarch's underground crypt one time, she had learned 3D marble spaces weren't always built for aesthetic purposes.

Common gangsters preferred rooms made of steel to house and torture their victims, so spilled blood and guts were easy to wash away with a simple hose, soap, and water. Some wealthy crime bosses used marble instead. It was much more pleasant to look at and just as easy to clean.

At her feet, Max whined. He cocked his head as if to ask what she was waiting for. His unguarded demeanor confirmed her conclusions. They were alone.

Tanya opened the door wider.

"Go, search, bud," she said in a low voice.

Max leaped across the threshold. He scurried down the hallway, his nose to the ground, his tail swishing from side to side.

Tanya pushed the door open all the way. Something told her their exit would be fast and furious.

After a quick glance behind her to make sure they weren't been followed, she hurried to catch up with her dog.

Max was twirling in place halfway down the corridor, his ears twitching and his eyes narrowed like he was confused.

He's lost the scent.

Tanya was about to pull Chantal's socks out of

her pocket, when he trotted over to one side of the hall. He sniffed the surface noisily.

"What is it, bud?" she whispered as she reached over and grazed the surface with her fingers.

As soon as she touched the marble, she saw the faint outline of the hidden door, just like the one in the main gates of the estate.

The door was camouflaged well, but a flat knob jutted out, cleverly concealed among the stone's patterns.

Max pawed at the wall and whined, as if to say, *Hurry.*

Tanya put her hand on the knob and pushed it, her Glock aimed forward, ready for whatever lay beyond the secret entrance. The heavy marble door opened an inch. She peered through the opening, her heart hammering.

It was dark inside.

Is Chantal here?

Is the Crimson King with her?

Max whined louder.

A movement on the far side of the darkened room caught Tanya's eye. She pushed the door open fully.

Max dashed through her legs.

The pale light from the chandeliers fell on the small figure slouched on the floor.

Her heart jumped to her mouth.

Chantal.

Chapter Eighty-One

"Aunty Tanya!" cried Chantal.

Tanya dashed toward the girl and dropped to her knees.

"Oh, my God. You... You're here."

She wrapped her arms around the girl's shoulders and squeezed her.

Her pulse pounded in her ears so loudly, she barely heard her own voice. She hadn't wanted to admit even to herself, but a small part of her had expected to find the girl's lifeless body on the grounds of Grimwood Estate.

"I wanna go home," said Chantal in a muffled voice.

"I'm taking you to your mom and dad right now," said Tanya, as tears rolled down her cheeks.

"There's nothing to be scared of. I'm here with you now."

Max twirled around them, his tail wagging in a happy frenzy. He poked his snout over Tanya's arm and licked Chantal's nose.

A faint odor of something sweet and chemical came to Tanya's nostrils. Hugging the girl close with one arm, she pulled out her flashlight and surveyed the marble room. It was sparse and empty, and no larger than a walk-in closet.

Max's wagging tail and happy whines confirmed they were alone, but the sooner they got out of this place the better.

She turned to the girl.

"We need to move fast. My Jeep's just outside. It's a bit of a walk, but it's all downhill."

Chantal shook her head.

"I can't."

"Are you hurt, hon?"

Tanya pushed the girl gently back and surveyed her with her flashlight. Her shirt and jeans weren't torn or bloodied, but there was a bruise on her left cheek.

Chantal made a face. "He hit me."

Tanya gritted her teeth, wondering when she'd get the chance to smash the Crimson King into a mess of blood and bones.

"He hit me because he wanted me to stop," said Chantal.

"Stop what?"

"Stop biting him."

Tanya's heart fell at the thought of what the girl might have gone through, but she had other priorities right now.

"Why don't you tell me about it when we get to the car, okay? Right now, I need you to come with me. I can carry you if you can't walk."

Chantal slouched and sighed a defeated sigh. "I already tried. I can't get out of here."

"Why not?"

"He told me he won't let me go, even when you come looking for me."

Tanya stared at her.

Max whined and thumped his tail like he wanted to comfort her. Chantal lifted her right arm to pet him. It was an odd, jerky movement.

Tanya frowned as the girl extended her fingers to stroke the dog, but couldn't reach him. That was when she realized why.

A steel cable shackled her hands.

Tanya's heart sank.

That's why she can't leave the room.

Chapter Eighty-Two

The cables wrapped around Chantal's wrists were tied to a U-shaped bar behind her.

Tanya aimed her flashlight on the bar. It was a solid metal post that seemed to melt into the marble floor.

She pulled out her Swiss Army knife and bent low. There were no clasps or screws, and the cables seemed to be made of the same steel as the front-mounted winch on her Jeep. None of the gadgets in her simple kit could cut through this contraption.

Tanya laid her knife on the floor, squared her shoulders, and placed both hands on the post. She tried to rattle it with all her might, but it didn't budge.

Chantal cried out in pain.

Tanya spun around to see the cables were twisting into the girl's skin.

"I'm so sorry."

She smoothened out the cables and rubbed Chantal's wrists.

Tanya glanced over at Max, who was sitting by the open doorway. He was on guard, his snout pointed at the hallway. He hadn't alerted her to anyone yet, but she knew that would only be a matter of time.

This was all part of the Crimson King's game. *Think, girl, think.*

She turned to Chantal.

"This man who brought you here, do you know where he is right now, hon?"

Chantal's lower lip trembled like she was trying hard to control her tears. "When I woke up, I was in this dark room all by myself. I don't remember a lot."

"It's okay. You're doing great." Tanya leaned toward the girl. "Can you tell me what he looks like?"

Chantal shrugged. "He had a weird mask, like from a Halloween shop."

So Olek had been telling the truth about the Phantom of the Opera lookalike.

"I was looking for Zak's ball on the other side of the playground," Chantal was saying. "He dropped it when he fell off the jungle gym. That's when everyone ran to him."

Tanya nodded.

"Then, this really weird man grabbed me. I tried to scream, but he put something on my face. I pushed him away, but he was choking me with like this towel. It was wet and smelled horrible."

Chloroform.

That was the sickly odor Tanya had smelled earlier.

"When I woke up, he was pulling me out of a car. So I kicked and punched him."

"Good girl."

"He told me to stop fighting or he'd tie me up, so I bit his hand. That's when he slapped me and stuck that wet towel on my face again. I almost threw up."

"You're super brave. Do you know that? Many people would freeze, but you fought back."

"You told me that in self-defense class. Bad people hurt you more if you don't shout."

Tanya drew Chantal in close, her heart sinking.

Bullies pick on the weak and vulnerable. Any other abductor would have let Chantal go because she wouldn't have been worth the fight.

But the Crimson King was no ordinary bully.

"You remembered your lesson. I'm super proud of you."

Tanya shone her flashlight around the room in desperation.

How do I get her out of those shackles?

By the door, Max shifted his feet but didn't

growl, bark, or get up. His ears weren't pricked and his stance wasn't tense.

Tanya furrowed her brow.

Where is everyone?

The Crimson King's silence meant only one thing. He was biding his time.

Where's Jack and his crew?

She pulled out her phone.

Jack typically checked in frequently during missions to give updates and ask about her safety, but all she'd heard was radio silence.

Her eyes fell on the top right hand of her mobile's screen, and a chill went down her spine.

All the bars had turned red. Someone had jammed cellular coverage in the building.

Tanya clenched her jaws, but she wasn't surprised.

The Crimson King has isolated us.

Chapter Eighty-Three

A peculiar silence had descended on the mansion. It felt like she, Chantal, and Max were the only occupants in this enormous house.

Tanya racked her brain.

Leaving Chantal chained in this room to go hunting for the killer wasn't an option. The Crimson King may be betting on her to do just that.

Her priority was to get Chantal and Max out of the estate quickly, no matter what. Even if she had to remain behind and fight the King alone.

But that meant she had to free the girl first.

Tanya jumped to her feet.

She stepped quietly toward the open doorway and took position next to Max, her weapon in her hand. Her eyes fell on the tiny black bulbs on the ceiling by the chandeliers.

Surveillance cameras.

She glowered.

He's watching us.

She glanced down at Max. He cocked his head and thumped his tail, like he knew she was up to something. Tanya stepped inside the room and closed the marble door halfway so it would shield his body.

"Good boy. Don't move."

With another glower at the closest camera, she whipped around and marched back to Chantal, a new idea rolling through her head.

She unbuckled her Kevlar vest and turned to the girl.

"Scoot back as far as you can."

Chantal gave her a wide-eyed look, but shuffled back on her knees.

"Now make yourself into the teensiest ball and stay completely still."

Chantal pulled in her legs, hunched her back, and sank her head in between her knees.

"Good job." Tanya paused. "You're the bravest girl I know. I can't tell you how proud I am. We're going to get out of here soon, okay?"

Chantal didn't reply.

Tanya draped her bulletproof vest over the girl, making sure to cover as much of her head and body as possible. She knew firing her weapon in this small chamber built of marble was risky. The bullet could ricochet in any direction.

What choice do I have?

She positioned her flashlight on the floor so it was aimed at the metal post. She pointed her Glock at the base and cocked the gun.

She placed her index finger on the trigger.

That was when she noticed something remarkable.

The angle of the flashlight cast a shadow on the floor.

She frowned, wondering if her eyes were playing tricks on her.

Where's that shadow coming from?

Chapter Eighty-Four

Tanya bent low and stared at the bump on the floor. It was right next to the post.

Just like the entrance in the gate and the door handle to this chamber had been camouflaged, the small protrusion blended into its surroundings.

Her heart ticked a beat faster.

This is how the killer slipped the cables on the post.

She looked up at Chantal, who was cowering under the Kevlar vest, trembling.

I have to get her out of here.

She scrutinized the knob.

This must detach the metal post from the floor.

She felt around the bump. It was a button, and a button was infinitely safer than an errant bullet.

I have nothing to lose.

She placed her Glock on the floor. She put her thumb on the button and pressed it.

The room rumbled and shook, like a massive earthquake had hit the mansion. The floor started to open underneath them.

"No!" shouted Tanya.

By the door, Max whirled around and barked.

"Help!" screamed Chantal.

Tanya grabbed the girl and wrapped her arms around her. They tumbled through the opening together.

Their fall ended as quickly as it started.

Something hard hit Tanya's back. She convulsed as a crushing pain rushed up her spine. She held on to Chantal, one hand protecting the girl's head in case of raining debris. But nothing fell down on them.

Tanya's head throbbed, like someone had hit her with a baseball bat. She tried to breathe, but it felt like the air had been banged out of her lungs.

She groped in the darkness.

Where's my flashlight?

Where's my gun?

Huddled on her stomach, Chantal was screaming in fright, her voice echoing in the darkness. Through the screams, Tanya heard another familiar voice.

Max?

He was barking in the distance.

Tanya blinked. Her heart sank as she realized what had happened.

The Crimson King had set a trap.
And she had fallen for it.
Literally.

Chapter Eighty-Five

Max's barks got louder, but he still sounded far away.

Tanya lifted her head to see something fuzzy high above them. She wished her vision wouldn't be so blurry. She felt the floor around her. It was cold and slightly damp.

What is this place?

It was dark down here, but a muted, unnatural light came from somewhere. Tanya blinked as her eyes adjusted to the semidarkness.

She turned her head up again. Max was poking his head through a square opening almost twenty feet above them.

He whined and pawed into the void.

Tanya's eyes widened as a paw slipped through.

Max caught himself just in time. He pulled back momentarily, but didn't abandon his spot.

She wanted to call out to him, to tell him to step away from the gaping hole, but her lips refused to part. Next to her, Chantal had sat up and was coughing, one hand on her chest.

Tanya struggled to sit up, forcing herself to ignore the claustrophobia threatening to overcome her. As she pushed back to lean against what felt like a wall, she kicked something. Whatever it was, it fell to the side with a dull clang.

She peered into the darkness.

It was the metal post that had imprisoned Chantal in the marble room. It now lay in pieces by her feet.

Where are we?

An underground chamber?

The mansion's basement?

Chantal turned to her and whispered in a trembling voice.

"Aunty Tanya? Are you okay?"

Tanya swallowed and cleared her parched throat.

"Couldn't be better, hon," she said in a cracked voice. "And you? No broken bones?"

"I'm okay. How do we get out of here?"

Tanya winced as a sharp pain spread through her lower back like wildfire. She had absorbed most of the force from the fall, unlike Chantal who had been cushioned by her body.

"We'll figure it out."

"What if we can't?"

"There's always a way out." Tanya reached for her neck and touched her mother's sunflower pendant. "We just have to try everything we can. Never, ever give up."

Chantal looked away, her face despondent.

Tanya nudged her gently.

"We're not just going to get out, we're going to get the bad guy who kidnapped you."

Chantal looked up. "You promise?"

"Remember I said you're the bravest girl I know? I meant it. Do you know what brave people like us do? We remain fearless. We get the job done."

"I'm ready to get the job done."

"I know you are."

Above them, Max was still barking.

Chantal gazed up at the ceiling. "He's going nuts up there."

Tanya lifted her chin up.

"Hey, Max?" she called out.

He barked rapidly in reply.

"Hush, bud."

Max stopped barking and pawed at the opening.

"Here's what I need you to do. Get away from the hole and get out through the same way we came."

He cocked his head to the side. Tanya's head throbbed in pain.

He needs the right commands.

She looked up again. Her dog was staring into the abyss, waiting for her to speak.

"Max?"

He barked once to hear his name.

"Go. Find. Jack."

He snapped his head back as if he got it. Relief coursed through Tanya.

Chantal waved her arms.

"Go, Max, go! Find Uncle Jack."

With another bark as if to say he was on it, Max twirled around and disappeared from view.

Tanya and Chantal sat quietly side by side, listening to his toenails click on the marble floor above them. Soon, the clickety clack receded. Tanya's heart ached to know she could be sending him off on a dangerous mission.

Stay safe, bud.

Suddenly, Chantal scrambled to her knees.

"No, wait!" she cried, waving her hands. "Stop!"

Tanya pulled her arms down. "He's going to get us help."

But Chantal was staring in horror at the ceiling.

Tanya lifted her head, and her heart skipped a beat.

The opening through which they had fallen was narrowing. Soon, all that remained was a sliver of light where the marble slabs joined together.

They were entombed.

In this grisly grave.

Chapter Eighty-Six

Tanya gazed into the murkiness.

She yearned to explore the space, but there was no saying what she would discover.

More booby traps?

Another abyss?

"I think it's getting lighter," whispered Chantal. "I can see bett—"

An unearthly noise came from somewhere in the darkness. Chantal clutched her arm in fright. It had sounded like a moan, but it had been so brief, it had been hard to distinguish.

Was that even human?

"Did you hear that?" whispered the girl.

Tanya put a finger to her lips and squinted into the void. An unnerving quietness settled around them. Tanya's heart pounded so hard it felt like her rib cage would burst.

Am I going mad or is there someone else in this space with us?

Next to her, Chantal started to shift uncomfortably. She rocked back and forth like she was sitting on something that bothered her.

"Look at this."

Tanya squinted in the dark.

The girl was holding something long and gangly. Tanya leaned closer and peered at the unusual object, wishing she had her flashlight.

What on earth is that?

Chantal waved the droopy thing back and forth. "It's totally squished."

Tanya's eyes widened as she realized what it was. It was a large flower, with petals longer than the width of Chantal's hand.

"It's a sunflower," said Chantal. "We fell on it."

Tanya stared at it mutely for about a minute. She kicked herself mentally for not making the connection before.

Yes, of course it's a sunflower.

Just like the ones the Crimson King had left in the hair of his murdered victims. A sunflower, just like her mother's pendant she wore around her neck.

Why didn't I see this before?

Tanya swallowed hard as the events of the past few days whirled around her head like a hurricane.

The Crimson King. ANON. The anonymous text messages. The killer's riddles. The innocent victims of Black Rock.

Her past was calling.

With a vengeance.

And it wasn't going to rest until it got its pound of flesh.

Chapter Eighty-Seven

Tanya rose to her feet.

Her legs were shaky from the fall, but rage spiraled up her spine, giving her energy she didn't think she had.

I'm not done with you, Crimson King.

Suddenly, a blinding white light erupted around her. Tanya put up a hand to protect her eyes.

She glanced up, half expecting to see the man who called himself the Crimson King watching through the opening. But the hole remained closed.

She glanced around her.

They had fallen into an underground bunker. Dull concrete walls surrounded them. The bright lights streamed from the low ceiling. The room was bigger than she had envisioned, but was as stark as the chamber above.

They were alone.

Did I imagine that moan?

"It was me," came Chantal's voice from behind her.

Tanya spun around to see the girl on her tiptoes, reaching a switch on the wall with her fingertips.

Tanya's eyes widened. "*You* turned on the lights?"

Chantal nodded.

"I was looking for a door or something when I touched it."

Tanya stared at the nine-year-old, her respect for her growing. "You're amazing."

"You said we have to try everything, right?" said Chantal. "Max is doing his part, and I'm doing mine."

Tanya stepped over to her and squeezed her shoulders.

Despite the kidnapping, chloroforming, being held captive in a cold room, and falling into a nightmare of a pit, the girl had shown more gumption than an adult.

"What do we do now?" said Chantal, a serious expression on her face.

Tanya stepped up to the wall and put her hands on the bare surface.

"We need to do exactly what you did. Keep looking for an exit." She paused. "You go left. I'll go right."

Chantal spun around.

"But I don't see a door anywhere."

"Remember the marble room upstairs?" said Tanya. "The door to that room was flush with the wall. Max sniffed out the entrance. That's how I found you."

Chantal's eyes widened.

"You see, this is a game." Tanya rustled up a smile, ignoring the painful spasm in her left leg. "We just have to win it, one step at a time."

"Like the scavenger hunt we do in school?"

More like a murderous sport set up by a vindictive psychopath.

"That's exactly it, hon."

Chantal started to tap the surface.

They worked silently, scouring the wall, inch by inch. Halfway down her side, Tanya started to sweat profusely. She gritted her teeth as her muscles screamed in agony.

Next time I hunt a killer, I'm getting the strongest painkillers from Dr. Chen—

"Aunty Tanya?"

Tanya whirled around.

Chantal was pointing at something hidden in a dip in the wall.

"What is this?"

Tanya stepped over to her and bent down to get a better look.

"A keypad," she whispered.

Instead of the usual "0" located at the bottom of

a keypad, there was a string of words. Tanya squinted to read them.

Open Sesame.

Chantal looked at her, her eyes shining.

"Do you know what this means? We're going to win this game."

Chapter Eighty-Eight

"There must be a secret exit here."

With her heart ticking fast, Tanya felt the surface of the wall, searching for a seam or a doorknob.

Chantal stood in front of the keypad, her eyes inches from the numbers, tapping a finger on her chin.

"The teacher's room has a lock like this."

Tanya felt a thin groove. Her heart raced. She traced the indent. It was a straight line that went from the floor to about a foot above her head.

"Found it," she called out.

"It's pretty clear to me," came Chantal's voice. "There's only one option."

Tanya glanced down. The girl's hand was hovering near the bottom of the keypad.

"Stop," said Tanya. "That could be a trick."

"But it says *Open Sesame.*"

"He's expecting us to take the most obvious next step. Remember, I said this was a game?"

Chantal nodded.

"That means we have to outsmart him," said Tanya.

"What if I press the number one?"

Before Tanya could say anything, Chantal pushed the button.

The key beeped once, then fell silent.

They waited, but nothing happened. Tanya relaxed her breath and dropped her shoulders.

"Please don't touch any more buttons, okay?"

Chantal turned to her. "But you said we have to try everything."

"Absolutely. But we have to be careful." Tanya narrowed her eyes. "There are booby traps and hidden doors everywhere in this house. We don't know what—"

A low rumble came from behind them.

They spun around. Chantal gasped out loud.

The wall on the far end was moving.

Tanya grabbed Chantal and pulled her to the back. They flattened themselves against the wall and stared at the scene unraveling in front of them.

The wall across from them was rolling up like a garage door, exposing a room behind it. A dark silhouette appeared, crouched on the floor.

It was a woman.

She was chained to a metal post, just like Chantal had been upstairs.

Chantal pointed and whispered. "She's got a flower, too."

Tanya took a sharp breath in to see the sunflower in the woman's hair.

Is she dead?

A lifeless body couldn't remain in a half-seated position unless the Crimson King, with his morbid sense of humor, had propped her up.

Tanya noticed the woman's chest heave.

She's alive.

A muffled moan came from the woman.

The moan.

Tanya's heart pounded.

What happened to her?

She stepped over to her, with Chantal at her heels, unsure what to expect.

The woman kept her face down, and her head buried between her knees. She had been stripped to her underwear and a white tank top that was drenched in sweat.

Tanya squinted at the stranger. All she could see of her was a crop of short brown hair, but she looked familiar.

Very familiar.

Chantal stepped ahead of her and jerked back with a surprised cry.

Tanya spun around.

"What happened?"

Chantal rubbed her forehead, her brow furrowed in confusion. Tanya reached over with her fingers and touched the invisible barricade the girl had bumped against.

A glass wall.

Tanya rapped her knuckles on the barrier.

The woman didn't move.

If I hear her moaning, she can hear me too.

She rapped the glass again, louder this time.

"Hello?"

The woman stirred.

Chantal pressed her nose against the glass. "Hi there," she called out. "Are you okay?"

The woman raised her head. Her face was lined in anguish and drenched in sweat.

Tanya's heart jumped to her mouth.

Officer Nicole Hall.

Chapter Eighty-Nine

Officer Hall stared back at them, her eyes glazed.

Rivulets of sweat dripped down her forehead.

"It must be hot in there," said Chantal. "How come we don't feel it on this side?"

Tanya shook her head.

"Temperature-controlled rooms, I guess."

Why would the Crimson King crank up the heat in the other room? Is this some form of torture?

She felt the glass wall, but it was cold to the touch.

Officer Hall shuffled forward, her eyes pleading. Tanya placed her palms on the glass.

"Can you hear me?"

The officer nodded feebly.

"We're going to get you out of there. Just give us a few minutes, okay?"

The officer slouched, and tears streamed down her face.

Chantal started feeling the bottom of the glass where it met the floor.

Smart girl.

Tanya joined in, and soon they were running their fingers across the glass, moving from one end to the other, feeling, pressing, and slamming their fists on the invisible barrier.

"Did you see that?" Chantal's voice came from the other end of the wall.

Tanya turned.

The girl was crouched at the farthest point of the wall, staring at something across the glass.

Tanya stepped over to her, and her throat went dry. The officer was sweating, not from heat, but out of abject fear.

Behind the post to which she had been tied, sat a small clock.

"Is that a bomb?" whispered Chantal.

Tanya frowned. It didn't look like any of the homemade detonation devices she had seen. It wasn't a sophisticated IED either. It looked like a common clock, one found in any home or a corner drug store.

But she now knew not to underestimate the Crimson King and his sick games.

The officer turned her terrified eyes to Tanya.

"Help me," she croaked.

"Stay completely still for me, Nicole. We're going to get you out. Hang tight, okay?"

The officer hung her head. She looked close to collapsing.

Tanya had two lives to save now. She needed to find out how to get them both far away from this house of horrors. She examined the glass again, trying not to let the panic gnawing at her overcome her.

She didn't know what type of bomb that was, how it would be triggered, or what impact it would have. A detonation in this underground chamber could result in their blood, bones, and guts splattering everywhere. The only way Dr. Chen would be able to identify them would be via DNA tests.

The officer moaned, like she was in pain.

"Hang on, Nicole," called out Tanya. "We'll get you out of there."

Is that clock really a bomb? Or, is it a ruse to rile us up?

The terror etched on the officer's face was a testament to how much fear the Crimson King had put in her. Tanya banged on the glass and hissed in frustration.

"I know what we should do," came Chantal's voice.

Tanya turned around to see her standing by the keypad.

"When I pressed the number one, it opened the wall." Chantal got on her tiptoes. "Maybe if I press the other numbers, it will stop the bomb."

Tanya shook her head.

"There are a million different combinations. You got lucky the first time. I wouldn't risk it."

"Shouldn't we try?"

Tanya clenched her jaws.

She was now almost certain it didn't matter what number they pressed, because the Crimson King was watching them and orchestrating every step. He was the puppet master, and they were the puppets.

Still, they couldn't take a chance on their lives.

"The wrong number could also trigger the bomb," said Tanya, "if that clock is a real explosive."

"What if I press Open Sesame?" said Chantal.

"Don't touch anything."

"We won't know till we try, and you said we have to try everything."

Before Tanya could stop her, Chantal punched the bottom button.

Chapter Ninety

Tanya grabbed Chantal and slammed to the ground.

She braced for an explosion.

But it didn't come.

A loud click sounded from somewhere.

"Look," cried Chantal.

Tanya spun around.

The hidden exit by the keypad had unlocked. The door was now ajar. Tanya held her breath as the opening widened, inch by inch.

Where's my Glock when I need it?

A dark tunnel appeared behind the doorway. Heavy footsteps came from the other end, like the person was dragging their feet. Soon, a bizarre apparition appeared on the threshold.

The stranger was in all black, from head to toe,

including his gloves and the ski mask. He was dressed like a Ninja, ready to blend into the background, except for his outlandish footwear. On his feet were a pair of red moccasins with a skull-and-bone design, crafted in silver thread.

Zoe had seen those shoes when she was attacked on the beach. That fatal day seemed a million years ago, but Tanya knew who this was.

The Crimson King.

Tanya got to her feet and squared her shoulders.

The man stood by the threshold, his deep-blue eyes penetrating through his mask. He carried no weapons, none she could see, anyway.

The piercing eyes were unsettling, but Tanya glared right back. It was hard to discern which of the crime bosses or warlords she had battled with this was.

The man turned to Chantal and tilted his head.

"You pressed the button, little girl?"

Chantal gasped out loud and scooted behind Tanya.

Tanya curled her hands into fists.

"Let the girl and the officer go."

He didn't respond, but she noticed him squinting. He was sizing her up, just as much as she was sizing him.

He looked buff and fit, like a Navy SEAL trained to fight. *Is he carrying concealed?* It was hard to say.

"If you want revenge for whatever I did to you or

your criminal pals," snarled Tanya, "your fight is with me. Don't you dare touch a hair of Chantal or Nicole."

The man didn't reply. But he didn't look away either.

Tanya locked eyes with him.

"You have destroyed enough. You've had your fill." She raised her voice, failing to keep the fury and contempt she had for this psychotic serial killer out of her tone. "Let them go."

"Why would I? They're my insurance."

Insurance?

A vein on Tanya's neck throbbed.

She wanted to lunge at him and smash him up. But she knew there would be consequences for her actions, and there were two others she needed to think of.

Her mind whirled.

If Max is getting help, Jack will be on his way. I need to keep this madman from blowing us up into pieces.

"Why kill innocent people? What kind of kick are you getting from all this?"

To her surprise, the man thrust his head back and cackled. It was the same harsh and hollow laugh she had heard through the intercom by the gates of this estate.

He stopped his laugh abruptly and turned, his eyes pointing at her like laser beams.

"You have no idea who I am, do you?"

Chapter Ninety-One

Tanya stepped forward.

"Show your face."

"We've been in contact for a long time, and you still don't know who I am?" The Crimson King shook his head. "Yet, you call yourself a detective?"

He spoke in a deep, low timber, and had a touch of an Eastern European accent.

"You call yourself an organized crime boss," snarled Tanya. "Yet, you're too afraid to show yourself."

He laughed, his cackle echoing through the underground chamber. Officer Hall whimpered from behind the glass wall, but Tanya didn't dare take her eyes off her adversary.

"You murdered women who have done nothing

wrong to you. You kidnapped a nine-year-old. Why target innocent civilians?"

"Because I heard you liked puzzles. I thought you would enjoy the challenges I sent your way."

The rage that had been boiling in Tanya's belly rose to her throat. But she knew she couldn't give in to her anger. This was the time to stay cool and calculating, just like the Crimson King had been, all along.

She went through the list of crime bosses she had tangled with. They were too many to count, but for this man to come after her with such vengeance meant she had caused major damage to him and his gangster friends.

"Who are you?"

"They call me the Crimson King." There was a touch of pride in his voice. "I leave a river of crimson in my wake."

"That doesn't impress me."

"You were never impressed by me."

Tanya raised a brow. She had hit a nerve.

This was personal.

A niggling feeling told her she had seen those piercing blue eyes before, but she couldn't place them. Her mind shifted to the men she had dated in the past, but none had the scorching eyes this man did.

"Why are you here?"

"The Bratva family was kind enough to let me stay in their home."

"They are the owners of the Grimwood Estate?" said Tanya.

"I thought you already knew that, detective."

"What is the Bratva Brigade doing in Black Rock?"

"This is their safe base. A haven from prying people."

"So, you are a Bratva."

The man shook his head. For a moment, Tanya thought she detected a flicker of sadness cross his eyes.

"They're not my family. I'm merely an employee. I'm the head of the Bratva Brigade's armament division."

"A merchant of death."

"If that's what you want to call it." He shrugged. "I call it a business. A very lucrative one."

Tanya racked her brain to recall all the arms dealers she had met during her travels. She wished she had her gun. A bullet into his left knee would get him to open up and stop playing these games.

"What are you most proud of?" she spat out. "Sudan? Myanmar? Haiti? Yemen?"

"All of them." He gave another nonchalant shrug. "If they don't buy from me, they'll get their wares from somewhere else and slaughter one another, anyway."

"You capitalize on human conflict." Tanya felt the taste of bitter bile in her throat. "It's people like you who fuel the fires burning in Ukraine."

He jerked his head back at that last word.

Bingo.

Tanya narrowed her eyes. She had hit another nerve.

So we met in the war fields of Ukraine.

The man sighed and dropped his shoulders.

"I thought you would recognize me by now."

Though his voice was muffled from the mask, his contempt for her seeped through.

Tanya clenched her jaws.

Stop playing games with me.

"Take off that mask and show yourself, coward."

He lifted a hand to his face, then dropped it, like he changed his mind.

"I don't think you would like to see what you will see, Agent Tanya Stone."

He paused.

"Or, should I say, Tetyana Shevchenko?"

Chapter Ninety-Two

Tanya's heart skipped a beat to hear her real name.

He knows who I am.

She fought to keep her face straight and her eyes steady. She took a deep breath in to settle her nerves.

She leaned toward him. "I don't give a damn what you look like."

"I think you do," said the man, his voice low.

Tanya frowned. This wasn't the conversation she expected to have with an international crime boss seeking revenge.

"Here's the deal. Chief Jack Bold and his team are outside the estate gates. You must safely hand over the girl and the officer to the chief. Then and only then can we have our reconciliation party."

The Crimson King stood silently, his shoulders

drooped, his hands limp, and his head slightly bent. He wasn't looking at her anymore.

A ball of frustration grew inside of Tanya. If she hadn't known the horror this man had inflicted on the entire town of Black Rock, she would have gauged him to be melancholy. Mournful, even.

"Did you hear me?" She raised her voice. "I'd be happy to duel it out. *Alone.*"

He hung his head.

Tanya suppressed the urge to lunge at him.

She was sure this was another ruse. He was acting weak and vulnerable, so she would let her guard down. One wrong move and he could blow up Officer Nicole Hall. Or open the floor underneath her and Chantal, and have them fall into a deeper and deadlier grave.

"Until these two are free, I have nothing to say to you."

He flinched, like those words stung.

"Nothing?"

Tanya stared at him, wondering if he was mentally unhinged.

His actions had been those of a diabolical man, who toyed with his victims. But his posture and words didn't match her vision of the intelligent serial killer who had evaded capture for so long.

He's got me cornered. Why hasn't he attacked me?

Tanya wanted to tear that mask off and rip every organ inside of him out.

"Your sick games are over," she growled, her anger boiling inside of her. "The fact that you hurt so many people means you're not getting out of here alive. I will make sure you pay for every one of your sins."

"You hated me." He whipped his head up and glared at her. "You hated all of us."

Tanya frowned.

"You were so ashamed of your origins," he said, "you even changed your name."

Tanya shook her head and sighed.

He's crazy.

He raised his right hand and reached for his other sleeve. Tanya stiffened, preparing to face a knife or a gun. But something shiny unfurled from his fingers.

The gold chain twinkled under the bright lights of the underground chamber. A pendant dangled at the end of the necklace.

She had seen it before.

It had been around her mother's neck.

Chantal gripped her shirt. Tanya heard her whisper from behind her.

"That's like your sunflower pendant, Aunty Tanya."

Chapter Ninety-Three

Tanya glared at the Crimson King.

"Where did you steal that from?"

"I stole nothing. I took it as a memento."

A memento? Like a serial killer does with his victims?

Tanya felt like vomiting.

Was he part of the gang that killed my mother?

The Russian militia rarely took things unless they were starving or desperate. Kremlin's orders had always been to torture insurgents for information, shoot to kill those who ran away, and terminate anyone who organized against the invading army.

Like her brave mother had.

A frisson of fear went down Tanya's back.

She had only been eighteen, but she remembered the day like it was yesterday.

She had come running through the kitchen door, panic-stricken. She had thought she had escaped the red thugs who had been chasing her through the woods.

But they had burst into her home, right behind her.

The men had stopped in their tracks the moment they had discovered the head of the local resistance unit in the kitchen.

All four, in unison, had raised their semi-automatic AK-12s, and gunned Tanya's mother down in cold blood.

The smell of gunpowder rushed into Tanya's nostrils. She squeezed her eyes to force out the bloodied memories that were erupting in her head like a volcano come alive.

But the image of her mother swirled through her mind.

There had been four bullet wounds in her chest. She had lain lifeless on the kitchen floor, one hand on her heart like she had said a prayer just before she got hit by the hail of unholy gunfire.

Her golden hair spread around her like an angel's halo. But this angel would no longer hug Tanya or sing a sweet song like she used to.

The assassins had departed as quickly as they had arrived, stomping back to their camp to report to their leader and celebrate the success of their mission.

One more dissident dead.

This was how they kept the villagers down.

Tanya had stood over her mother's body, too numb to see the blood splatter seeping through her embroidered white blouse. She had wanted to scream in terror, but no sound had come out. The militia gang had silenced her as well as her mother.

Tanya didn't know how long she stood frozen in horror, but she eventually fell to her knees, sobbing. She crouched next to her mother's bleeding body, emptying every ounce of teardrop from within her.

When she could no longer cry, she reached over to her mother's neck and removed the blood-splattered choker.

Her legs had shaken, and her hands had trembled, but her mind had hardened that day. That was the day she had decided to fight. Fight for the underdog. Fight for justice. Fight for her mother.

It was only when she had stepped out of her home, her neighbors had told her the militia had kidnapped her kid brother. Tanya had gone right back in the house and picked up her mother's rifle, with one goal in mind.

Rescue Yevhen.

The Crimson King swung the gold necklace back and forth, like he was attempting to hypnotize her.

"This was her special necklace for special

occasions." He pointed at her neck. "That choker you're wearing was what she liked to wear on weekdays."

Tanya automatically put a hand on her neck, touching the golden sunflower pendant she had taken off her mother's body.

The thugs who had assassinated her mother would be in their fifties or sixties, but the man in front of her was much younger. His voice and eyes gave his youth away.

"She kept this one in her jewelry box in her bedroom," whispered the Crimson King, swaying the gold necklace like a pendulum. "She wore this one to church."

The room spun.

"How...," Tanya croaked. "How do you know so much about my mother?"

The man clasped the necklace in his hand.

Tanya stood still, too petrified to move. Though she had blurted out the question, she already knew the answer.

The Crimson King leaned forward as if he was about to tell her a secret.

"Because she was my mother too."

Chapter Ninety-Four

Yevhen.

Tanya swallowed hard, but her throat had gone bone-dry.

She hadn't seen her brother for more than fifteen years. He had been a lanky teen whose voice had barely been broken. She remembered him as the kid who ran around the fields, showing off his model rockets to the village girls, thinking it would impress them.

She stared at the crisp blue eyes behind the ski mask.

These were older, colder eyes, the kind you get from a life filled with terror and hate. But they were the same.

How did I not see it?

She choked up.

"Yevhen?"

He nodded silently.

"I thought you were dead," whispered Tanya.

"Do you know what they did to me?"

Tanya shook her head, too stupefied to speak.

His eyes turned colder. "You betrayed me. You abandoned me."

Tanya stared at him.

"I saw you get shot, just like...like our mother got shot."

"You didn't stop to check?" Yevhen's voice rose. "You didn't care to see if I was dead or alive?"

Tanya licked her cracked lips, trying to reconcile the hideous memories that were clashing inside her head.

"I thought—"

"If you thought I was dead, why didn't you return to claim my body?"

Tanya closed her eyes.

It had happened so long ago, and she had tried so hard to erase that fateful day.

"Bullets were flying around me...," she whispered. "It happened so fast...."

Her vision had become pinpointed now, and all she could see were those furious blue eyes, accusing her.

"You ran away to save your own skin." The eyes behind the mask narrowed. "You left me at the mercy of the men who murdered our mother."

Tanya's head whirled like a tornado.

The underground chamber had become claustrophobic, like the walls were closing in on her. She could feel Chantal by her, clinging to her. Officer Hall had turned silent behind the glass wall.

Yevhen took a step closer to her.

"I asked if you knew what they did to me."

Tanya shook her head, mute in shock.

"They burned me, raped me, then beat me," he snarled. "That's what they did every day I was at that camp. And this is how they left me."

He pulled off his mask.

Chantal screamed.

Chapter Ninety-Five

Tanya stared at her brother, her pulse racing.

A grotesquely disfigured face stared back at her.

Burn marks, knife cuts, a shattered nose, and scars left over from who knew what else. The red thugs had done their worst.

She placed her hand on her mouth to stop herself from retching.

Even through that mutilated face, she saw her little brother. He was the cute boy whom all the girls in the village had a crush on. He was her kid brother she had read bedtime stories to. He'd had his whole life ahead of him.

But that was then.

Tears welled up in Tanya's eyes.

"Yevhen," she whispered.

He pointed at his face.

"This is what happened after my big sister ran off like a coward."

"I'm... I'm...," Tanya whispered through her tears. "I'm so sorry...."

He scoffed.

"Sorry? And you dared to call *me* a coward?"

Tanya swayed on her feet. The only thing that kept her upright was Chantal holding on to her from behind.

"The Bratva family rescued me," said Yevhen. "They took care of me. They became my family. Without them, I would have died."

Tanya listened, feeling like she was trapped in a horror-filled nightmare she would never wake up from.

"You were my blood family," he hissed. "But you took off and left me with those thugs."

Tanya wanted to say something, but the words dried up in her throat.

He pointed a finger at her.

"You brought the Russians to our door. It was your fault Mother got killed. It was your fault they took me away. All of this is your fault!"

His furious voice rang through the underground chamber.

"I should have stopped them," she whispered.

It hurt her to see his deformed face, but she knew the horror she was feeling now was nothing compared to the terror he had experienced as a boy.

"You're right," she said. "I should have come back for you. I've been carrying this burden ever since. I feel—"

"I don't care how bad you feel!" Yevhen screamed, spittle flying from his mouth. "You left me to die like a dog!"

His face contorted in a fury, making him look even more terrifying than before.

"When I started to look for you, what did I find? You've run off to America. You have a cushy job. A safe home. You even got yourself a new family."

He swallowed hard.

"Did you think of me even once?"

"Every single day," whispered Tanya. "I think of you and Mother—"

"Don't lie! You never had time for me then. You never cared for me."

"Mother was fighting to save our village," said Tanya. "So I worked, cooked, cleaned... Maybe I didn't do such a good job. I was just a kid too."

"You found me a burden. You couldn't wait to get rid of me, could you?"

"That's not true, Yevhen—"

"Don't speak my name!"

Yevhen whipped something out of his sleeve. It happened so fast, even Tanya didn't see it coming.

Chantal screamed.

"Watch out!" cried Officer Hall from behind the glass wall.

Tanya stared down the barrel of a silver pistol.

It was pointed right at her face.

Chapter Ninety-Six

Tanya put her hands up slowly.

"Please put the weapon away."

Yevhen's eyes narrowed into slits.

"You can't order me around like you used to. You stopped being my sister the day you betrayed me."

"Even if I had a thousand elephants to pull back time," said Tanya, "I can't change the past—"

She thought she heard running steps from up above. They seemed distant.

Is Jack finally here?

Or is it Yevhen's goons?

"I understand what you've gone through," she said, turning her attention back to her brother. "I understand your need for revenge—"

"*You understand me?*" Yevhen laughed that mirthless laugh. "How dare you?"

He stepped closer, the barrel of his pistol inches from Tanya's face.

Chantal called out in a shaking voice from behind her.

"Please don't hurt her."

Tanya wanted to reach back and squeeze the girl's arm, but she couldn't. She pointed at Officer Hall trapped behind the glass wall.

"Don't you realize how far you've gone? You build a house of horrors and these deathly machinations to entrap me."

Yevhen cackled again.

"I'm just house sitting for the Bratva family while they're on vacation. This is all theirs, built for their biggest operations. I just used what they had already set up."

Tanya's stomach lurched.

Human trafficking.

Of course.

This was what the FBI Director, Susan Cross, had been chasing all along. This was the Bratva Brigade's primary operations, part of a 150 billion dollar underground industry.

Yevhen's lips turned into a scornful scowl.

"Seems like the Bratva family had exactly what I needed to bring you inside here."

Tanya's mind spun at the irony.

This was my FBI mission.

She turned to her brother.

"You have had your pounds of flesh and your gallons of blood. Isn't it time to stop this madness?"

"You're going to have a painless death, big sister," snarled Yevhen. "A death you don't deserve. But I can't bear to see you gallivanting in freedom when mine was snatched from me so brutally."

He took another step closer. The barrel of his gun grazed her nose.

Tanya thought she heard a bark. Her heart leaped. It had come from somewhere deep within the massive mansion.

A vein in Yevhen's neck pulsated in anger. His eyes bored into hers. He was so focused on her, she wondered if he even heard the faint commotion above them.

Her eyes flickered toward the dark tunnel behind him.

Keep him talking.

"If you want to shoot me," said Tanya, "shoot me. But let Chantal and Nicole go first."

"I want them to witness your death. They can live to tell the world what happens to real cowards."

"Yevhen—"

Tanya stopped as she spotted a furry outline at the end of the tunnel.

Max!

Max bolted toward her like a missile.

He burst through the open doorway and leaped

into the air, higher than Tanya had ever seen him jump. He sank his jaws into Yevhen's shoulder and brought him crashing to the ground.

The pistol flew from Yevhen's hands and clanged against the glass wall.

Max shook him like a rag, growling madly.

Yevhen screamed in rage, kicking and punching. Max held on with his massive jaws, all four paws planted firmly on the ground like he knew what was at stake.

Tanya sprang on top of her brother and grabbed his arms. With sweat pouring down her face, she reached for her handcuffs in her belt, giving her dog a silent thanks.

You saved three lives, Max.

She clicked the handcuffs into place when she heard a child's voice from behind her.

"You're a bad man."

Tanya swiveled her neck to see Chantal had picked up Yevhen's pistol. She was pointing it at his head, a ferocious intensity in her eyes Tanya had never seen before.

"You killed Aunty Nicole!" Chantal's voice rang through the chamber.

Yevhen lay still on the ground, his dark eyes on the girl. Max held on to him, growling from his belly.

Tanya stared at Chantal in disbelief.

"Put that down. This isn't a game."

"You murdered Mrs. Durant!" cried Chantal.

Tanya blinked. It took her a second to remember Mrs. Durant had been the school principal.

Chantal's trembling index finger was on the trigger.

This was no game.

Chapter Ninety-Seven

Tanya rose to her feet slowly so she wouldn't startle the girl.

"Hand me the gun."

Chantal stamped her foot and flashed her furious eyes at Yevhen.

"I hate you!"

Tanya's voice hardened.

"Give that to me, young lady."

"No!"

The running steps from above were louder. It sounded like an army was swarming the mansion. Tanya didn't have time to wonder how Max had found his way to the underground chamber while the others hadn't.

She glanced at her dog.

Max was holding on to Yevhen's shoulder and

hadn't stopped growling. She knew how powerful his jaws were. One quick yank and he could rip his prisoner's arm right off.

Yevhen seemed to know that too. He remained perfectly still, but his darkened eyes were on Chantal, like he was channeling all the evil inside of him to spark terror in her.

"Good job, bud," said Tanya, glad to have Max by her side again. "Don't let go."

She turned back to Chantal, knowing one wrong move on her part could be dangerous to them all.

"Listen to me, hon," she said. "You can't shoot that gun. You'll feel really bad afterward."

"He deserves it!"

The girl's face was flushed and her cheeks were wet with tears.

Tanya's mind spun.

How do you explain the unassailable regret you feel after taking the life of another human being? How do you make sense of the nightmares that terrorize you for the rest of your life?

To a nine-year-old, no less.

"We can't play with people's lives, no matter what happened."

Chantal shot an angry side-eye at her.

"You told me we were going to get the bad guy. You promised me." She turned back to Yevhen, waving the pistol back and forth. "He hurt everybody!"

Tanya hadn't realized how much easier it was to face an adversary who knew how to handle a gun. The danger would still be present, but at least their next move could be anticipated to some extent. A distressed, emotional child holding a deadly weapon for the first time was completely unpredictable.

Tanya took a small step toward her.

"I know how you feel. I'm angry too. He hurt so many of our friends."

"You said sorry to him. You said sorry to this bad man!"

Tanya's heart flamed. Chantal had gauged her correctly. Before Yevhen had pulled the gun, she had considered letting him go.

How can I kill my own brother?

"Yes, he did horrible things," said Tanya, catching something in her throat. "But if you shoot that gun, you'll be hurting yourself more than him."

The running steps above them were getting louder. Tanya couldn't tell who it was, but she knew she had to take control over the situation before they arrived. Whoever they were.

"Do you know what will happen if you pull that trigger?"

Chantal didn't reply.

"The force of the recoil will throw you back. You'll hit your head on the glass wall. You could crack open your skull. You could bleed to death, hon."

"I don't care. He killed Aunty Nicole. He hurt Zak's mom. He—"

"The bullet could hit Max, sweetie."

Chantal glanced at Max. Her eyes flickered.

Good.

Tanya offered her palm.

"Please hand me the weapon."

Chapter Ninety-Eight

Tanya reached over and grabbed the gun. Chantal let go and staggered back with a cry.

Tanya clamped the pistol with both hands and turned to her brother.

She stared at her only blood sibling, memories of them playing in the sunflower fields of Ukraine swirling through her mind.

"What happened to you, Yevhen?" she whispered.

He glowered at her.

"You made me who I am."

The image of Zoe bound and left to drown in the ocean sprang to Tanya's mind.

She choked back her tears.

She recalled the lifeless bodies of Nicole on the

beach and the principal at the theater. She could almost hear the sound of the crackling fire as Asha's car burned from an explosion that could have killed her.

"How could you turn into this monster?"

"If you hadn't betrayed me," said Yevhen, his jaw tightening, "maybe I would have become the scientist you always wanted me to be."

"You can't blame me for the choices you made."

Yevhen laughed, his voice reverberating through the dungeon.

"Accept the facts, big sister. I am the Crimson King now. I'm proud of my work." He narrowed his eyes. "I'm glad I didn't turn into a two-faced cowardly traitor like you."

Tears streamed down Tanya's cheeks. She squinched her eyes as horrific images from her past flashed across her head like a slide show.

She had stumbled across a mass grave of villagers in Ukraine once. She had seen the aftermath of a suicide bomber blowing up a hospital in Israel, right under her nose.

Once, she had opened up a metal container in a port of West Africa only to find it filled with orphans of war. They had been shackled, ready to be shipped to the Middle East where they would be sold to the highest bidder.

Young girls and boys. Innocent men and women.

These are the true victims of the Merchants of Death.

How could you?

The furious cacophony in her head refused to go away. The more she tried to silence them, the louder they got.

I dedicated my life to justice. You dedicated it to terror and vengeance.

Tanya lifted the pistol and aimed it at her brother's head. It was like someone else was moving her body in slow motion.

"You joined the most notorious crime family in the world. You killed all the innocents in Black Rock. *You* made these choices."

She wanted to drop the weapon, but something inside of her couldn't.

"I did what I did to survive!" Yevhen's voice echoed through the space. "Because the only family I had abandoned me."

Tanya shook uncontrollably.

"You have the entire Bratva Brigade and their powerful legal team behind you. If I let you go, they will get you out. You'll never stop the horror you have unleashed around the world."

Someone was running down the tunnel, hollering.

A smirk broke out on Yevhen's face.

"You won't do it. You don't have the guts."

Max growled, but maintained his hold.

Tanya placed her finger on the trigger.

Yevhen held her gaze, like he was challenging her.

"Kill me, then," he said. "Go ahead, shoot me, big sister."

Chantal whirled around and screamed.

"Uncle Jack!"

Jack burst through the doorway, his weapon drawn.

He stopped dead in his tracks, taking in the handcuffed man on the floor, immobilized in the massive jaws of Max. He spun around to Tanya, and his face turned dark.

He shook his head, but Tanya couldn't move.

She didn't notice him step around Yevhen.

Jack gripped the gun and pried it from her shaking hands. He pulled her in.

"It's over."

Tanya dropped her head and fell sobbing into his shoulders.

~ *Two Weeks Later* ~

Chapter Ninety-Nine

"Blood is not thicker than water."

Sahara took a sip from her cup of Ceylon tea.

"Take it from us. If ever a myth needed to be busted, this is it," said Ocean, pushing an errant white hair behind her ear.

Tanya squeezed the sides of her forehead. She was still reeling from the events in the subterranean chamber of the Grimwood Estate. A pounding headache had overcome her since Jack had carted Yevhen away in handcuffs with chains attached to his feet.

Max lay by her, his massive furry head nestled against her boots, giving her much-needed comfort. She felt the warmth of Chantal and Zak beside her.

The kids had flanked her at the largest table in

Lulu's café, but their attention was on an online game. They had their noses stuck to their tablets and their thumbs moved at lightning speed. Chantal's sighs and Zak's whoops told her who was winning.

Both of their parents had banned electronic devices at the dining table, but Sahara and Ocean seemed to believe they needed this distraction.

Tanya had learned a valuable lesson. Kids absorbed everything. Chantal hadn't hesitated to mimic her. She had seen her wield a sidearm and had done the same, with near disastrous consequences.

The girl had been unusually quiet for the past two weeks. She had undergone more terror than most rookie cops did in their first year. Tanya knew it would take therapy and time, but Sahara and Ocean thought kids needed to be exposed to the truth, no matter what.

How else will they learn about the world? Ocean had said.

Peace was at home from the hospital, recuperating from the plane crash with Katy by his side. Zoe and Deputy Fox were also at their home, making arrangements for Nicole's funeral.

Tanya was glad the kids' parents were taking them later that day. They needed to return to their stable, peaceful lives again.

The sweet aroma of coffee and cinnamon buns wafted from the back of the café. Something clanged in the kitchen. Lulu barked at her teenage nephew, Troy, the reluctant server in her small establishment.

Lulu's café was kitty-corner to Black Rock's police precinct and was where Tanya retreated to when she needed to wind down and reflect. Like she was now.

Her brother's scarred face flashed to her mind, and a sharp pain cut through her heart.

I almost killed him.

She felt sick to her stomach. She looked away, hoping her face didn't give away the horror that still throbbed in her veins.

Sahara rapped sharply on the table, arousing her from her troubled thoughts.

"Do you think my family gives a care? After all I sacrificed for them?"

Tanya shook her head.

"I changed their diapers. I stayed up all night when they got sick. And what did they do to me when I got a few gray hairs? They pushed me out of my own home. The beautiful, oceanfront Malibu house my husband and I built with our own two hands."

"Families." Ocean slurped her tea and grimaced. "Mine tried to trick me into changing my will. Ha. Everything I own will go to the cat sanctuary. I just wish I could see their faces when they read my last testament."

Sahara reached across the table and squeezed Tanya's arm.

"It's time to let your past go, my dear."

Tanya nodded feebly.

"You have us," said Ocean. "Asha, Katy, Peace, David, Jack, Zoe, Shawn, Lulu, the kids…. We're your family now."

Zak glanced up at her and smiled before turning back to his screen. Tanya put her arms around the two children and pulled them in for a hug. Neither of them looked up from their tablets, but didn't object.

"Buns are done!"

Lulu's singsong voice came from the kitchen.

She sashayed over to their table with a tray of cinnamon rolls. Troy shuffled after his aunt, precariously balancing a tray of hot mugs in his hands.

Lulu turned to him. "Bring the cheesecake out when you're done, would you? These girls deserve a treat."

Troy groaned. "But it's all the way in the back of the fridge."

"I'm not asking you to bake the cake, boy." Lulu gave him a sharp look. "Just move everything from the front and take it out. Don't forget to put everything back in place once you're done."

Troy rolled his eyes and turned to Tanya. He made a face as if to say, *Look what you make me do.*

423

He plunked the tray down and waddled back to the kitchen.

Tanya smiled quietly, knowing there was only one reason he was working for his aunt. Tanya had given him two choices, help out at the café or get taken to the precinct on charges of petty theft.

"He's got a good heart," said Lulu, setting the mugs and small plates around the table. "He's still learning. I'll make a responsible man of my boy yet. Just you all wait."

Tanya's phone buzzed in her pocket.

Her heart jumped.

It took her a second to realize ANON would never message her again. She hadn't realized how much her brother's texts had impacted her mental health.

She pulled the mobile out of her pocket and glanced at the screen to see who the caller was. Her throat tightened.

She scraped her chair back and stepped away from the table quietly, worried.

Will I have to say goodbye to everyone?

No one seemed to notice her, too busy oohing over the warm and gooey cinnamon rolls.

Tanya clicked to take the call from FBI Director Susan Cross.

Chapter One Hundred

"Congratulations, Agent Stone." Director Susan Cross's voice came through the airwaves, as crisp and clear as if she were in the café with Tanya.

"I'm glad we finally secured the Grimwood Estate. Good work."

"Thank you, ma'am," said Tanya, feeling more burned-out than accomplished.

"Too bad we didn't apprehend the Bratva members at the same time. The news is the family is vacationing in Italy." The director scoffed. "Vacationing, my foot. They're chatting up with the Sicilian mafia, if you ask me. Interpol's tracking them as we speak."

"Glad to hear that, ma'am."

"I've set up a joint task force to analyze

425

everything you uncovered at the estate. I believe we'll have enough on the Bratva Brigade to hold them liable on several accounts."

Director Cross paused.

"This is a coup for us, Agent. A coup for our field office and a coup for the bureau."

Tanya had never heard her this voluble. The Director normally spoke in short, sharp sentences, which Tanya had to decipher after she hung up.

And a major coup for your political aspirations too, she thought.

"I'm delighted to have the head of their weapons trading arm," continued the director. "We've been after him for a decade, but he was as slippery as an eel. Excellent work pinning him down."

Tanya swallowed hard.

"How is he, er, doing?"

"He's lawyered up as expected, and isn't talking. But we'll see about that."

Tanya's heart sank.

"What about the other suspect?"

"He's a small pawn who happened to be in the wrong place at the wrong time. There's not much we can charge him with, to be honest, but he's as talkative as a parrot. He signed an agreement to spill everything he knows in exchange for witness protection."

"I'd like to see him, ma'am. He's my cousin."

"You must stay away from both parties, especially

given your connections." The director's voice hardened. "That's an order, Agent Stone."

The director stopped and murmured something to someone on her end. A gentle thud and a rustle of papers came next, like she had placed the phone on her desk to read something.

Tanya waited patiently for her boss, but she couldn't ignore the sadness creeping into her heart. Her only living blood relatives were in custody, and she might never see them again.

"Tanya?"

Tanya snapped her head back. It was a different voice.

"Ray?"

"Do you realize how much evidence was in that mansion?"

Tanya nodded, though he couldn't see her.

"I saw the FBI teams pack boxes and boxes into the vans."

"Our Seattle HQ is the most popular intel branch at the moment. Everyone wants to talk to us. The NSA. The CIA. The IRS. Even the State Department. Good timing, too. Director Cross couldn't be happier."

Tanya squeezed her forehead to stop the headache overcoming her.

I just wanted to save Chantal and stop the killer from taking more innocent lives.

"When we first met, I told you your job was to

427

make the bureau and your boss look good," said Ray. "You've achieved it a hundred fold."

Tanya sighed.

"You know I don't care about any of that, don't you?"

"I know," said Ray. "But there are some things we need to do if we want to keep playing the game, young Padawan."

"I wasn't playing anything." Tanya gritted her teeth. "I was only trying to do the right thing for Nicole's sake, and for the sake of the other victims."

"The perpetrator and his people will be charged. The camera surveillance he had set up at the estate has enough footage to prosecute them to kingdom come. It's nice to use a crime boss's methods against him."

Tanya swallowed hard.

What will happen to my brother?

"Cross didn't just call to say good job, did she?" Tanya paused. "Is she sending me on another mission?"

Please don't say yes.

"There's a lot of stuff to sift through at the Grimwood Estate. You are to remain in Black Rock." Ray paused. "For now."

Tanya sighed in relief.

"Did you manage the favor I asked you?"

"I did, indeed. Young officer Nicole Hall has an

information interview with a cyber security team lead next week. Will she be up for it?"

Tanya smiled to herself. "I think she'll impress the bureau."

Murmurs came from the other end of the phone, followed by heels clicking on the floor. They receded to the background. Tanya gathered the director had left the room. Ray's voice came back on.

"She just signed the papers."

Tanya raised a brow.

"What papers?"

"Is our K9 hero with you?"

Tanya turned to check on her dog.

Max was under the table, positioned strategically between Chantal and Zak. As Tanya watched, the girl slipped a cookie to him which he chomped down in seconds. Chantal leaned over to embrace him, and Max happily licked her face.

Tanya shook her head, thinking of how many times she had warned them to not feed her dog. Chantal would get a pass, though. Max, too. For now.

She turned back to her phone and narrowed her eyes.

"Don't you even think of taking him away from—"

"Relax," said Ray. "I just wanted to be the first to tell you. He's getting the K9 Valor Medal for apprehending one of the biggest criminals in the world."

Tanya smiled a sad smile.

My dog is getting awarded for catching my brother.

How life turns.

"He'll be happy to get the attention," she said. "As long as you give him a dog treat with it."

"You get one, too, Agent," said Ray. "A medal, I mean. But you don't care about that, do you?"

Tanya blinked away a tear.

"I don't."

Chapter One Hundred One

The café's wind chimes clanged and the front door opened.

Everyone whirled around to see who the newcomer was.

With a joyful bark, Max scrambled from under the table and darted over to the chief, wagging his tail a million miles a second. Jack bent over to ruffle his head.

Lulu placed one hand on her hip.

"I haven't seen you in days, Chief. Where were you?"

Jack removed his cap and walked over to the table where everyone was sitting.

"Been a bit busy."

Lulu wagged a finger at him.

"Just because you're in the middle of a national news story doesn't mean you can forget us."

With a smile at the café owner, the chief pulled a chair and sat down. Lulu leaned across the table and plopped a cinnamon bun in front of him.

Jack shook his head.

"Thank you. Just a black coffee for me, please."

Lulu frowned.

"When was the last time you had anything to eat?"

Jack rounded his shoulders like he was afraid to answer the question.

"How are you going to do good work on an empty stomach?"

"I, er...."

Lulu slapped his shoulder.

"I have a chicken pot pie bubbling in the oven. You sit right here, you hear me?"

Muttering to herself, Lulu walked back to her kitchen. Soon, the sound of pots banging came from the open doorway.

Tanya stepped over to the table and took the empty seat next to him. Jack lowered his voice like he was about to share confidential news.

"The FBI's taken the lead on the case," he said. "The Feds have him in custody now."

Tanya nodded, but kept her eyes averted. He didn't know she was part of the "Feds."

"All the three-letter agencies are arguing over

where he'll be detained," said Jack. "Our riddle killer was more than just the average serial. Who knew?"

Tanya didn't reply.

"They're doing everything to put him behind bars for good," he continued. "He's no longer our problem."

He's my brother. He will always be my problem.

But Jack didn't know that. And according to Director Cross, he couldn't know.

The last Tanya had seen of Yevhen had been when her FBI colleague escorted him into a heavily tinted, bulletproof SUV. She had watched the unmarked vehicle drive out of the Grimwood Estate with a heavy heart.

Tanya took a deep breath in, trying not to let the sadness creep into her heart. She turned to Jack.

"How is Priscilla doing?"

"Better. She's out of the coma and under observation. I'm glad Bob's coming in today."

"Bob?"

"Her fiancé. I called him from the library as soon as I saw her. He was in Florida visiting family. The hurricane shut down the airport, but he finally caught a flight. "

Tanya felt a strange sensation go through her.

"So, you know Bob?"

Jack nodded.

"I introduced him to her. He's a good man."

"And you don't resent him?"

Tanya's face turned red the minute she spoke the words. She kicked herself for letting her mouth run before her brain realized what she was saying.

Jack looked up from his coffee cup and smiled.

"Everyone expects a divorce to be a cat fight, but when we separated, I wished her well. And she wished me the same. Life's too short for grudges. We just moved along. We even get together for some Christmases. Bob, Priscilla, her parents, her brother, and his family...."

Tanya noticed a pink flush creep up his neck.

"I'm the only single guy at the family gatherings."

Tanya's shoulders relaxed.

So he's unattached?

Jack nudged her in the elbow.

"Hey, so how are you faring?"

She gave him a wavering smile, unsure how to even begin to respond.

"I'll survive," she said. "This has been a...." She blinked a tear away and swallowed hard.

Jack leaned in.

"You did a great job. You tracked down a serial killer and uncovered an international crime ring the Interpol was after. I'd say you deserve a break. Take all the time you need. You'll always have a place here in Black Rock."

"Thanks, Jack."

He reached over and put a hand over hers. Tanya

flinched but didn't move her hand. Her heart fluttered, a feeling she hadn't felt in a long time.

"I'll always be here for you," he said in a soft voice. "You know that, don't you?"

Tanya nodded. She was about to reply when the front door's wind chimes clanged again.

Lulu popped her head out of the kitchen door.

"Cafe's closed for a private function," she called out. She turned her face to the side. "Troy, didn't I tell you to put a sign up and lock that door?"

But the person on the other side was already pushing the door open.

Chapter One Hundred Two

"Aunty Asha!" cried Zak and Chantal at the same time.

Lulu waved her over.

"Just in time for tea, my dear. Pull up a chair. I'm glad you haven't become too big to patronize my little corner café."

Asha plopped on the free chair next to Ocean and dragged the teapot toward her.

"Do you know how many calls I got this morning? Everyone wants to know what's going on in our town. My throat is so dry. "

"Seems like your podcast has blown up, sweetie." Sahara gave her a genial smile. "Don't forget us when they invite you to *The Daily Show*."

"That'll be the day." Asha poured herself a cup of

tea. "It's all good for my download and view rates. That's for sure."

She picked up a cinnamon roll and exclaimed as a drop of melted sugar fell on the table.

Chantal poked her arm.

"You have to lick that now. Or Max will do it for you."

Tanya watched the girl giggle and felt her heart lighten a little. Chantal still acted like a kid despite what she had gone through, and that meant things weren't as dark as Tanya had thought.

Asha lifted the bun to her nose, closed her eyes, and breathed in the aroma.

"This is what heaven smells like."

Ocean wiped the mess on the table with her napkin.

"What would you people do if we weren't here to clean up after you, huh?"

Asha turned to her.

"That's why I came. Ladies, I need your help."

Sahara narrowed her eyes.

"What kind of help?"

Asha stared at her bun for a moment, like she was choosing her words.

Ocean squared her shoulders. "You want us to hide a murder weapon? Bury a body? Kill a bad guy. We're your gals."

Sahara leaned in, put a hand against her mouth,

and whispered loudly. "We just can't guarantee Jack here won't stick you in his stinky jail."

Jack shook his head and smiled into his coffee mug.

"It's about these calls that are coming in," said Asha.

Ocean and Sahara's faces turned serious.

"Everyone has a sordid story to tell." Asha paused. "Most callers want to get on the show for their five minutes of fame, but I'm also getting... requests."

Tanya raised a brow.

"Requests for what?"

Asha sighed.

"One guy lost his three-legged lizard while camping. Who takes a lizard camping? Another woman wants me to find her husband who ran off to Florida with her nanny, who also happens to be her sister. It's a crazy world out there."

Sahara turned her mouth down in disappointment.

"Are you asking us to chase cheating husbands and catch lost lizards?"

Ocean threw her arms in the air. "Here I thought you had something exciting."

Asha put her bun down and wiped her mouth.

"I do."

Her eyes gleamed.

"It's a cold murder case that was hushed up a long time ago."

Ocean and Shara sat up in their chairs. Jack looked up from his coffee, a concerned expression on his face.

Asha turned to him.

"This was way before your time, Chief, so you have nothing to worry about."

Jack screwed his eyes like he was withholding judgment on that.

"Fifteen years ago," said Asha, "our mayor's sister-in-law supposedly poisoned her husband and three adult sons at Thanksgiving dinner."

Sahara gasped. "I remember. I saw that on the news."

Ocean leaned in. "Wasn't there a girl who survived?"

"The daughter got stuck in a freak snowstorm and didn't make it to supper."

Asha sat back with a smug expression on her face.

"The daughter called me this morning."

Everyone was listening now, even Troy who had snuck out of the kitchen.

"What did she say?" said Ocean.

"She wants me to figure out exactly how her mother killed her family members. And why she did it."

Jack shook his head.

"If that had been a suspected multiple homicide

case, I would have a file on it. I can assure you, I don't."

"That's because the mother called her doctor before the police. The physician, not Dr. Chen's father mind you, marked it off as food poisoning. The four death certificates state the culprits were the morel mushrooms in the gravy."

"What happened to the mother?" said Tanya.

"She's at the psychiatric hospital on the hill," said Asha. "She hasn't spoken a word since that day, and she refuses to see her daughter."

"This sounds like a hoax," said Jack. "The caller's probably not even related to the family. You'll be hunting ghosts that don't exist."

"Oh, yeah?" Asha turned to him. "Then, why did she wire me a cash retainer of twenty thousand dollars?"

Jack's eyebrows shot up.

Sahara and Ocean exchanged a glance. "Wow."

Asha turned to the two ladies.

"My usual retainer is ten grand, but she wanted me to dedicate all my time and resources on her case." She paused. "The only thing is I can't do this alone."

A sly look came over Ocean's face.

"We work on a commission basis."

"How much?" said Asha.

"Twenty-five percent."

"That's extortion. Fifteen percent."

"Twenty, and that's fair."

"Deal," said Asha.

Chapter One Hundred Three

Max barked, making them all jump. He scrambled out from under the table and darted toward the front entrance, barking.

Lulu stepped out of the kitchen with a large pot in her hands. She scowled to see the silhouettes through the frosted glass doors. A handful of people had gathered on the front steps of the café and were peering inside.

"You'd think people can read," hissed Lulu as she placed the pot on the table. "I made it clear I'm closed all afternoon. Good thing Troy locked the door, or I'd have my hands full."

Max turned back at Lulu and barked.

"Chase them off, Max. There's a good boy." Lulu

wagged a finger at Zak. "Don't touch the pot. It's hot."

Tanya got up and headed to the front entrance. Max's happy whines told her he knew who was huddled outside. She unlocked the door and pulled it open, making the wind chime tinkle.

"Tanya!"

Tanya reached over to hug Katy.

"I thought Lulu had banned us," muttered Peace as he hobbled inside, using a cane for support. He put a hand up as Tanya turned to him.

"I look a lot worse than I feel."

Zoe and Deputy Fox trooped in after them. With an excited shriek, Zak tore across the room and jumped on his parents, almost bowling them over.

Lulu came out with a stack of plates, yelling at her nephew in the kitchen.

"Didn't I already tell you? No phone until your shift ends. Now, bring the forks and knives."

Troy shuffled out, a fistful of cutlery in one hand and his mobile in the other. Jack and Tanya pulled over a second table and connected it to the main one so they could all sit together. Soon, the sound of chairs being scraped back came as they took their seats.

Tanya pulled a chair out for Peace. He sat down, wincing, and leaned his cane against the table.

"I'm not stepping foot on another aircraft for the rest of my life," he announced.

Ocean patted his arm.

"Quite understandable. We're just happy you're in one piece, my dear."

Jack turned to Peace.

"Seriously? You won't even get on a big jet plane?"

"I'll be taking clients within driving distance from now on," declared Peace. "I'm not getting tumbled around in an air-borne death trap again."

"You won't even fly to London to watch Manchester United?"

Peace smiled a satisfied smile.

"That's exactly why the Internet was invented, Chief."

Katy shot her husband a look.

"And why the surround sound system, the 150-inch screen, and the man-cave were invented too, it seems."

Peace grinned at her. He turned to Jack.

"Once I set it all up, come on over to watch the Seahawks or the Seattle Mariners."

Jack nodded. "I'm a hockey guy myself, but I'd be up for that."

Tanya slipped into the chair between Jack and Katy. Asha got up to serve more tea. Troy poured water from a jug into a bowl, placed it on the floor, and scratched Max's ears.

Satisfied everyone was where they were supposed to be, Lulu began to serve her pot pie.

"If you all had given me proper notice," she grumbled, "I would have cooked a proper meal. Now all you'll have is chicken pot pie leftovers and cinnamon rolls. This is embarrassing."

Asha grinned. "I love mashed-up late lunches. They're the best."

"Me too," piped up Zak.

Chantal licked her lips and picked up her plate. "Yum."

"Don't forget the cheesecake," said Ocean, turning to Troy. The teen's face turned red.

Ocean pulled him up by the arm. "Come on. I'll help you get it out. We can raid the fridge."

"Lulu, you need to stop worrying about everything and nothing," said Sahara, handing her plate to the café owner. "Don't you know company is more important than the meal?"

That just made Lulu grumble even more.

Max trotted over and settled by Tanya's feet, with a loud doggy sigh. She sat back in her chair, feeling his furry head on her feet.

Her entire world had collapsed in the dungeons of Grimwood Estate.

Discovering her brother was alive should have been the happiest moment of her life. Instead, she was overcome by a strange numbness. Her heart felt heavy that she, of all people, was responsible for his possible incarceration for life.

But sitting here, surrounded by her found family,

listening to them chatter, laugh, and tease each other, made her feel a tad lighter.

As if he knew what was roiling through her mind, Max leaned against her leg, and licked her hand. Tanya bent down to kiss him on the nose.

A small warmth wormed its way into her heart. The hole in her heart was healing.

Thank you for reading HER GRISLY GRAVE. I hope you enjoyed this story.

Don't forget your exclusive bonus!

Download the short bonus chapter which I wrote as a prologue to this novel, but realized it gave away too many spoilers. So here it is for you, now that you have reached the end of the story.

Get the bonus chapter here.
Murder in the Air

https://www.tikiriherath.com/murderintheair

Join my VIP reader club and download your exclusive gift today.

Happy reading!

A Note From Tikiri

Dear friend,

Thank you for reading this book. Did you enjoy the story? Did you catch the sentence near the end that had the book's title?

My promise is to give you an exciting escape with every book I write, and I sure hope I have done so.

Would you like to help other readers meet Tanya and Max and join in their adventures like you have? If you do, tell your reader friends about this book and share on social media. Leave an honest review on Goodreads, BookBub, or your favorite online bookstore.

Just one sentence would do.

Thank you so much.

Have you heard of the Rebel Reader Club?

This is an exclusive reader club, where you get early access to my new mystery thrillers before they're published. You also receive bonus content, reader stickers, bookmarks, personalized paperbacks, and even a postcard from K9 Max himself, sent to your home.

If you'd like to learn more, join the wait list to get an invitation when the club opens to new members next. You'll find the secret door to the club on my website.

https://www.tikiriherath.com

You might have to sleuth a bit to find the entrance, but by now, you've become a good detective, haven't you?

My very best wishes,
Tikiri
Vancouver, Canada

PS: Download the short bonus chapter which I wrote as a prologue to this novel, but realized it gave away too many spoilers. So here it is for you, now that you have reached the end of the story.

Get the bonus chapter here: Murder in the Air

https://books.tikiriherath.com/ murderintheair

PPS: If you didn't enjoy the story or spotted typos, would you drop a line to let me know?

Or just write to say hello. I would love to hear from you and personally reply to every reader who writes to me.

My email address is: Tikiri@TikiriHerath.com

Debate This Dozen

Twelve (plus one) Book Club Questions

1. Who was your favorite character?
2. Which characters did you dislike?
3. Which scene has stuck with you the most? Why?
4. What scenes surprised you?
5. Did you catch the sneaky sentence that had the title?
6. What was your favorite part of the book?
7. What was your least favorite part?
8. Did any part of this book strike a particular emotion in you? Which part and what emotion did the book make you feel?
9. Did you know the author has written an underlying message in this story? What theme or life lesson do you think this story tells?
10. What did you think of the author's writing?
11. How would you adapt this book into a movie? Who would you cast in the leading roles?
12. On a scale of one to ten, how would you rate this story?
13. Would you read another book by this author?

The Reading List

The Red Heeled Rebels universe of mystery thrillers, featuring your favorite kick-ass female characters. Available in e-book, paperback, hardback and large print editions, globally.

Start Reading

~

The Tanya Stone FBI K9 Mystery Thrillers

This pulse-pounding series stars Tetyana from the Red Heeled Rebels as undercover federal agent Tanya Stone. With her is FBI-trained K9 Max, her loyal and lovable German Shepherd dog. Serial killers prowl the wealthy small towns along the coast of Washington state. Can Tanya and Max hunt them down before the killers turn on them?

Her Deadly End

Her Cold Blood

Her Last Lie

Her Secret Crime

Her Perfect Murder

Her Grisly Grave

This series is now complete.

❧

The Asha Kade Private Detective Murder Mysteries

This series contains standalone murder mystery books featuring Asha Kade and Katy McCafferty, the sassy smart Red Heeled Rebels. A secret benefactor's estate deposits one million dollars into their favorite children's charity every time Asha and Katy solve a cold case. But do they know the deadly the odds stacked against them?

Merciless Legacy

Merciless Games

Merciless Crimes

Merciless Lies

Merciless Past

Merciless Deaths

This series is now complete.

❧

The Red Heeled Rebels International Mystery & Crime - The Origin Story

This is the award-winning origin saga of the Red Heeled Rebels. Meet the Rebels in their youths, a ragtag group of trafficked orphans who unite to form a found family and fight for their lives. For freedom. For justice. The books in this origin series must be read in order for your best enjoyment.

The Girl Who Crossed the Line

The Girl Who Ran Away

The Girl Who Made Them Pay

The Girl Who Fought to Kill

The Girl Who Broke Free

The Girl Who Knew Their Names

The Girl Who Never Forgot

This series is now complete.

❧

Tikiri's books are available globally in e-book, paperback, hardback, and large-print editions. They are also available in libraries everywhere. Ask your friendly librarian or your local bookstore to order a copy for you via Ingram Spark.

The Tanya Stone FBI K9 Mystery Thrillers

Some small-town secrets will haunt your nightmares. Escape if you can...

A brand-new FBI K9 serial killer thriller series for a pulse-pounding, bone-chilling adventure from the comfort and warmth of your favorite reading chair at home.

Can you find the killer before Agent Tanya Stone?

www.TikiriHerath.com/thrillers

~

FBI Special Agent Tanya Stone has a new assignment. Hunt down the serial killers prowling the idyllic West Coast resort towns.

An unspeakable and bone-chilling darkness seethes underneath these picturesque seaside suburbs. A string of violent abductions and gruesome murders wreak hysteria among the perfect lives of the town's families.

But nothing is what it seems. The monsters wear masks and mingle with the townsfolk, spreading vicious lies.

With her K9 German Shepherd, Agent Stone goes on the warpath. She will fight her own demons as a trafficked survivor to make the perverted psychopaths pay.

But now, they're after her.

~

Small towns have dark deceptions and sealed lips. If they know you know the truth, they'll never let you leave...

The Book Collection:

Her Deadly End

Her Cold Blood

Her Last Lie

Her Secret Crime

Her Perfect Murder

Her Grisly Grave

This series of six books is now complete.

~

Each book is a standalone murder mystery thriller, featuring Tetyana from the Red Heeled Rebels as Agent

Tanya Stone and Max, her loyal German Shepherd. Red Heeled Rebels Asha Kade and Katy McCafferty and their found family make guest appearances when Tanya needs help.

There is no graphic violence, heavy cursing, or explicit sex in these books. The dogs featured in this series are never harmed, but the villains are.

To learn more about this exciting series and find out how to get early access to all the books in the Tanya Stone FBI K9 series, go to www.TikiriHerath.com/thrillers

Sign up to Tikiri's Rebel Reader Club to get the chance to win personalized paperback books, receive postcards from K9 Max, chat with the author, and more.

Available in e-book, paperback, and hardback editions in all good bookstores around the world. Print books are available for free in libraries everywhere. Just ask your friendly local librarian or your local bookstore to order a copy via Ingram Spark.

The Asha Kade Private Detective Murder Mysteries

How far would you go for a million-dollar payout?

A newly minted private investigator, Asha Kade, gets a million dollars from an eccentric client's estate every time she solves a cold case. Asha Kade accepts this bizarre challenge, but what she doesn't bargain for is to be drawn into the dark underworld of her past again.

The only thing that propels her forward now is a burning desire for justice.

~

The Book Collection:

Merciless Legacy

Merciless Games

Merciless Crimes

Merciless Lies

Merciless Past

Merciless Deaths

This series of six books is now complete.

~

What readers are saying in reviews:

"My new favorite series!"

"Thrilling twists, unputdownable!"

"I was hooked right from the start!"

"A twisted whodunit! Edge of your seat thriller that kept me up late to finish it, unputdownable!! More, please!"

"Buckle up for a roller coaster of a ride. This one will keep you on the edge of your seat."

"A must read! A macabre start to an excellent book. It had me totally gripped from the start and just got better!"

❧

Read this murder mystery series for a pulse-pounding, bone-chilling adventure from the comfort and warmth of your favorite reading chair at home. *Can you find the killer before Asha Kade does?*

To learn more about this exciting series, go to www.TikiriHerath.com/mysteries.

❧

Each book in this series is a standalone murder mystery thriller featuring the Red Heeled Rebel, Asha Kade, and her best friend, Katy McCafferty, as private detectives on the hunt for serial killers in small towns, USA.

There is no graphic violence, heavy cursing, or explicit sex in these books. What you will find are a series of suspicious deaths, a closed circle of suspects, twists and turns, fast-paced action, and nail-biting suspense.

Available in e-book, paperback, and hardback editions in all good bookstores around the world. Print books are available for free in libraries everywhere. Ask your friendly local librarian or your local bookstore to order a copy via Ingram Spark.

The Red Heeled Rebels International Mystery & Crime - The Origin Story

In the award-winning Red Heeled Rebels international mystery & crime series—the origin story—you'll find out how Asha, Katy, and Tetyana (Agent Tanya Stone) banded together in their troubled youths to fight for their lives against all odds.

~

This is an epic international crime thriller saga that spans four continents and features a maverick group of spunky, sassy misfits who have only each other for family.

www.TikiriHerath.com/RedHeeledRebels

~

The Book Collection:

Prequel Novella: The Girl Who Crossed the Line

Book One: The Girl Who Ran Away

Book Two: The Girl Who Made Them Pay

Book Three: The Girl Who Fought to Kill

Book Four: The Girl Who Broke Free

Book Five: The Girl Who Knew Their Names

Book Six: The Girl Who Never Forgot

The series is now complete.

In a world where justice no longer prevails, six iron-willed young women rally to seek vengeance on those who stole their humanity.

If you like gripping thrillers with flawed but strong female leads, vigilante action in exotic locales, and twists that leave you at the edge of your seat, you'll love these books.

Go on a heart-pounding international adventure without having to get a passport or even buy an airline ticket.

What readers are saying in reviews:

"Fast-paced and exciting!"

"An exciting and thought-provoking book."

"A wonderful story! I didn't want to leave the characters."

"I couldn't put down this exciting road trip adventure with a powerful message."

"Another award-worthy adventure novel that keeps you on the edge of your seat."

"A heart-stopping adventure. I just couldn't put the book down till I finished reading it."

~

Literary Awards for The Red Heeled Rebels:

• Grand Prize Award Finalist - 2019 Eric Hoffer
Award, USA

• First Horizon Award Finalist - 2019 Eric Hoffer
Award, USA

• Winner First-In-Category - 2019 Chanticleer Somerset
Award, USA

• Winner in 2019 Readers' Favorite Book Awards, USA

• Winner in Suspense Category - 2018 New York Big Book
Award, USA

• Finalist in Suspense Category - 2018 & 2019 Silver
Falchion Awards, USA

• Honorable Mention - 2018-19 Reader Views Literary
Classics Award, USA

• Publisher's Weekly Booklife Prize - 2018, USA

~

This series is best read in order. There is no graphic
violence, heavy cursing, or explicit sex in these books.

To learn more about this addictive series, go to www.
TikiriHerath.com/RedHeeledRebels and receive the
prequel story - *The Girl Who Crossed The Line* - as a gift.

~

Available in e-book, paperback, and hardback editions in all good bookstores around the world. Print books are available for free in libraries everywhere. Ask your friendly local librarian or your local bookstore to order a copy via Ingram Spark.

Acknowledgments

To my international club of beta readers who gave me their frank feedback, thank you. I truly value your thoughts.

- Michele Kapugi, United States of America
- Kim Schup, United States of America.

⌇

To Rebel Reader Sharon Marks, whose dear husband has a character named after him in this book. John Marks is the Fire Chief in this story!

⌇

To all the kind and generous readers who take the time to review my novels and share their frank feedback, thank you so much. Your support is invaluable.

~

I'm immensely grateful to you all for your kind and generous support, and would love to invite you for a glass of British Columbian wine or a cup of Ceylon tea with chocolates when you come to Vancouver next!

About the Author

Tikiri Herath is the multiple-award-winning author of international thriller and mystery novels.

Tikiri has a bachelor's degree from the University of Victoria, Canada, and a master's degree from the Solvay Business School in Brussels, Belgium. For close to two decades, she was a risk management specialist for the intelligence and defense sector in the Canadian Federal Government in Ottawa and at NATO in Europe.

Tikiri is an adrenaline junkie who has rock climbed, bungee jumped, rode on the back of a motorcycle across Quebec, flown in an acrobatic airplane upside down, and parachuted solo.

When she's not plotting another thriller scene or planning an adrenaline-filled trip, you'll find her in her kitchen, cooking up a storm with a glass of Shiraz in hand and vintage jazz in the background.

A fifth-culture kid who grew up across four continents, Tikiri now calls Canada home.

To say hello and read more adventures and thrillers, go to www.TikiriHerath.com